Gouster
Girl

Gouster Girl

A NOVEL BY

David E. Gumpert

LAUSON
PUBLISHING

Publisher: Lauson Publishing Company
Contact via: goustergirl.com

Book Design: wordsintheworks.com and Lauren Grosskopf

For Tim Black—
Chicago historian, civil rights activist, community organizer,
and high school social studies teacher par excellence.

The idea of race is a construct without any basis in science
at all. Yet look at the immense amount of suffering that has been
caused by people buying into that mental construct.
—*Joseph Goldstein, meditation teacher and cofounder of the Insight Meditation Society*

In 1950, fifteen years before my parents moved to South Shore,
the neighborhood had been 96 percent white. By the time
I'd leave for college in 1981, it would be about 96 percent black.
—*From 'Becoming' by Michelle Obama*

1

July 1963. As oppressive as the mid-day summer heat feels, the furniture from our apartment looks deathly cold and uninviting sitting naked along the street curb. For the first time, I notice the holes and dirt worn into the beige cloth arms of the long couch that sat elegantly in our living room. I don't remember ever feeling the small springs in the seating areas of the two orange and brown easy chairs, now clearly visible as the furnishings lie on their sides. Same with the many chips and dings in the brown formica kitchen table.

It's amazing how completely the coziness and familiarity that furniture exuded not too many hours earlier, when it served our everyday lives, has vanished. Now the outdoor brightness is exposing the furniture's depressing raggedness.

When the two movers, trim muscular white guys in sleeveless undershirts and blue jeans, had begun bringing the furniture down from the third floor a couple hours earlier, I had wanted to caution Mom and Dad to make sure someone was always present curbside, to discourage theft by one of our many Negro neighbors. But as the movers wordlessly maneuvered the furnishings down the wide stairwell, through the open glass and mahogany-framed main doorway, and out the white-tile-floor entryway of the apartment building, I realized the sad collection likely wouldn't be tempting, even to the poorest of our dark-skinned neighbors.

So Mom and Dad and Emily and I occupy ourselves emptying the apartment of things we can easily carry—books and lamps and boxes of plates and silverware and plants and board games. Such a wonderful apartment, easily the nicest of the five places we lived in during our fifteen-year journey to stay ahead of the Negro wave inundating Chicago's South Side.

Just another move I tell myself as anxiety floods my gut. But I know it's not just another move. This is the final move. After several false starts, we're finally leaving the South Side.

I know, rationally, it's only old and dumpy furnishings exiting our building, maybe not even deserving of decorating another apartment, yet watching the stuff parade out, I am the one being emptied out.

Back on the third floor, in the void of what once was my first solely occupied bedroom, and the inviting eat-in kitchen and the vast living room where guests gathered on Sunday afternoons, the echo of voices seems harsh, even jagged. The excited chirping of Pretty Boy, our pet parakeet bought at a nearby Woolworth's five years earlier, can't dispel my gloom as I carefully place his square steel cage onto the floor by the apartment entrance, so he won't be forgotten. It's becoming ever more difficult to keep at bay the tears that well up in my belly and chest.

As I tear a fraying black-and-white newspaper photo of the Chicago White Sox pennant-winning team of 1959 from my bedroom wall, my younger sister Emily surprises me from behind. I can tell she is trying hard to be kind. "Think you can ever become a Cubs fan?"

I hadn't gone that far in my thinking, but my younger sister's question jolts me back to the present. The South Side is White Sox territory. The North Side, where we are headed, is Cubs territory.

"I'm not sure," I reply softly, still staring at the now bare pale-green chipped wall where the newspaper photo hung. I don't want to start in on how pathetic the Cubs are, with star infielder Ernie Banks their only decent player, and how they'll always be a last-place team.

She shifts. "Are you going to be okay at Sullivan High, starting as a senior?" I turn from the wall and face her. The concern is genuine, not only in her high-pitched voice, but in her gleaming brown eyes and furrowed brow of her pale round face, set off with short black hair that is especially curly and unkempt in the summer day's humidity. She looks genuinely worried for a twelve-year-old who's often on guard against her teasing brother.

"I don't know. It's not going to be fun, though." I stop myself from speculating any further because I fear losing control, that the wave of tears will exit my belly and chest and convulse me uncontrollably.

She doesn't argue. "I still have another year, so I don't mind so much having to get used to a new school and making new friends. I can't begin to think of doing what you'll be doing."

Before I can nod my agreement with her, another voice intrudes—that of Dad's cousin Werner. He has a high-pitched voice for a man, made distinctive by his clear German accent, and he is chattering away like it is some kind of day of celebration. I'm not sure why he's made the trip here from the North Side, except that Dad has apparently accepted his offer to "help out," even while knowing he'd be an annoyance. I have to assume Dad thought Werner could help enough that we might cut a half hour or hour off the movers' time and save a few dollars.

Looking at Werner now, breathing heavily and his thin remnants of white hair matted to his dome of a head just from the simple exertion of carrying a few books, he strikes me as a definite health risk. He is so fleshy and out of shape. How could he help except to demoralize everyone more than they already are?

He's not giving up his Saturday, when he could be with his family at the beach, because he sincerely cares about us. Maybe he sees our situation as a rescue mission, since he's been after my parents for years to abandon the South Side to the growing hordes of Negroes. Or maybe he gets personal satisfaction from bringing more relatives to the glory of life on the North Side.

"You guys are going to love Devon Avenue," he chirps, his Germanic accent more noticeable than usual to me, as he reaches the open door of our third-floor apartment with the book box under one arm. "It's just like 71st Street was five years ago, full of kosher hot dog places and delis and movie theaters. None of the wig stores or fried-chicken choints you see now." Germans have trouble with the "J" sound.

When no one answers his monologue about the wonders of the North Side, Werner pauses at the wide open door to our apartment and sets the book box down so he can grab at the bottom portion of the sleeveless white t-shirt clinging to his sweaty body and use it to wipe his face. In the process, he unselfconsciously exposes his rubbery gut over his low-lying Bermuda shorts. He then continues obliviously on, as if everyone has expressed surprised amazement about his description of Devon Avenue. And without regard that the Negro neighbors in our apartment building might be offended by his talk, by his references to them in the demeaning Yiddish slang as "schvartzes."

"On Saturday mornings during the summer, everyone gathers at the Belmont Harbor, and watches the sail boats moving in and out of the harbor. It's beautiful. It makes you forget about Rainbow Beach."

"It can't be as nice as Rainbow Beach," Emily says in thin-voiced objection, as she stands just behind Werner, holding a small table lamp by its neck.

But even a twelve-year-old girl's mild dissent can't be allowed to stand. "At Belmont Harbor you have everything you had at Rainbow," Werner counters. "You have the beach, the rocks, the tennis courts, the softball fields." He hesitates. I know what he wants to say, and I am half tempted to fill in the void about what's missing, but I don't.

Emily is silent as well. Having dispensed with the little girl, Werner moves on to Mom. "Esther, I know Hilde can't wait for you to arrive. She's already talking about how she's going to take you to her favorite bakery and kosher butcher on Devon. And they'll even gift wrap whatever you buy, no questions asked."

Werner fancies himself a comedian. One of his favorite joke lines is to buy a piece of pastry at a bakery or some pencils at Woolworth, and then tell the checkout clerk: "You don't have to gift wrap that."

He had a series of running jokes like that—jokes that were sort of cute the first time you heard them, but became stale. Like when he describes his work as a manufacturers' rep selling women's clothing to retailers: "I am in and out of women's underwear." I used to watch his wife, Hilde, a beautiful raven-haired woman, for her reaction to one or another of his jokes, and I never caught even the slightest hint of a smile. It was almost as if she stopped hearing them years ago.

Mom's mind is definitely elsewhere. "I just hope there's a good shul near our new apartment. A good Reform shul. Now that our shul has been turned into a Nation of Islam temple, whatever that is."

The mention of Nation of Islam is a signal to Dad, who has been silent as well, until now. "We don't know if that means it's for the schvartzes or the Arabs," he says to Werner, with a tone of sincere exasperation in his voice.

"It's for Negroes," I say softly. "Negroes who are Muslims, who want to live separately." I decide not to elaborate about how they are led by Elijah Muhammad, a Negro leader who refers to whites as "the devil," and how I learned about the group. Not a productive shift for our conversation at this stage of the game, in any event.

It really doesn't matter because Werner, along with my parents, act as if I didn't say anything. "Nation of Islam, Nation of Pislam," he chortles. "Nothing like that on the North Side. You'll have so many real shuls to choose from, nice Reform shuls, because I know you like Reform, though I'm not sure why. There are even more Conservative shuls, if you change your mind and want to join us at our shul. Hilde loves the rabbi there."

He almost makes it sound as if we are moving to another country, when we're just going a few miles, from one side of Chicago to the other.

He's not finished. "Kurt, no more worrying about the schvartze punks pushing you around when you get off the El on 63rd Street, or walk home from the bus. Those days are over. The North Side is punk free." Dad is looking away from Werner, lifting a bulky thick-wood-framed oil painting of a German country scene off a wall hook in the living room. But I can tell he's been listening because a slight smile creases his long normally serious face in acknowledgment of Werner's clumsy attempt at humor.

The smile reveals the dimple on his chin, the dimple that Mom sometimes half jokes is what first attracted her to Dad when they met at a dance in Chicago back in the late 1930s—"much more than his dancing, I'll tell you that." If relatives or friends are present, she'll sometimes continue the story by saying I have Dad's long face, including the dimple, except my dimple is more prominent because I smile more than Dad. No doubt "the girls will be after him" as a result, she usually continues, as I blush in embarrassment.

While it's true, I do have a younger version of Dad's angular face, including the prominent nose, and his once-full mop of black hair, I'm probably an inch or two taller than his five-feet-seven, but likely a few pounds lighter because I don't have his expanding midriff. But what kid wants to have his mom speculating about his dating, before he's even started dating, and has no idea how it's all going to go?

At last, as we all stand silently and with teary eyes looking back over the empty apartment, Werner seems to give Mom, Dad, Emily and me a final scan, and then says something that actually makes some sense: "The Stark family doesn't look very excited to be starting a new life."

Dad and Mom stare at him, disbelieving. Then Mom speaks softly. "Nothing against Hilde. But we hate to leave. We love South Shore. It's the most wonderful place we've ever lived. This beautiful apartment. Wonderful neighbors. Well, maybe not so wonderful any more. A

5

wonderful shul. The most beautiful beaches in the world. And now we're being chased out of our own home, our own neighborhood." I can tell from the contorted half smile that dominates her pretty round face and has her piercing brown eyes blinking rapidly that she is trying hard to suppress sobs.

Werner is undeterred. "Believe me, I know just how you feel. Don't forget, five years ago we were the ones who were running, when the schvartze pushed me out of my store on Stony Island, forced us to give up our beautiful apartment. What I'm trying to tell you is that you're going to a place as wonderful as South Shore used to be. Montrose Beach is as beautiful as Rainbow Beach. Devon Avenue is as great as 71st Street. Lincoln Park is as pretty as Jackson Park. And Wrigley Field is much nicer than Comiskey Park, even if the team is lousy."

Mom and Dad lock eyes, their sad faces glistening with sweat, and their eyes with tears. Emily and I glance at each other and look away. No one says anything, but we are all thinking the same thing: nothing can be as wonderful as South Shore used to be.

I can feel the heat rising from my chest, into my face and out the top of my head. What a jerk, I think for maybe the tenth time this day. Finally, I can't resist. "It sounds like the promised land, Uncle Werner. Great beaches, lots of delis, wonderful shuls…" I hesitate, as Werner did earlier, except this time I fill in the void. "…and no schvartzes." I give the word "schvartzes" special cynical emphasis.

"That's no way to talk to Uncle Werner!" Dad exclaims, truly incredulous. "Don't forget, his father helped get me into this country when everyone was saying no to our family. His father signed the government papers and committed money they didn't have. He did that when our rich relatives were pleading poverty. We might never have made it, otherwise you might never have been born. Never forget that!"

I've hit a sore spot, one I've hit before when I've confessed nasty thoughts about Werner and one I can't counter in any kind of rational, or cynical, way.

Rather than join in the get-Jeff-free-for-all now taking shape, Werner stays fixated on North Side glories. "Let's just think about fun, Jeff. You know as well as any of us that the most fun thing about the North Side, the thing none of us will ever get tired of…" He looks expectantly at me with an excited half smile, as if I'm inhabiting his mind and should shout the answer.

When I remain silent, he holds out his arms and hands. "Riverview! You'll be able to go to Riverview any time you want. All of us can go together. You remember the weekend you spent with us, when we took you and Richard and Beverly to Riverview?"

I have to keep myself from smiling. It truly was a wonderful weekend a couple years back, with his two kids, who are about my age. Any time at Riverview was the absolute best. For a kid in Chicago, visiting Riverview was the funnest thing you could do, beginning with the decisions about which rides to do and when—should The Bobs, the fastest and scariest roller coaster in the world, come first, or last? What about the Parachute Jump, the Rotor, the Chutes? Riverview was so vast and had so many rides and shows and games that you could spend a whole day there, and not have done everything you wanted.

Werner interrupts my thoughts. "You know, now that you've grown so much, I bet you could get a lot of bulls eyes at the African Dip." Werner would have to reminisce about the dunk, one of creepiest corners of Riverview. It was a row of three or four cages, each occupied by a Negro man sitting on a platform dressed in a big coat. They acted good humored, teasing the white patrons—"You couldn't hit the broad side of a barn"— to throw a ball forty feet at a metal disk target to release the platform and dunk the Negro into a pool of water below.

But Dad seems not to have heard any of this, or at least he's pretending not to have heard Werner's shift of the conversation. Dad's mind remains stuck on my insult of Werner.

"He's sore because he has to leave his schwartze girlfriend. He doesn't understand he'll be much better off on the North Side, meeting nice Jewish girls."

Now I've lost any pretense of control. "You can say her name!" I yell back at Dad. I pause as his narrow face seems to lengthen, maybe from the stubble of dark beard that has spread on his chin, and he takes on a pained expression. "You don't even know her name, do you?" Without letting him dangle more than a few seconds in the silence of humiliation, I answer. "Well, it's Valerie."

I use the shocked silence that ensues to turn and bolt out the door and skip down the stairs. Angry as I am, I feel a slight sense of relief, not only for having let Werner know how annoying he is, but for having let Dad know how hurtful he is and has been. We'd bumped heads over Valerie before, but this was the first time he brought her up to someone outside our immediate family. I know he's unaware of Valerie's injuries, that have had her stuck at Lying In Hospital at the University of Chicago, and more recently at her home, but still.

It's a short skip and jump from the apartment entrance to the moving-truck, and finally some luck is on my side. My old JC Higgins bicycle, bought at Sears Roebuck, is the first item I encounter in the truck, so I can easily roll it down the steel gang plank and hop on, riding toward Jackson Park. As heavy as the August air is, the breeze I've created by riding feels cooling.

2

"Running." For all the many upsets of that moving-out morning, it is Werner's weird description of our impending departure from South Shore that ricochets through my mind as I pedal my bike east toward the lake along 67th Street, the grand trees of Jackson Park on my left.

It isn't as if the idea of us fleeing an enemy is new. In the never-ending moaning and complaining by my parents and their friends about our racially changing South Side neighborhoods, we are invariably "running" or being "chased" or "forced out" or "pushed"...or our neighborhood's "getting darker" or being "taken over," by Negro hordes who refuse to "stay in their own neighborhoods." It is as if we are hapless victims, powerless to do anything but pack up our clothes and furnishings, again and again, and move a few blocks or even a few miles onward to another white enclave, before the inevitable pursuit begins yet again.

I should point out before going much further that there was one big positive in all the "running": It made possible my meeting Valerie.

Without getting too deeply into the sociology of living in a racial cauldron, let's just say that my family's hand-to-mouth existence prevented us from ever vaulting too far ahead of the poor Negro areas that were expanding in our direction. In other words, our poverty kept my family in the school district where I had to attend Hyde Park High School, which had a mixture of Negro and white kids, rather than in a more distant neighboring district that was wealthier, and completely white.

Werner's chatter about Riverview and the African Dip rekindled the strange circumstances under which I first encountered Valerie. We were both students at Hyde Park High, though we knew nothing about the other.

I usually got over to Riverview about once a year. As Werner mentioned, I went with his family a couple times when I was in elementary school. Once I got to high school, I would go with my best friends, Nate Higgins and Lee Springer. It was a long trip on the elevated, subway, and buses from South Shore to Riverview, which was on the North Side. Even as I got older, the excitement of Riverview didn't dim. If anything, it became stronger. It always began with the sighting, from a mile or two away, of the towering parachute tower. Then, on arrival at the vast grounds came the smells, of hot dogs, burgers, and cotton candy.

It was late August on this particular trip, a couple weeks before the start of school and the start of my junior year. I had just gotten off the Rotor, and I felt this awful urge to puke. I had made the unforgivable mistake of eating one of the wonderful hot dogs before going on the Rotor, a big metal cylinder that took maybe fifty people at a time who stood with their backs against the curved wall. It then began turning, slowly at first, gradually becoming a rapid spin, and after a minute or so, the floor dropped down, leaving everyone pinned in place with the power of centrifugal force. After a couple more minutes of spinning, the floor came back up, and the riders were deposited, dizzy, some on their hands and knees to get their bearings.

I stumbled out into the bright sunshine, and caught sight of two Negro teenage girls looking our way. They stood out because they were pretty, but more so because they were Negro. I realized at that moment how unusual it was to see Negroes at Riverview among the throngs who always crowded the place.

A minute or so after this sighting, the nausea overtook me.

I moved to some grass at the edge of the walkway exiting the Rotor and deposited the hot dog remains, right there in bright daylight and in public. I then kept walking as if nothing happened. I hoped the girls weren't still looking my way.

I did feel better after throwing up my lunch. Nate and Lee had a good laugh, especially because they had been smart enough to resist the hot dog temptation. We continued on our way, hitting our favorite rides in the order in which we had negotiated them over the nearly two hours we spent on the elevated and bus to get to Riverview. Next came the Pair O Chutes, where you sat on a bench in a wood-and-rope basket, and were hoisted up for what seemed forever—probably 200 feet or so on the tower that marked the amusement park from afar. That was the thrill of the thing, that you kept inching up and up to a creaky sound and, finally, when the basket was released, you were jolted up for a few seconds until the big parachute attached by cables above the basked opened fully and smoothly eased the basket down.

After that came Aladdin's Castle, a maze of slanted floors and distorting mirrors that always had a crowd of guys near the entrance. I had never taken much notice of the crowd, except this time I saw why they gathered, when a powerful burst of air from below the fourth step leading to the entrance blew up the dresses of a few women ahead of us, to their surprised giggles and embarrassment. That was apparently a regular thing every fifteen or twenty seconds, part of Riverview's crazy entertainment.

Then came the Chute the Chutes, a water ride in which a big carrier, kind of like a military landing craft, zoomed down a long slide into an artificial pond. The fun part came when it splashed into the pond, and the driver in back of the carrier began gyrating the boat so everyone got splashed and tossed around as the boat wobbled from side to side.

Finally, the roller coasters—The Comet, The Silver Flash, and The Wild Mouse—all leading up to the main attraction, the most terrifying roller coaster of all, The Bobs.

I at once loved and hated The Bobs. I loved how it was billed as the fastest roller coaster on the planet, at ninety-five miles per hour, but hated it, hated myself for having decided to get on the ride, when I was seated in a red cushioned seat in one of the bright green cars, and it was creaking up to the top in preparation for a nearly ninety-degree dive that would leave my still-sensitive stomach not far from my mouth.

3

It was as Nate, Lee and I were still laughingly reliving the roller coaster terror, walking past the freak show, which we always wondered about but never witnessed, that I saw Valerie again. "I think those girls go to Hyde Park," Nate nudged me as the two walked about twenty-five feet in front of us. "I'm pretty sure one of them was in my home room last year."

Even now, five years removed from that moment, in the comfort of my college library, it feels like only yesterday. But it really was true—in that moment my life began changing in ways I never could have imagined. Because just then, two tall slender white guys in white t-shirts and jeans, who looked to be a few years older than the girls and us, approached them from the side and began walking with them.

As the girls slowed, and we came closer, I could hear one of the guys: "My friend Vinnie, he's got his convertible here. Wanna take a ride with us? There's a party close by, we'll stop, have some fun."

The two girls didn't seem to have answered, or if they did, it wasn't the answer they were looking for, because the two white guys moved a little closer to the girls, and Vinnie was talking in a raised voice. "Whatsamatter, we're not good enough for ya? You rather have one of those darkies over there?" He motioned toward the African Dip, and the Negro men sitting on the stools in each of three cages.

At that moment, one of the girls, whom I would eventually learn was Valerie, stopped in her tracks, and turned to face the two white guys. Her bouffant hairdo looked smart and fresh, her tight blue pedal pushers accentuated her blossoming small body, her bright brown eyes flashed, and the smooth light brown skin of her delicate face creased in a seemingly incongruous near snarl: "Can't you boys take a hint? We have to spell it out for you? We don't want a ride in your car. We don't want anything to do with you. Just turn your white asses around and go back to where you come from."

My jaw dropped and my eyes widened. Not only because she had stood up to them, but how she threw their racial slurs right back at them.

Vinnie and friend seemed even more shocked than I was. So much so that they stood frozen in their tracks, as the girls continued walking, though at a faster pace than before. With confused looks on their faces, the two white guys looked at each other and retreated to the midway's sidelines, and joined a group of four or five other white teens, also in white t-shirts, who were guffawing. I presumed they had witnessed Valerie's putdown, and were teasing their pals about their bungled pickup effort.

I motioned to Nate and Lee that we should veer left, toward the African Dip. I sensed the whites would be plotting revenge against the girls, and I was right. They were discretely passing around a paper bag, each taking a short swig from the bottle inside, their voices growing louder as the bottle passed from lips to lips.

"They need some hard white cocks, that's what they need," said Vinnie, who had greasy blond hair combed back.

"Let's get Vinnie's car, meet them outside, stuff 'em in," said another.

A counter-plan quickly hatched itself in my mind. Without saying anything to Nate and Lee, I approached the group, and spoke directly to Vinnie. "Hey, $3 says I can knock those guys off their stools more than you in a couple rounds." I motioned toward the Negro men in the African Dip.

Vinnie looked me up and down, and with encouragement from his friends ("This pipsqueak don't got nothin'," said one) broke into a smile that revealed nice teeth, punctuated by a gold tooth just off to the right of his top front teeth.

"Okay, shorty. You're on. Just don't go cryin' to mommy when you lose your money."

What Vinnie and his friends didn't know was that I had been playing a lot of softball in the previous few weeks, playing third base, and getting practice making throws to first base. Vinnie was tall, but didn't look especially athletic, and that became even clearer when he began awkwardly throwing the forty feet or so at the target on a curtain adjoining one of the African Dip cages.

I fingered the single dollar bill that remained in my pocket after the roller coaster rides. I figured, or hoped, that Nate and Lee had enough left if I needed help paying Vinnie.

We each had five tosses per twenty-cent round. Vinnie's first four throws missed the target, though each came a little closer. Finally, on the fifth toss, he hit the target and dunked the middle aged Negro fellow. The man didn't seem fazed "Ya got lucky!" he shouted as he climbed back on his board and blew water from his mouth. "I bet ya can't do it again. Hey, I know ya can't do it again."

I realized at that moment that the Negro men in the cages were like actors, trying their best to irritate the white customers, to create more business. I wondered if they got some kind of bonus based on the number of tosses that were purchased.

I remained confident I could do better than Vinnie. I also reminded myself to not rush my throws, both to help my chances of an accurate toss, and to give Valerie and her friend more time to depart the grounds.

My first two tosses just missed the target. But number three clanged the metal disk, and dunked the man. Once he was back up, number four missed. I took an extra long time on toss number five, so much so that Vinnie got impatient. "Yer stalling!" he razzed.

Bingo, throw number five hit the target, and I was now ahead, two to one. The next round went exactly the same, so I finished ahead four dunks to two for Vinnie.

Before I could bask more than a few seconds in the glory of winning $3, Vinnie and his friends were departing the scene. "Hey, you owe me $3!" I called to Vinnie.

He looked over his shoulder and sneered. "Ya gonna have to come get it from me, asshole!" Vinnie and friends continued walking down the midway.

I stifled my anger. I had accomplished my main goal of giving the girls time—probably about fifteen minutes. And I still had enough money to get home. Not a terrible outcome, given where things were headed fifteen minutes earlier.

4

On the second day back to Hyde Park High, a couple weeks after the Riverview episode, Nate told me he had figured out that the two Negro girls we had helped were Tanya Gray, the girl in his home room the previous year, and Valerie Davis.

He didn't know much further about either one, and that was the end of the subject...for him. I found myself on the lookout for her, in the hallway between classes, in the cafeteria at lunch, outside after school.

Whenever I saw her, I just became more intrigued, and captivated.

I had had crushes on girls before. There was Debbie Barton at the temple youth group that occasionally had Saturday evening dances. I enjoyed dancing with her because she was cute and chatty, not standoffish like a number of the girls. Brushing up against her big breasts made dancing especially entertaining. Unfortunately, lots of other boys were drawn to her as well, probably for similar reasons, and it became difficult even to dance with her because of all the competition. Then there was Jen Golden, whom I knew from grade school, and whom I became infatuated with enough that I asked her to a temple youth group hay ride event, where we went to a farm and then were taken by a horse-drawn wagon out onto dark fields, where some of the kids made out. Jen and I kissed a couple times, but it felt awkward and rushed. She seemed embarrassed when I saw her at school the next week, and things just petered out.

There was something about Valerie that was different from the other girls I had been attracted to, and I don't just mean her race. There was something about her energy and confidence that made her seem more mature, and sexier, than other sophomore or junior girls I knew.

That sense of her ratcheted up a few notches when she appeared at a basketball game later that fall, as a cheerleader. It happened to be at an afternoon game against our arch enemy, South Shore High School, just a few miles to the south. Because it was located in what was still an all-white neighborhood, the school, and its basketball team, were all white. And the community seemed determined to keep it that way; one story that made the rounds at Hyde Park High was that the South Shore students turned their backs at their lockers as the school's first Negro teacher walked into the school that September. Hyde Park for a number of years had had several Negro teachers, without any signs of racial resentment.

Anyway, Hyde Park's team was all Negro, except for one white who played reserve. Nate, Lee, and I rarely went to basketball or football games, partly because of the racial and gang tension that was often part of the events. It wasn't just that the teams played especially hard to beat the guys of the other race, but that the student fans got so worked up during the game that there were occasionally brawls when the competition ended. Sometimes these were race based, such as when we played South Shore High School. Sometimes they were based on gang or other clique rivalries.

There was even a saying at Hyde Park High, "We don't always win the game, but we win the fight after the game."

We went to this game because Nate had a cousin playing on the South Shore team, and Nate practically pleaded with Lee and me to come along with him. We just made Nate agree that we wouldn't cheer for his cousin during the game and risk drawing the ire of our Negro classmates.

To my pleasant surprise, Valerie appeared as a cheerleader during the intermission between periods. She was on the freshman-sophomore cheerleading squad, which got second billing to the regular cheerleaders, but she stood out as the most animated, and sexy, cheerleader of her all-Negro group, jumping around and doing cheers—"Gimme an H, gimme a Y..." and then "Go Indians!"—with her dark blue pleated skirt flying all over the place, showing off her shapely legs. Her friend Tanya was a cheerleader as well, and though she was a little chunkier and not quite as agile on her feet, she was clearly inspired by Valerie's enthusiasm.

I pointed out Valerie and Tanya to Nate and Lee, and they remembered the girls from Riverview. As the squad's intermission routine built up in its enthusiasm, reaching a crescendo when the six-member squad made a pyramid with Valerie on top, groups of Hyde Park students got up and joined in applause and cheering. Nate, Lee, and I joined in, and I nudged them by intensifying my applause and cheering at the end, so much that we were the only students still standing even though their routine had ended. Negro and white students alike looked over at us, as did Valerie and Tanya. They smiled broadly, clearly appreciating the positive feedback, though I thought I saw a bit of confusion in their expressions—perhaps wondering if we were from South Shore High School and what we were doing cheering for them. Nate definitely wasn't pleased, fearing we had potentially made targets of ourselves to the Negro majority. "Way to go, Jeff," he whispered loudly, and sarcastically, out of the side of his mouth as we sat down following my gesture.

At the start of the final quarter, South Shore took a sizable lead, and I nudged Nate and Lee to leave before the end, to avoid us becoming targets in a possible "fight after the game." Lo and behold, Valerie had departed around the same time. She was with a group of five or six Negro girls who looked to be cheerleaders—they had changed out of their uniforms—and when I waved at her in front of school, she grinned and waved back.

15

I was smitten. I started fantasizing about being with her, holding her and kissing her. I tried to catch myself, and tell myself how unrealistic I was being.

Whites and Negroes just didn't date much. It was as if whites and Negroes had enough trouble just getting along day to day that we didn't want to inject sex and emotional attachment into the whole equation. So white guys generally avoided Negro girls, even if they were cute and pretty and intelligent, and bronze skinned, like Valerie, and the Negro girls did the same with white guys, regardless of whether they were popular and handsome or, like me, studious and nerdy. Negro boys with white girls seemed even more remote. The only example of interracial dating I knew of, and it wasn't a good one, was when Nate got it into his head to ask Yoshana Bradley for a date. Lee and I were shocked.

Yoshana looked like a model—slender, sharp nose, high forehead, and nearly straight shoulder-length hair—who held herself erect and tall and dressed in obviously expensive dresses and blouses. She was in our French class, and while all the boys, white or Negro, couldn't help but drool over her, she seemed aloof. Word had it that she was dating a Negro boy from another school.

Nate was brave enough to not only pursue Yoshana, but also to tell Lee and me about the unfortunate outcome. She said she was really busy for the next couple months doing modeling, and couldn't go out.

I just wanted to get to the point where I could even think about asking Valerie for a date. And then, amazingly, at the start of second semester that January, I found myself in the same geometry class with her.

We sat in different parts of the classroom, but one day after class, I managed to catch her on the way out and inquire if was going to be cheerleading at an upcoming basketball game. "No, I had to quit being a cheerleader because of all my school work," she said, and she looked sad.

"Gee, that's too bad, because you were so good," I said. "You were a real natural when I saw you at that game against South Shore High."

She looked directly at me, seeming genuinely pleased. Before she could respond further, two friends of hers came by calling her name, and she was off with them, though not before she gave me a big smile and breathed a "gotta go."

I thought I'd catch her after another class, and somehow steer the conversation to that day at Riverview a few months earlier, so I could let her know what happened after she and Tanya departed, and she could see me as a hero and protector.

But alas, I didn't get another chance to talk with her again before The Fight.

5

It was late on a Tuesday morning in early April, about six months after the Cuban Missile Crisis of October 1962, and maybe an hour after the weekly 10:30 a.m. blare of air-raid siren testing across Chicago that was supposed to warn us of a nuclear attack and its threat to incinerate us all in a nuclear holocaust.

On this day, as on most other Tuesday mornings, teachers ignored the siren and the recommended response that we pull down classroom window shades and hide under our desks. We just continued about our gym activities, which consisted of lethargic jumping jacks, followed by an uneventful kickball class. It was just as gym class was letting out that the fireworks began.

I was walking out with Nate, and we were lamenting how we were each struggling to complete a paper about Theodore Roosevelt due in AP history in a few days. Nate, who was on my right, was saying he thought we should visit the main public library on Randolph Street downtown to find some impressive resources we could cite in our papers. "They usually have some old biographies and history books with good stuff."

I was half listening to Nate, because the other half of my listening was focused on my left, where I was being targeted by big bad Booker Walsh. Booker was a gouster—don't ask me where the term for Negro tough guys who spoke in crude street talk came from—and one of the huskier gousters at that, with muscular forearms and shoulders which seemed to make him much bigger than me, even though in reality he wasn't more than an inch or two taller.

Booker was in a very bad mood. I could tell because he and I went back three or four years. He was in my eighth grade class at Parkside Elementary School, and early on seemed like a smart kid who cared about school. He'd raise his hand with answers when the teacher put arithmetic problems on the blackboard. But then he disappeared from class for days at a time, and when he returned, he'd be out of synch with what was happening in class. I remember a couple times the teacher would call on him to answer some question or another about reading we had done, and it was obvious he had no idea what the answer was. There'd be snickers from those of us who were up on the reading assignments, and I could tell from the confused look on his face that Booker was embarrassed, and angry. There would be more embarrassment when Booker didn't have homework ready to be turned in when a teacher called for it from each student by name. By the second half of the year, he seemed like he had changed a lot, as if he no longer cared much about school. He'd sit in class slouched at his wooden desk, with his legs stretched out, looking up at the ceiling, or out the window—anywhere but at the teacher.

During gym, he and a few of his friends targeted me in games of dodge ball. At first, it had been sort of good natured, and I had kind of asked for it by being a wise guy and taunting them that they could never come close to hitting me with the pink rubber ball. And usually they couldn't, though Booker was the most accurate thrower. They even took to calling me "the white flash."

After games a couple times, he and one of his friends, Maurice, pushed and tripped me for no reason I could see.

I assumed it was because of his many absences that Booker was forced to repeat eighth grade. When he arrived at Hyde Park High he was one of the huskiest freshmen, since he was a year older than most of the other freshmen. He also had a very big chip on his shoulder, especially for white boys. Maybe in his mind, it was white boys who had laughed at him when he struggled in class, but whatever the reason, on this day he was in an especially foul mood.

Walking slowly down the wide stairs from the second-floor gym, I tried to stay focused on my conversation with Nate, to my right, in hopes Booker would get bored with talking to the back of my turned head and find others to bother. Nate was about my height, but with disheveled dirty-blond hair and a round face whose pug nose somehow made him look more relaxed and smiling than me, even as Booker's abuse was escalating. But Nate's seeming nonchalance had no noticeable effect on Booker, and as we all approached the second-floor landing, I could sense Booker's continued presence to my left. And his energy remained laser focused on me, his monologue rapidly degenerating.

"I know yo mama. She a ho'. Who she sleep with last night? Bet I know."

Booker and two or three of his friends, who were immediately behind him, doubled up in laughter.

Even though I continued talking to Nate, I can't remember at this point what I was saying. I was just hoping, praying, that Booker and friends would leave, and they weren't leaving.

As we neared the first-floor landing, Booker had shifted his monologue to my little sister. How did he even know I had a sister? Emily was still in eighth grade at an elementary school.

"My friends tell me youz sister just like yo mama, only better! Ooee! I can't wait!"

I could feel heat and anger rising in me, competing with mortal fear. I turned my head toward Booker, not sure what, if anything, I could say.

No way I could have gotten a word in, because Booker was still going strong. "Ooh, he lookin' at me. You want some of that pussy, don't you, honky?"

Something deep down inside told me there was nothing I could say, that I had to do something, anything, to stop his verbal assault. And that, in any event, his verbal assault was about to become a physical assault. As if possessed by some outside force, I told him to fuck his own sister if he thought that was so cool. Two stairs before the first-floor landing, he shoved me against the stair railing.

Before I knew it, we were wrestling, stumbling down to the first floor landing, and I was smelling something that resembled Campbell's vegetable soup on his breath. Amazingly, I had him in a headlock—I couldn't believe I had any kind of advantage since he was so much huskier than I was.

But I had been taking wrestling classes at the YMCA on 71st Street on and off over the past few months, and one move I'd learned pretty well was a headlock. If you leaned in and kept your legs back, your opponent couldn't grab you and get loose.

In fact, he was usually helpless, even if much bigger than you. My friends and I practiced putting each other in headlocks, and working at freeing ourselves, sometimes by tickling our opponent in the neck and ribs.

One problem with holding Booker in a headlock was that his kinky hair felt like Brillo rubbing against my left elbow cradle and the inside of my upper arm. I wished I hadn't decided to wear a short-sleeved shirt that spring day. Plus, my legs were trembling, no doubt from my fear.

My biggest problem, though, was that the sight of me gaining an advantage on Booker wasn't bringing the crowd, the thirty or so mostly Negroes who had quickly gathered around the two of us, to my side. Instead, it was prompting all kinds of taunting, mostly of Booker by his friends. "Lookie Booka, gettin' his ass kicked by a honky. Shee-it."

6

Holding Booker in a headlock on the first floor landing, with the crowd rooting against me, was worsening my budding queasy feeling. It was panic, coursing through my body over the inevitable outcome if I continued with my advantage over Booker. One of his friends could give me a shove or a punch. Or something worse. It quickly became clear as day there was no way I'd be allowed to walk out of this melee the "winner."

I suspect it was those "winner" fantasies that caused me to lose my concentration just long enough for Booker to push me backwards and lose my balance so he could break free. Suddenly we faced each other, standing crouched, arms nearly in boxing poses, trying to figure out what to do next.

His answer came first, as he almost nonchalantly put his right hand into the pocket of his baggy gray pants, and pulled out something light-colored and shiny. He was holding a curved off-white piece of what looked like ivory at the front of his large brown fist. A push-button knife.

The panic that had enveloped me earlier was replaced by a sense of having been transported to a new realm. I had been in fights before with white kids, usually over a trip or a shove in touch football or basketball, but there was never any serious worry about how it would all end. Even if someone got the better of me, pinning me to the ground, the fight always ended with a sense of relief, of anger having been purged, and moving on. Here on this landing, there was no such reassurance.

I had seen a push-button knife just once, at the home of a white classmate I knew only from Boy Scouts, but it made a huge impression. He was a cop's son, which may explain why he had the knife. I remember being amazed, then awed, when he pushed the small stainless steel button near the front of the knife, and a narrow glistening blade sprang out, a soft spring-like echo accompanying the release. It was riveting entertainment that Saturday afternoon months earlier for a group of teenagers standing around in a living room. On this Tuesday morning, surrounded by adversaries, I could sense only a gathering sensation of nausea in my gut. That was all I needed, to puke in front of this crowd. Or maybe it would gross them out enough that everyone scattered in disgust.

I quickly scanned the crowd for Lee. Please, Lee, be around. Because he was one of few whites in the "average" classes—the classes just between remedial and accelerated in our school's tiered system, and populated mostly by Negroes—and he had become friendly with some gousters. Desperate times called for desperate measures.

I harbored the hope that a single voice raised on my behalf from someone respected or trusted by the crowd could turn this situation around. I fantasized that Lee or one of his gouster friends was on friendly enough terms with Booker to persuade him to put the knife away.

I saw Nate and another white friend, George, on the fringes of the circle of spectators, looking around, as if searching for adult help, or trying to anticipate the danger to themselves. George was, if anything, even more useless than Nate. He was a kid made round by too many of his mom's gooey chocolate brownies and chocolate chip cookies, and a math genius who built amazing science projects like pretend robots, but he had no idea how to pacify gousters. And there was no sign of Lee.

As the prospect of help from my friends faded in short order, my mind was doing new calculations. Maybe I should just tell Booker I was giving up, that he was the winner. My gut responded badly, with even more uncomfortable churning. While the tactic seemed logical in the abstract, this scene on the first floor landing wasn't abstract. My gut's more desperate turmoil let me know that giving up wouldn't play well. I sensed it would simply whet Booker's and the crowd's lust for some sort of revenge fulfillment, like beating or stabbing me.

So I stood there seemingly paralyzed as I watched Booker's right thumb move along the switchblade's ivory housing, in search of the button that would spring the blade loose.

"Youz made a big mistake, white boy," he said matter-of-factly, his dull dark eyes looking directly into mine for the first time since our fight began. The darkness of his eyes seemed to make them blend into the darkness of his skin and his closely cropped black hair. I barely took note of the nearly elegant light blue and yellow Italian knit shirt that clung tightly to his muscular chest and arms and gave a strange color contrast to his appearance, almost making him look like what I imagined of a Mafioso. His thumb continued to scan the switchblade's ivory. "You dun messed with the wrong nigga."

His thumb was just settling on the stainless-steel button. My focus on that tiny image seemed to have blocked everything else out—the catcalls, the placement of Nate and George. I awaited the sound of the blade springing out as a matter of natural inevitability. How could it be any different?

I remember feeling envy for my white friends on the periphery. It was as if I was imprisoned in this new realm, without options, and could only observe them in their freedom. All I could think to do was move into dodge-ball mode, dancing around to avoid Booker's thrusts with the knife. That might be good for a very brief time, till either Booker or the crowd-turned-mob got me.

So disordered was my mind that I didn't even recognize the possibility of deliverance when it arrived. It came from directly behind Booker, in the form of a soft but full female voice that barely registered on my panicked psyche. "Put it away, Booker."

The voice couldn't have been heard very widely what with all the taunting and shouting, but alas, the noise level noticeably diminished.

In retrospect, it must have been the calm in the voice, in a sea of agitation. I don't know. All I know is I saw Booker hesitate, his confident stare-down replaced by a building look of bewilderment. His once-dull eyes were now nearly sparkling, darting around, blinking, his glowering suddenly less confident and menacing, his demeanor more cautious. He looked everywhere, it seemed, but not right behind him, to the source of the voice.

It was Valerie. I don't know why I hadn't taken notice of her earlier in the fight, but there she was, slender and bronze skinned, her small pretty face highlighted by large bright deep-brown eyes, and the bouffant hairdo. Maybe it was because her current persona seemed so completely out of character with the animated upbeat girl I knew from geometry class. Standing behind Booker, bent forward slightly from the waist, not only was she the only Negro who seemed to be not cheering him on, but she wore a grimly serious and intense expression.

She was also probably the only one among the thirty or so Negroes in the crowd dressed like an Ivy Leaguer, our term for an upscale middle class Negro. That meant she was wearing bobby socks and black loafers together with a plaid green and red wool skirt and white blouse that made it difficult to tell how shapely or well endowed she was. As the importance of her presence gradually intruded into my consciousness, it occurred to me she was studying Booker's right hand nearly as intently as I was.

Ever so slowly, as if he was hoping no one would notice, Booker's right hand, complete with unopened knife, retreated back into the front pocket. I instinctively took the pause as an opportunity to step back, letting my arms and shoulders drop. I quickly made a quarter turn away from him as if I was ready to continue my way into the first-floor hallway.

"Sheeit, I don't got time for no crazy honky," Booker said softly, so only those near to him could hear his weak excuse for ending the fight. To my expanding relief, he went about straightening his Italian knit shirt, which got rumpled and shifted out of place during our wrestling. As quickly as the crowd gathered, it dispersed. Only three or four minutes had elapsed, but it seemed as if hours had gone by. Only then did I become fully aware of how quickly my heart was racing and how short of breath I had become.

Nate scampered quickly over alongside of me. His round face, usually dominated by a nonchalant expression, now looked pained, confused. His dirty blond hair, normally at least nominally neat, was now nearly disheveled. And he seemed to be having trouble catching his breath as he spoke: "That was close, man...what were you thinking? Or were you thinking?"

Jeez, I thought. I was the one nearly getting carved up, and you're looking and acting like you went through a fight. I wanted to shake my head in amazement and say something nasty, but I caught myself.

I could kind of see where Nate was probably pretty scared himself.

Neither of us had the bearing to intimidate angry gousters, nor had either of us ever taken a course or read a book on managing hostile crowds of a different race.

"Damn," I muttered between quick breaths. "I shouldn't have reacted to all his shit about my mother…he just kept digging. and digging…this time it got to me."

"What made Booker quit?" Nate asked, sounding slightly less breathless. "I didn't see how it ended."

"You mean you didn't see my sucker punch?"

Nate looked at me seriously for a moment, as if he was trying to remember having seen me punch Booker, but then he smiled. "Ha ha, very funny. You still haven't answered my question. How did the fight end?"

I wanted to sidestep the question, because I thought revealing what happened could get Valerie into trouble with the tough guys, but I decided to clue Nate in. He was my best friend, after all. "Promise you'll keep it to yourself, because Valerie could get into trouble for helping a white boy." He nodded.

"Only Booker and I could hear it, but Valerie told Booker to put the knife away, and he did." Nate looked at me, genuinely impressed. "Wow. That's amazing."

7

In the cavernous lunch room, sitting at our usual table with the badly chipped formica top, I was still on edge. What if other friends wanted to know the real story of why my fight with Booker ended so suddenly? There was no way I could ask each of them to keep the explanation quiet, like I did with Nate.

I was also afraid of what might come next from Booker, or one of his friends. I half expected we might even see some kind of ruckus at this day's lunch. Every once in a while, when there was tension between the white and Negro students, it was at lunch that the sound of drumming on tables started up, nearly undetectable at first, and gradually picked up around the expansive cafeteria. For me, it was like Gene Autry or The Lone Ranger cowboy-and-Indian television shows, where the Indians communicated via drum and smoke signals. Then, on cue, three or four plates or cups or metal spoons came flying from different directions toward one or another of the tables where the white kids congregated.

Most of all, I worried about whether Nate would be able to keep his mouth shut about Valerie's role in the fight.

Nate and I had been best friends since the seventh grade at Parkside. We became close when we placed one-two in a public speaking contest our teacher ran to get everyone to do research about the Chicago Fire in 1871. I focused on Mrs. O'Leary's cow, which was blamed for kicking over a lantern that ignited the devastating fire, and Nate focused on how one family survived through the heroics of a neighbor. The teacher rated Nate's five-minute talk the best, and mine the runner up, and then asked just the two of us to give our speeches at a special parent-teacher evening event. It was a huge honor, and both our parents were very proud.

That was just the tip of our academic success, and I'm sure it made some of the gousters at Parkside jealous. They'd sometimes take out their jealousy by pushing one or another of us around during recess, or after school. We'd look out for each other, trying to distract the bullies by inquiring into some unrelated matter, or just grabbing the other by the arm and walking away before things could get too hot and heavy.

What other kids, gousters and non-gousters alike, didn't see was Nate's and my unspoken competition over grades and any prestige associated with grades. It tended to make me nervous, yet I was a willing participant. I just hated the part of him gossiping and poking fun if I got a bad test grade and he got a good one. So, sitting at the lunch table right after the fight with Booker, I waited nervously to see how well Nate would do with the potentially explosive Valerie-as-my-savior story.

I didn't have to wait long. White upperclassmen I didn't even know approached me at the lunch table where I sat with Nate, Lee, and George. I didn't have much appetite given my still-churning stomach, but I tried to look busy munching on the egg salad sandwich Mom had made for me.

Not only had the seniors heard about the fight but they treated me like a hero. They spoke in soft tones so as not to stir up gousters who might be nearby. Like Mel Graham, a dark-haired broad-shouldered handsome senior who also happened to be captain of the swim team, president of the honor society, and had pretty Shirley James as his steady girlfriend.

"Way to stand up and fight, Jeff, I heard you gave it to that mother." The admiration in his bright and glowing baby blue eyes was sincere. "Very groovy."

"I don't know about that," I responded, feeling awkward, since he was one of the coolest white kids in school and I had never before had a real conversation with him. What was the cool thing to say, to do? I tried to be valiant despite my personal shakiness. "Who knows, maybe some of them will think twice before picking a fight."

The swim team was the only varsity sport dominated by whites. I assumed that was because whites tended to gravitate toward water during the summer—parents sent their kids to summer camp, where they had swim lessons, or retreated to summer houses at the Indiana and Michigan Dunes on Lake Michigan. Nate, Lee, and I had gone together to a YMCA camp on a small lake in a tiny town in Michigan for month-long periods each of three summers beginning when we were ten. The Negro kids, meantime, spent most of their summers hanging around city basketball courts or baseball fields.

I had no idea if it was the cool thing to do, but so long as I had Mel's attention, I decided to inquire about his college plans. I had heard he was headed to Brown University in the East after graduation.

"I hear you're going to an Ivy League school next year," I offered. I could see the surprise flash in his blue eyes that I had such inside information.

"Yeah, I'm going to Brown. They want me to be on their swim team."

I don't know what made me ask him my next question, except that it fit into my own worries about the disintegration of our neighborhood: "Is your family moving out of South Shore after you graduate?"

Now he was looking at me in a serious way, almost as if he was trying to look inside me. "Who told you that?" he asked.

"No one. I was just wondering. So many people are leaving South Shore, I just wondered if you were, since you are graduating."

"Yeah. My parents want out. I'm the youngest in my family, last to graduate. So it's a good time to be leaving. I can't say I'll be real sorry. Maybe if more people had stood up to all this crap, like you did today, we wouldn't be running. But not many stood up, so here we go."

I wanted to ask him more about what he meant about people standing up to all the crap. But he was now looking down my body and I could see a horrified expression gradually take over his movie-star face as he stared at my left bicep. "What did he do to your arm?"

I looked down and saw a big red welt that had taken shape on my elbow. I must have banged it on a stair railing when I put Booker into the headlock. I just shrugged, resisting the temptation to overplay the evident violence of the encounter.

The good news was that, amid all the congrats, no one inquired about how the fight ended so suddenly, or said anything about Valerie's interference on my behalf. And Nate kept his mouth shut.

As lunch ended, and I went to my afternoon classes, the events on the stairs with Booker churned in my mind, including how differently things could have turned out if Valerie hadn't come to my rescue—that I might be a few blocks away, at the University of Chicago's Lying-In Hospital on 59th Street, fighting for my life. I hoped the lunchtime congrats from upper classmen were the end of the gossip.

Moreover, I was still uncertain about all that transpired, and why. I was so intent on leaving the scene of the encounter as quickly as I could, I didn't notice interactions between Booker and Valerie, or between her and others, after I departed. All I knew was what I had seen of her at Riverview at the end of summer, and during our brief and tentative interactions at the basketball game and after geometry class.

Could she and Booker be related? That was the only reason I could imagine for the rapid-fire chain of events that saved me—her command to him and his decision to obey it. Otherwise, their interaction didn't make any sense.

In the school's three-tier social order, Booker, by virtue of being a gouster, was at the bottom rung academically and economically. She? Valerie was definitely in the middle tier, an "Ivy Leaguer." She mostly dressed the way she did that Tuesday—plain white blouse, V-neck sweater, plaid skirt, white bobby socks, and flat black loafers. Gouster girls wore the white blouses, but generally avoided the sweaters, plaid dresses, and bobby socks of Ivy Leaguers in favor of black dresses and nylon stockings.

I didn't want to think about another possibility—that Ivy Leaguer Valerie could be dating gouster Booker. I don't know exactly why, but that seemed improbable—even more improbable than the possibility that a white guy like me could be dating Valerie. Smart Negro girls like Valerie didn't have time for losers like Booker. Or so I assumed.

8

Even as I sat down to dinner with Mom, Dad, and Emily that evening in the cozy hutch at the end of our spacious kitchen, I had this feeling of things being out of kilter. It was almost as if my body was still vibrating from the clash with Booker. I felt hyper-sensitive to ordinary sounds like the dropping of kitchenware or the slamming of doors. I was aware of my heart still beating more rapidly than usual.

I did feel hungry as Mom served up a piping hot meatloaf and mashed potatoes dinner. I barely had a chance to dig in, when Dad announced he had been harassed yet again on his way home from the bus stop by a group of gousters. Apparently, they tried to shake him down for a few dollars. When he refused, they taunted him by calling him "grandpa honky," and threatened to "kick yo ass" at some time in the future.

"Gee, you don't look like a grandpa," I joked, partly to ease my own rising sense of anxiety. "You only have a little gray hair." I definitely didn't want to share my own more harrowing tale from school. Besides, to me, he still looked fairly youthful. His black hair was graying, as were his bushy eyebrows, but he was still slender and had a smaller paunch than a number of my friends' dads.

Dad wasn't smiling and his Germanic crooked nose and narrow face just accentuated his serious demeanor. He generally didn't have a great sense of humor, but he at least tried this time. "I chase them at Goldblatt's, they chase me home." He was referring to the chronic gouster shoplifting problems at the store. The way Dad told it, they'd arrive in groups of three or four at Goldblatt's, the department store where he managed the men's clothing section on the third floor. As one or two tried on leather jackets or cashmere sweaters, another acted as the lookout who distracted the sales person with some inane question about where to find socks and shoes, while those wearing the goods slipped away.

The cops never came in a timely way in my father's experience. He blamed Goldblatt's for refusing to pay the weekly cash bribes that other merchants shelled out to keep the uniformed cops hanging around their stores and occasionally nabbing shoplifters.

"I don't know what we are going to do about this neighborhood," he said, shaking his head.

Now it was Mom's turn. "It isn't going to get any better, Kurt. I heard at the office today that schvartzes are moving in on Paxton and Crandon." Those were streets immediately east of us in our area of South Shore, toward Lake Michigan. Since our neighborhoods had been changing racially from west to east, the news that Negroes were moving in east of us suggested we and the other remaining whites on our block were becoming more surrounded, more isolated.

"Each day, someone seems to be leaving. This morning, it was Edith Murphy on the first floor. You know, the widow with the two little children. I just happened to see the moving truck as I was going out about eleven. She never said anything, even though we used to talk in the building, or when we were out shopping. It only took them an hour or so to load her things up. And then she was gone. And you watch. Tomorrow or the next day, a big schvartze family will move in."

Emily and I looked knowingly at each other. I was sure she felt as deflated as I did, because we had heard this conversation from our parents more often than we liked to think about. Emily at 12 was more effusive and gregarious than me, taking after our mother. She looked a lot like our mother as well, with a small nose set on a small pleasingly round face, highlighted by sparkling brown eyes and barely shoulder-length curly black hair. I knew from talking with Emily alone that, like me, she was experiencing racial tension at the O'Keefe School, the local elementary school a couple blocks away. She was in the seventh grade, just about the age where the tough Negro kids began asserting themselves.

The dinnertime conversation was yet another reminder of how significantly our living situation had deteriorated over the past three years. When we moved to this apartment on Clyde in time for me to start as a freshman at Parkview, the neighborhood had been all white and the expectation had been that we'd be able to live here at least four years without racial upheaval, in time for me to graduate Hyde Park High and Emily to graduate O'Keefe. If things had stabilized racially, Emily might even have gone to Hyde Park, or at least started in there as a freshman.

I tried an upbeat approach with Mom and Dad as we poked with our spoons at the plain red Jell-O that completed our dinner. "We played dodge ball in gym," I offered. "I was the winner because I was the last kid standing."

Neither of them said anything as they began clearing the dishes, as if they were lost in their own sea of anxiety. I excused myself to do homework in my room. I loved my room. It was large and airy, with a single bed and an old beat-up wooden desk, but what I liked most about it was that it was private. I even had my own bathroom.

9

My problem was that while my body was settling into my bedroom's desk chair ready to crack the books, my mind was back on the first-floor landing at school. In the movie playing out on the big screen of my mind, Booker's switchblade knife had opened, and I was nowhere to be found, except that I noticed an intensifying sense of wanting to sob.

Then the scene switched to Mom and Dad in our synagogue, presumably at my funeral, where they were all dressed up, arguing in front of a group of mourners. They were blaming each other for my attendance at Hyde Park High. Mom, normally upbeat yet deferential to my intense father, was crying loudly that, "The schvartze killed my boy. Why did he ever go to that God-forsaken Hyde Park? I was always against it. But no one listened to me. Who was I? Just his mother."

Pangs of guilt intruded on my feeling of upset as I imagined the exchange, as if I was responsible for the mess because I had lobbied for them to not leave the Hyde Park High district when we moved three years earlier. I wanted to be with my friends from elementary school. While the families of some were moving away, to the North Side or various suburbs, a decent chunk, including my friends Nate and Lee, were staying and would be going to Hyde Park.

Anyway, Mom hadn't finished her sad monologue. "And you!" She was looking at my father. "I wanted to move to the other side of 71st Street, so Jeffery could go to South Shore High School. What did you do? You said it would cost too much. Always trying to save money!"

From the time our family began to discuss which high school I would attend, as I began eighth grade, Mom wanted us to flee our once-cozy and comfortable neighborhood in the Hyde Park High district and move a few blocks south, across 71st Street, to the South Shore High School district. The Hyde Park High district had become mostly Negro over the previous two years, while the South Shore High district was still lily white, and heavily Jewish, like us.

In the film reel of my mind, Dad was facing Mom, head bowed, and had his arms around her shoulders, trying to comfort her as she sobbed against his broad chest; his slicked-back hair was tousled. Normally assertive, he was telling her in a soft voice that he agreed about moving, but we just couldn't afford it. His job as manager of the men's clothing department at Goldblatt's didn't pay enough. "What could I do, Esther?" he asked, sobbing.

In the real-life debates raging at home, I didn't say much, to avoid inflaming the escalating tension between my parents. I never raised the question that always tugged at me: If we and other white families just stayed where we were, wasn't it possible that everyone, Negroes and whites, could learn to live peacefully together? Then, we wouldn't need to be having all these family arguments. Negroes and whites wouldn't have to eye each other with nervousness and fear.

It was just as well I kept my mouth shut, because they had a seemingly endless inventory of arguments and accusations, like one particularly nasty after-dinner exchange at our previous apartment on Ridgeland, while Mom was washing and Dad drying the dishes.

Mom started it. "Kurt, we owe it to Jeffrey and Emily to move to a safe area. Let's face the truth, this neighborhood isn't safe anymore, even for us. If you and I can't walk around without worrying we're going to be attacked, you know it's not safe for the children."

"So, what are you suggesting?" Dad inquired. "That we move south of 71st Street, where we can't afford the rents?"

Mom replied, "There has to be something there we can afford. Maybe it will be a little small, so Jeffrey and Emily will share a bedroom."

Dad, raising his voice. "Jeffrey is going to be a teenager, Esther. He can't share a bedroom with his sister."

"So, we'll stretch a little. I'll see if the real estate people can use me full time. Or maybe I can take in some typing from a few professors to earn extra money." She was referring to University of Chicago professors, who were often in need of outside typists for their research papers and books.

"I don't want you having to take work from those arrogant professors. And how do we know the other side of 71st Street won't turn schvartze right after we move there? We thought this area around Ridgeland would be okay for ten years. Now here we are three years after moving, with the schvartze all around us like a gun to our heads and we have to run again."

"Maybe that area will hold up better than Ridgeland," Mom said. "You know, there are so many rich Jewish families over there. They have their shuls. They have Rainbow Beach. They don't want to leave so quickly."

"You're dreaming, Esther. You know as well as I do what happens when a family like ours wakes up one morning to a schvartze family with six or seven children across the hall. Nobody is bringing anyone a welcome apple pie. The white family panics, then all their white neighbors panic. It's everyone for themselves. No, once the speculators get in there, and start spreading rumors about the schvartze invading, those rich Jewish families will run as quickly as the poor Jewish families on Ridgeland."

"So you want Jeffrey to go to that Hyde Park all-schvartze high school? And get beaten up, or worse?" Mom said.

"Maybe it's time for Jeffrey to toughen up. If it was Emily, okay. But Jeffrey is a boy, he can fight back, take care of himself."

"He can't fight back against some of these schvartzes. They are bigger than you, Kurt. And they don't care about who they beat up. They just want to grab money for drugs, or buy fancy clothes."

"Listen, we just need to ride it out here for four years, until Jeffrey finishes high school. Then when he graduates and Emily is ready to go to high school, we'll have more money saved, we can buy a house in Skokie or Lincolnwood way north."

Mom was exasperated. "So what are you suggesting?"

"I'm just suggesting we think about moving further east, on the other side of the Highlands, toward the lake. That's still white. One more move. Let's see what we can find."

Mom: "And let Jeffrey go to Hyde Park? We'll never get out of this jungle. Who says we can last four years? What if we have the same situation over there in two years? Looking over our shoulders whenever we go out, worrying about being out after dark. It's no way to live, Kurt!"

Dad: "Who knows, maybe the city will move the boundary for South Shore High School down to 67th Street from 71st Street."

Mom: "You're dreaming, Kurt. You think the rich people on the other side of 71st Street want the schvartze in their neighborhood and high school any more than we do? They'll never allow it. They'll pay off the aldermen if they need to. Get real. Stop trying to save some money, and think about the bigger picture. Think about the safety of your children."

Dad, almost moaning: "It's just not fair, to make the school boundary at 71st Street. Four blocks further north, and we'd be fine."

Mom: "Who's talking about fair? You know as well as I do the rich real estate people move the boundaries around to keep the schvartze out of their own neighborhoods, and then make big money selling buildings to schvartze in our neighborhoods."

Dad suddenly shifted his tone, to a softer, warmer approach: "Listen, Esther, let me just start looking around at apartments further east. Let's see what things look like over there. How nice people are. Whether any schvartze have moved there."

Mom, still talking loudly: "Yeah, sure, and you'll see how cheap the rents are. You think you'll get a bargain over there, and that will somehow solve our problems?"

Pause. Mom stared straight ahead.

"Maybe you have to go there without me."

That led to a first, my dad stunned into silence.

So was I.

The idea that my parents could split up over the school and living situation had never occurred to me.

Off to the side, Emily was sobbing. "I want to go to Hyde Park. I always wanted to go to Hyde Park. I don't want to be with all the snobs at South Shore High. The girls wear fancy jewelry and makeup. A lot of the boys have their own cars. I've even heard they have fraternities with Greek names and a rush each fall for the freshmen. I don't want to be in any rush."

Dad was pleading in a soft voice: "Please, Esther, let's just give it a try."

I took her silence for assent.

10

And so, we were running again. Mom was busily lining up a mover, which wasn't a simple task, since so many people were moving around and out of South Shore. Dad was negotiating with landlords, seeing who would do the best deal for what length of lease. Because so many whites were fleeing our northernmost slice of South Shore, which lay in the Hyde Park High district, Dad was finding some good deals from landlords desperate to rent to whites—a few were actually willing to paint their apartments if he committed to a two-year lease.

But all that activity couldn't obscure the nervousness I so often felt. If it was like all the other times we ran south during my growing-up years—from Chicago's Near North Side to the Hyde Park neighborhood in 1950, and then south again to South Shore, and then another place in South Shore, and another.

There was a depressing pattern about it. Life would be nice for a while, with all white kids around to play fast pitch or penners with, and then gradually white families moved out and Negro families appeared to replace them, and Mom and Dad would be on edge and arguing yet again about where and when to move.

In my parents' telling, and that of their friends and neighbors, it was "the schvartze and all their kids" that were responsible for the undoing of our pleasant urban neighborhood, wherever it was. They spoke fearfully and vividly about Negro families moving into our neighborhood in the middle of the night, and neighbors waking up to dark-skinned strangers across the way with six or eight little kids scampering about. In this telling, the newcomers didn't know, or care, about keeping things tidy and clean, so garbage would be strewn about in apartment hallways and even thrown out of second and third-floor windows.

I had this vision of a dark-skinned Negro mother, and perhaps a father, or perhaps not, with all these two, three, and four-year-olds chaotically scampering around and between their legs. That was mostly in my mind, because I didn't see a lot of what the adults described.

I saw racial changes at school, and at least at first, they were small changes. In fifth and sixth grades at Parkside elementary school in South Shore, the few dark-skinned children mostly seemed like kids anywhere, and we'd all play tag or marbles at recess. It was by seventh and eighth grades that I noticed a correlation between an increase in the number of Negro kids and an increase in the problems in my life…like who got to be a patrol boy.

You wouldn't think getting to wear a white cloth belt that looped over your right shoulder and around your waist and standing on a street corner each morning and afternoon to let other kids pass during breaks in traffic would be such a big deal. Nor would you think it could highlight racial problems.

Being a patrol boy always was a prestige position, as such things sometimes are for young kids. But it seemed to be a position available to any seventh or eighth-grade boy who wanted to volunteer. Somehow that changed when Tommy Sullivan, a skinny brown-haired neighbor kid also in the seventh grade, set himself up as the patrol boy kingpin. The thing I remember most about Tommy's appearance was that he walked pigeon toed. Because it looked a little strange, it might have become something to make fun of for some kids. But Tommy had a certain attraction, call it charisma, that made his strange gait part of his coolness.

Tommy used his coolness to accept or veto patrol boy candidates. To become a patrol boy, you had to be on Tommy's good side or he'd pass you over, no matter how badly you wanted the job.

Maybe I remember it so well because of what Tommy did to Tyrone Lamond, who was in my class. Tyrone was a smart Negro kid, a budding Ivy Leaguer, who hung out with Nate and me during recess and gym. When Nate and I became patrol boys, Tyrone decided he wanted to be one as well. Usually it was just a matter of one or two patrol boys giving Tommy the word that a friend wanted to be a patrol boy and, presto, a fresh rolled up white belt appeared and a street corner was assigned.

But when I mentioned Tyrone wanting to be a patrol boy to Tommy, he didn't just grin and nod his ascent the way he usually did, but instead hesitated.

"I'll think about it," he said, and walked off in his pigeon-toed walk.

Over the next couple weeks, I savored being a patrol boy. It's difficult to explain the boost in status I felt standing on the street corner down the block from our apartment, proudly wearing my white belt and signaling other kids to either stop or walk ahead.

35

One of the kids I'd wave through each morning was Tyrone.

"We need you patrolling over on East End," I'd tell Tyrone.

"Yeah, that would be neat," he nodded, and a broad smile creased his light brown face, made handsome by a broad forehead and high cheekbones.

But when no word came from Tommy during those two weeks, I inquired again about Tyrone, this time with Nate at my side in the gravel school yard. "I told you I'd think about it," he said to me, looking down and kicking gravel around, a hint of irritation in his voice. "I'm still thinkin'." And off he walked in his awkward gait.

I must have been pretty naïve, because it wasn't until that last brush-off that I realized all the patrol boys were white, that there wasn't a single Negro patrol boy at a street corner, even though our neighborhood had become probably one-third Negro.

When I first told Tyrone that Tommy was "thinking about it," suggesting it was just a formality, Tyrone nodded his head and smiled in agreement. But the day after Tommy's brush-off, Tyrone inquired on his way to school about when he was going to assume his patrol boy duties.

I gave him the update that Tommy was "still thinking." Tyrone no doubt heard the hesitancy and doubt in my voice. I felt embarrassed, maybe a little ashamed, as I watched his smile fade, and a knowing look come into his sparkling dark-brown eyes—a look of hurt and resignation.

I contemplated challenging Tommy, even suggesting to Nate that we do the challenge together. But, like me, Nate was uncertain how to do that, what to say, whether we'd be making a mountain out of a molehill. While it was left unsaid, we worried on some level that Tommy would strip us of our patrol boy belts as he had done to one or another kid who got on his bad side. Besides, Tyrone never mentioned it again as he seemed to drift away from Nate and me to spend more time with other Negro boys at recess. Over the ensuing months, that look of hurt and resignation evolved into a nearly permanent scowl.

By eighth grade, Nate's and my concerns had shifted away from patrol boy matters to worries about being confronted by big tough Negro boys. Many of the Negro boys seemed bigger and older than my friends and me. Like Booker, they often missed days at a time at school and had difficulty keeping up on homework. Then they'd face the humiliation of having to repeat a grade or two. They seemed to know each other, and recess sometimes turned into bullying matches, with the Negro boys threatening or shoving us white kids.

One of those boys was Booker Walsh. He was still about my size, not especially muscular. But becoming a presence with his menacing glare. I remember once Booker threatening Nate that "I'm gonna kick yo' butt after school." When Booker followed up, and asked me as we left school where he could find Nate, I intentionally misdirected him.

I would come to wonder if Booker remembered my bit of deviousness.

11

I wanted to tell Valerie in those days immediately following the fight how much I appreciated her coming to my aid. I'm not sure exactly what reaction I expected from her, but it definitely wasn't the one I got.

Several times in those days immediately following the fight I tried to walk out of geometry class alongside her. My plan was to pretend I didn't understand something the teacher said during the class, and ask her to explain it to me. Then hopefully in the conversation, I could tell her how grateful I was for her help, and cleverly explain how her action made us "even," since I had saved her from a bad situation at Riverview. But it wasn't working out, as she always seemed to be with a couple of Negro girlfriends, in animated discussion, sometimes laughing gustily as they exited the classroom. She never so much as glanced my way, let alone made eye contact.

It wasn't until almost two weeks after the fight that I received an unexpected opportunity to approach her. Classes had kind of settled back from what I would call an on-edge atmosphere into a normal routine. In gym class, Booker, along with his pals, appeared to have stepped back, as if they suddenly feared being suspended or even thrown out of school. He wore a grim, almost pained look, like he was on some kind of enforced good-behavior routine.

Around school, it seemed as if I was seeing Valerie everywhere. In the halls, in geometry class, even at lunch sometimes at a neighboring table. She was often smiling and laughing and nearly dramatic in her demeanor with other Ivy-League-type girls in her class, as if someone had just told the greatest joke, or made the most interesting revelation.

I even noticed her hanging around with a small group of Ivy League boys. I didn't know two of them, but the third was Tyrone Lamond. He had matured from the sometimes awkward eleven-year-old I knew at Parkside into a handsome six-foot fifteen-year-old, slender with closely cropped hair and nice teeth. Yet even though he was smiling some, the smile looked nearly forced and he seemed somewhat stiff, ill at ease, as if his friendliness with Valerie and the others was forced, as if he wished he could revert to the standoffishness that generally marked his demeanor.

Still, the whole scene, especially of Valerie and Tyrone enjoying each other's company, made me jealous and sad. I wished in that moment that I was Tyrone, that I didn't have the barrier of white skin separating me from her. I wished that I had stood more forcefully against Tommy over his blackballing of Tyrone as a patrol boy. At least then, I might have remained friends with Tyrone. Unlike now, where he usually rushed on, glowering when he and I came face to face in the hallways or at lunch; the patrol boy rejection clearly hadn't subsided for him.

My opportunity to finally approach Valerie came unexpectedly on a Monday, when I received an official note in home room that I was being penalized with two extra study periods that week for "creating a disturbance in the hallway." That meant I would have to stay at school for an extra fifty minutes on two days, sitting in a room with similar "problem" students.

At first I was upset—I'd never been punished this way, and I was afraid it might affect my college application process, due to begin the following fall.

It was clear at the first study hall that these penalty periods were gouster affairs. I was the only white student of the maybe twenty-five present.

Booker sat near the back, looking as sullen and distant as in gym. Near the front was Valerie, the only Ivy Leaguer I could identify, and one of just three or four girls.

It didn't make sense that she was being penalized, since she was the one who saved the event from becoming a catastrophe. How did her involvement in the fight even get noticed?

My upset turned to nervousness as it dawned on me that this was my big chance to make a move on Valerie. I sat about halfway back in the room of mobile wooden desk chairs, at the end of a row, with Valerie in the front and Booker in the back. Valerie was a study in concentration as I watched her from a side angle, intently focusing on some homework, not glancing up or around. The air was heavy, stale, from the dozens of students who had been in and out of the classroom over the course of the day, and she looked as tired as the room felt, her normally buoyant wavy hair limp, and nearly drooping. She didn't look like she welcomed contact with anyone.

I pulled out a notebook with blank 81/2 x 11-inch sheets of white paper. I had homework as well—a few geometry problems, some reading about World War I for social studies, and an English composition essay to write based on readings we had been doing about Ralph Waldo Emerson. But instead, I retrieved some colored pencils from a case and began sketching Valerie's profile.

While most of my friends saw art classes as a waste of time, I usually enjoyed assignments to draw or paint country and city scenes. It helped that I had some artistic talent. A few months earlier, I had taken the liberty of sketching the art teacher's portrait. She was matronly looking, with short curly graying hair and a plump face. I made her face appear a tad thinner and younger than she appeared in person and she blushed when I showed it to her.

"That's very nice work, Jeff," she said. But I was uncertain she really liked it, because she didn't pick it up and ask the rest of the class to view it as she did with some drawings from other students.

The immediate challenge with sketching Valerie was how dark to make her skin. I decided to err on the lighter side. I'm not sure exactly why the issue was prominent in my mind, except that it seemed as if gousters tended to be darker-skinned than Ivy Leaguers. If gousters were at the bottom of the economic and social hierarchy, then darker skin must be less desirable as well, I reasoned.

I couldn't even imagine Valerie would ever see the drawing, but I suppose I could fantasize she might. In the fantasy, I assumed she desired lighter skin, and I didn't want to offend her by going too dark.

As the jolt of the loudly ringing school bell signaled the end of the study period, and the end of the school day, I noticed a large-boned Negro girl who was sitting in back of me during the study period approach Valerie and point toward me with a slight smile. I recognized that girl, Brenda, from my home room class, where we sometimes commiserated about having too much homework.

She was gesturing with her right hand in a drawing motion. Uh-oh. I was pretty sure I read her lips correctly: "I think he likes you." I waited for Valerie to smile or blush, but she showed no obvious interest, didn't even look at me.

I decided to proceed with my original plan, and take this penalty period as an opportunity to approach Valerie just after Brenda headed off. I had to ignore the warning signals from my gut, which suddenly began churning.

"I'm Jeff," I said. "We're in geometry together. I was the guy fighting with Booker a couple weeks ago."

She stared blankly, which felt strange because she nearly always had an animated expression, smiling and engaging, for everyone else. "Yeah, I remember you. You were the guy pretending you were Wyatt Earp at the OK Corral, who almost got his self killed."

She began walking out of the classroom, not waiting for me. I immediately realized that her ignoring me over the last two weeks since the fight was no accident—she blamed me for starting the blowup.

Should I just accept the rejection, appreciate the calming of my gut, and go on my way? Another part of me rejected the option as I scampered to catch up with her. "Hey, I wanted to thank you for what you did there."

She still had the blank look, as if she was bored, except now she was looking straight ahead, not doing me the courtesy to stop while speaking to me.

"I didn't do that to help you. I wanted to keep Booker from getting into a heap of trouble he didn't need."

She picked up her pace, walking faster toward the main exit to the street, clearly not desiring an extended conversation.

I decided to shift gears as I caught up with her yet again. I couldn't believe I was pursuing her so aggressively, more aggressively than I ever had any other girl. Was I intentionally heading into forbidden territory, as I occasionally did taking bicycle rides into Negro neighborhoods with Nate and Lee?

I was just even with her in the hallway. "Say, Valerie. I have a question for you, about geometry, about the class yesterday on trapezoids. I didn't understand the last part, about calculating the area of a trapezoid."

She didn't even slow down. "Why don't you ask one of your smart friends about that?" She didn't say, "Why don't you ask one of your smart white friends," but that was her clear suggestion. She peeled off without waiting for an answer, and was out the front door. There was no mention of my drawing.

The only good news was that Booker had apparently gone his own way, and was nowhere to be seen.

12

Sitting on the number 27 city bus that went from nearly in front of our high school into central South Shore, I was alone on a double seat, near the back, and free to focus fully on feeling sorry for myself. Beyond the obvious embarrassment and the crushing of my wonderful fantasies, Valerie's harsh rejection seemed to send an ominous message, that the next time Booker or one of his friends came after me, I was on my own if she happened to be around.

I didn't pay much attention when a group of four or five white teens climbed onto the bus one stop after mine. This was the stop for Mt. Carmel High School, a small Catholic boys school just a couple blocks from Hyde Park High, except unlike Hyde Park, it was practically all white.

They were talking loudly to each other, laughing, clearly still revved up about some activity at school. They all were wearing brown and gold school jackets that said "Mt Carmel" on the back, in gold lettering. I think they were ribbing each other about how one or the other was responsible for losing a basketball game. Mt. Carmel students usually kept to themselves on the bus. I was generally with Lee or Nate or George on the bus, and each group pretty much ignored the other.

One thing I noticed about the group that had just gotten on was that one of the boys was Tommy Sullivan, the patrol boy maven from Parkside, my elementary school. Like Tyrone, he had blossomed from a skinny kid into a filled-out teenager, nearly six feet tall with brown wavy hair and intense hazel eyes. I noticed him because of his pigeon-toed walk down the bus aisle toward the back, where I was sitting. Because he seemed so engaged with his friends, I didn't even try to make eye contact or say hello as he passed and sat on the bench seat that ran along the back of the bus, a couple rows behind me.

As the bus made its way up Stony Island Avenue toward 67th Street, I found myself wondering idly whether Tommy's pigeon-towed walk interfered at all with his basketball prowess. Not that I really cared, but the thought did get my mind off feeling sorry for myself about Valerie.

Just as the bus was about to turn onto 67th Street, I sensed an object whiz by my ear from behind, and land in the bus aisle. Then I heard Tommy's voice behind me, almost a husky whisper: "Hey Jewboy, aren't you going to get that penny I just dropped?"

My chest and stomach immediately clenched, more powerfully than in study hall when I contemplated approaching Valerie. I had heard second-hand accounts about Mt. Carmel boys harassing Jewish students traveling alone from Hyde Park High. In the telling, the Jewish students ignored the Mt. Carmel bullies, although occasionally there was some pushing and shoving. Now I had a first-hand situation to deal with.

Part of me was ready to go at it with Tommy. As terrifying as the fight with Booker had been a couple weeks earlier, it had also given me a new confidence. Something told me Tommy would be easier to handle than Booker, that he wasn't as strong, or as experienced a fighter.

But my fight with Booker had also educated me on the importance of doing some planning before beginning to wrestle and punch. I worried about Tommy's friends. And being on a moving bus seemed to enlarge the risk—I could easily lose my balance and bang into a seat or a window. I also couldn't imagine any of the dozen or so other passengers, a mixture of Negro and white adults, intervening to help if Tommy's friends jumped me to help him. So I decided reluctantly to ignore the Mt. Carmel crew.

I could hear them laughing among themselves. "I thought the Jews went crawling for money," one boy, not Tommy, said. "Try it again."

Another penny was tossed into the bus aisle, and then a third. I could feel myself getting hot with anger. More laughter.

Then Tommy's husky whisper. "Those are for you to give to your colored friends."

As the bus began a gradual slow down, the whining of its engine lowering an octave or more preparatory to a stop along 67th Street, Tommy's voice again. "It's been fun, guys. I bet he'll grab the pennies on the way out."

I could sense movement behind me. Off to my side, I could see Tommy emerging into the aisle, his pigeon-toed first step the big tipoff.

Completely on a lark, I scooted over into the empty aisle seat and stuck my foot into the aisle a fraction of a second before Tommy walked by. At the same moment, the gradual bus slowdown became much more pronounced, as it braked sharply for the upcoming stop. Tommy went shooting down the aisle toward the front. I watched him desperately trying to catch himself, but unable to as the bus slowdown steepened. He was running out of room, and went down just before the front entrance. I could hear the soft clang of his head hitting some metal backing along the lower front of the bus.

I don't think Tommy's friends realized why he lost his footing, because they were laughing hysterically at the sight of him flying down the aisle head first. But Tommy, stunned as he was, knew exactly what had happened.

He got up, rubbing his head, and glared back at me. I looked down, pretending to read a book. He then exited the bus without a word.

I felt a tad uneasy that I had just made another enemy. But my main regret when I exited the bus a few stops later was that I hadn't reminded him during his clumsy exit that he had forgotten his pennies.

13

The late May sun felt warm, nearly soothing, as I smoothed the dirt around me. I tried to be careful not to let any into the small tear worn into the top of my left Converse sneaker.

I was anchored a few feet off third base on the Rainbow Beach softball field. It should have been a welcome bit of Saturday morning fun, a pickup game with a bunch of friends, after the tense last couple weeks at school.

But then Eddie Gulden showed up, and before we even picked teams, he was popping-off about "the darkies" he had heard were coming to

Rainbow Beach that afternoon, and how they were "pushing their way into another place they're not wanted."

Eddie's popping-off was an unpleasant reminder of the intensifying racial tensions popping up in more and more places around South Shore, including Rainbow Beach. The expansive beach sat on Lake Michigan about two miles south and east from our apartment, an easy bicycle ride for me through safe white neighborhoods.

While the name sounded idealistic, a plaque near the entrance explained that the beach got its name from a World War I Army division known for its bravery and fighting ability. The beach extended for about a half mile south from 75th Street, to its main entrance at 79th Street, a broad expanse of soft inviting beige sand.

There was always a special excitement about playing softball there, versus some of the schoolyards or parks nearer our apartment. The complex was mammoth and busy and well maintained. It had a big refreshment stand and even a building with showers at the main beach entrance where you could change your clothes.

On any sunny spring Saturday morning, it was a beehive of sporting activity, with its tennis courts, softball fields and wide-open grassy space to play Frisbee. Near the entrance, visitors often became entranced by intense games of handball between grunting and huffing men of all ages raging in half a dozen white-walled courts.

There was another beach further north, closer to our apartment, which might have been comparable to Rainbow Beach—the 63rd Street Beach. But I had no idea exactly how comparable, because I had never been there. It was the Negro beach—the beach I assumed Booker and Valerie and Tyrone hung out at on weekends.

I wouldn't have minded looking for Valerie at the 63rd Street beach, but biking or walking there would have been seriously risky because I'd likely be one of the few, or maybe even the only white person there. I didn't know for certain, but I imagined lots of gousters like Booker and his friends would be hanging out there, without even the minimal adult supervision we had at Hyde Park High.

I figured Negro kids had similar racial fears, viewing Rainbow Beach as the white beach. You didn't see any Negroes at Rainbow Beach, probably for the same reasons you didn't see whites at the 63rd Street

Beach. No one wanted to risk being a racial target.

I'd come to Rainbow Beach this Saturday morning together with Nate and Lee. I'd been up since seven mowing the lawns of two elderly homeowners in a prosperous island of South Shore homeowners. The one dollar I earned was all the extra money I had in my pocket at game time. Unlike Nate and Lee, whose fathers gave them weekly allowances, I had to earn all my spending money. "Nobody ever gave me anything," was my father's terse rationale regarding allowances and pretty much anything that involved him sharing his hard-earned dollars.

As Nate, Lee, and I crafted bases using some cardboard and paper bags from a trash can to signal we wanted other guys to join us in a pickup game, I filled them in on my bus encounter with Tommy Sullivan the previous afternoon.

"You like living dangerously, don't you?" Lee remarked. "First you're fighting Booker, and then you're tripping Mt. Carmel punks when they get off the bus."

"I was just sitting there minding my own business," I replied. Lee could be irritating that way, challenging me for getting back at a bully, when I had no doubt Lee would have tripped Tommy as well. In fact, he probably would have followed Tommy down the bus aisle as well to give him a kick, he was that much of a wise guy.

Now Nate was joining in. "You did trip Tommy on his way off the bus."

"Gee, you guys are making it sound like I started it. The guy threw pennies at me and called me 'Jewboy'."

They were silent, so I told them what was really on my mind. "I'm a little worried Tommy could show up here this morning, and that could be a problem. We have to stick together if that happens. That's where I got in trouble on the bus, by being there alone."

Nate piped up, that winning smile having blanketed over the worried look. "Don't worry, we'll look out for each other. Besides, I don't think I've ever seen Tommy here on Saturday mornings." Nate was correct. I couldn't remember Tommy ever joining in one of our pickup games. I felt a slight bit of relief.

Better Eddie Gulden's racist taunts than Tommy's anti-Semitism, though only slightly better.

14

I had become friends with Eddie a year earlier, during the summer of 1962. It was three years after the Chicago White Sox had won their first American League pennant in forty years, and the glow of that magical season was still strong.

We discovered during a pickup softball game at Rainbow Beach that we were both huge White Sox fans when he saw me imitating star White Sox second baseman Nellie Fox. Like Fox, I batted left-handed, and often hit the ball the opposite way, to left field. "Hey, Nellie!" he shouted when I came to bat.

Even though we were on opposite teams—his teams were mostly guys from south of 71st Street, South Shore High School, and my teams were mostly guys from north of 71st Street, Hyde Park High School—we both quickly realized we knew more about the White Sox than anyone else present. A couple weeks later, he told me he had an extra ticket to a White Sox Sunday doubleheader and did I want to come along. Sunday games were almost always doubleheaders—two games for the price of one.

My parents weren't thrilled with the idea because Eddie was already a senior at South Shore High School and I was only a sophomore at Hyde Park High.

"Why does a seventeen-year-old want to spend the day with a fifteen-year-old?" Mom inquired. "Doesn't he have friends his own age?"

I didn't know the answer, except that I assumed he wanted someone along who was nearly as rabid a fan as he was. Eddie did look a little different from most of my friends, wearing his dirty blond hair very short in a military-style crew cut that accentuated his pale complexion, angular nose, droopy eyelids, and big ears.

I used to wear my light brown hair in a crew cut during the summer as did other kids. But in this new decade, with a president, John Kennedy, who disdained hats and seemed to show off his hair, crew cuts became less and less fashionable.

I only knew Eddie from our pickup softball games and he stood out for getting worked up about the score, making more noise cheering for his team or booing opponents, than anyone else. He got especially upset when he made an out or an error.

"Damn you!" he said, talking to himself in the second person.

At the White Sox doubleheader, one incident on our way to the ballpark was bothersome. I was uncertain how much of it was the stress of getting to Comiskey Park, the White Sox's ancient stadium, or Eddie's personality.

Because it was located at 35th Street and Shields Avenue, Comiskey Park was situated smack dab in the middle of one of the toughest Negro areas of the South Side. The main way for teens like us to get there was to take the elevated train, from near Hyde Park High School, at 63rd and Stony Island, and then get off at the 35th Street station as the train made its way north toward downtown.

The train ride was always tense, as the few white passengers on board at the start dwindled quickly, and the number of Negro passengers increased. You never knew when some gousters would get on and begin trying to shake down the few whites.

No gousters were on this particular ride, fortunately. But the train let us off five or six blocks east of the ballpark. Those few blocks looked like forever to white guys like us. Even though the police usually patrolled the stretch on game days, you couldn't count on their presence, so the walk from the train past ten-story public housing projects was a test of nerves and sometimes of sprinting ability. There were occasionally reports of random gunfire from the projects. Muggings weren't uncommon.

On our late-Sunday-morning walk to the ballpark, we saw a white man being shaken down by three Negro teens as he emerged from his shiny late-model car. Without hearing the conversation, Eddie and I knew what was being said. The teens wanted cash in exchange for "watching" the man's car while he was at the game and they were negotiating a price. The teens pointed to another car further up the block, actually, a rusting car body hulk, which was sitting on four small piles of bricks in place of the tires—presumably an example of someone who didn't pay the protection fee. I knew the routine from having gone to games a couple times with my dad, who quickly paid the five dollars. It was still cheaper than parking in the huge stadium parking lot and, equally important, it saved waiting an hour to get out of the crowded lot after the game.

"Those darkies better not come into my neighborhood," Eddie said softly to me. "If they do, they won't make that mistake twice."

It was his use of the word "darkies" that jarred me more than his threat of violence. I wondered if that was how the kids at South Shore High School spoke about Negroes. Because as afraid as our minority of white kids at Hyde Park High was of racial violence, I had never heard any of them use racially charged expletives, even when in our own neighborhoods. Maybe because we went to school with Negroes, had them as friends, the racist slang of our parents or relatives hadn't rubbed off on us.

I was afraid Eddie would start quizzing me about how I put up with all the "darkies" at Hyde Park High, so I ignored his racial epithet, and changed the subject. "Who do you think will be playing center today for the Sox?"

"Probably Landis," he said, looking surprised I had shifted the conversation. "I hope so."

Watching a doubleheader, you get to know the person you are with, because there are long periods when very little is happening on the field. I thought I knew a lot about the White Sox players, but Eddie knew more. It was clear he lived and breathed baseball as we talked endlessly about not only the stars like infielders Nellie Fox and Luis Aparicio and pitchers Billy Pierce and Early Wynn, but also lesser known players. He even claimed to know that the daughter of one of the White Sox pitchers was about to transfer to South Shore High School. "And I hear she really puts out." It wasn't clear where he heard it, but his simple reference to a girl and sex somehow eased my uncertainty, that he wasn't weird the way Mom had worried.

I felt badly when I asked him about whether he had any brothers or sisters, and he went from talking about his older sister to how destitute his family had become. I figured, from Mom's and Dad's arguments about moving, that everyone who lived in the South Shore High School area south of 71st Street must have a lot of money to be able to afford apartments there, but it turned out his situation was anything but financially secure.

He told me the story about how his father owned an apartment building on the western edge of South Shore in the late 1940s and early 1950s, when it was an all-white area. His father also had a men's clothing store on a main street nearby, selling suits and ties and dress shirts. It had been a comfortable life.

"All of a sudden, in the late 50's, almost from one day to the next, the darkies are pouring in from the South. The whites are gone in no time, and the darkies, they can't afford to pay their rent. Before you know it, there are two or even three families sharing a two-bedroom apartment. The parents come in drunk late at night, and smash the hallway doors and walls. They're throwing garbage into the halls and out the windows. And then they're always late with the rent, if they even bother to pay the rent."

He paused and looked away, toward the baseball field, where the infielders were taking practice grounders between innings. "They were like animals. They live like animals, and they like having lots of kids."

I had heard stories of slumlords getting rich off of poor Negroes, but I definitely didn't want to say that to Eddie, sitting next to me practically in tears. Maybe those landlords had lots of buildings and could easily evict troublesome tenants. For a man like Eddie's father, who owned one building, it sounded like a different story.

Anyway, Eddie wasn't finished. "When the tenants didn't keep up on their rents, Dad couldn't pay the bank or the taxes."

"Did he try to sell the building?" I asked

"Yeah, try selling a building full of darkies where half the tenants aren't paying their rent," he said, with a combination of exasperation and anger in his voice. "On top of that, business at Dad's store was dying...speaking of dying, one day he just dropped dead at the store. Mom had to shut it down, and try to sell the building. Huh. Some kind of sale. She practically had to give it away. Imagine that, a nice piece of real estate where the value goes down over ten years. That never happens in real estate, except when my family gets involved."

I couldn't think of what to say, except I figured things must have improved from those terrible times a couple years earlier. "Have things gotten better?"

"The one thing that saved us from being completely wiped out was that Dad had bought a good life insurance policy when he opened the store. It also helped that Dad had almost paid off our house in South Shore."

Eddie didn't say how much the insurance policy was, but from the way he talked, it wasn't a fortune since his earnings from part-time after-school and summer jobs had become an important part of the family's income.

"I'll never forget what those darkies did in tearing Dad's building apart and not paying their rent. When he was alive, we used to go on trips to

Cuba during the winter, but now we don't go anywhere."

The only thing that upset him more than Negroes moving into a neighborhood was white speculators who scared white homeowners into selling en mass with rumors that lots of Negroes would be living on their blocks. "Those white traitors are the lowest of the low."

15

Eddie only turned upbeat when the conversation shifted to his job as a caddy at the South Shore Country Club. It was a beautiful piece of land, with a nine-hole golf course and expansive beach that hugged the Lake Michigan shoreline, and sat smack dab between the all-Negro 63rd Street beach to the north and the all-white Rainbow Beach to the south.

"Nobody believes me when I tell them I make four dollars and five dollars an hour being a caddy," he bragged.

I was certainly amazed, not only by the earnings, but where he was making his money. I tapped on his forearm to interrupt him.

"Whoa, wait a minute, Eddie. The South Shore Country Club is restricted. You're Jewish, right? How can you be working there?"

Eddie smiled. "Yeah, it's restricted. But that only means Jews can't join the club. They don't mind if Jews do dirty work, be caddies or dishwashers."

Mom and Dad hated the South Shore Country Club, as did most of their Jewish friends. "I don't go anywhere I'm not wanted," Dad once remarked when a friend of his visiting our apartment wondered if the ban on Jews joining might someday be lifted.

So I adopted that sentiment with Eddie. "Don't you feel a little funny working there, knowing you or your relatives could never join as members?"

The smile faded, and Eddie turned serious. "I admit, I did feel funny at first. But everyone's been nice to me. Lots of the golfers give big tips. When I started leaving there with $25 or $30 for six hours of work, just for carrying bags of clubs around a beautiful golf course, I felt less funny. The money is great, and that is what I'm worried about these days, making good money, to help my mom out."

"Does anyone call you Jewboy or kike or anything like that?" I asked.

"No, nothing like that. I'm not even sure they know I'm Jewish. It's never come up. As long as I don't try to join. And my family could never afford to join anyway."

I couldn't think of any other objections to raise. It sure sounded like a good idea to me, carrying golf bags around a tree-lined course right on the lake and making good money.

It was almost as if Eddie could read my mind. "If you want to apply for a job, I'll put in a good word for you. It would be nice to have a friend or two over there."

"I even know something about golf," I offered. "I live practically across the street from the Jackson Park golf course. I sometimes play over there with a few friends. So I won't embarrass anyone."

Eddie smiled again. "That's good. You definitely have to know what clubs to give the members in different situations on the fairway. But you also have to stay serious. You can't laugh when they keep hitting slices or hooks or can't get out of a sand trap."

A pause, and then his expression turned serious. "And don't go bringing any of your darkie friends from Hyde Park High to try to be caddies. It won't go well."

I took the bait. "You mean they'll allow Jews to work as caddies but not Negroes? We're disgusting, but not that disgusting?"

He gave me a quizzical look. "Very funny. I don't know how you do it, going to school with all of them. I just hope they don't kick your ass too bad."

This wasn't going in a good direction. I wasn't going to tell him how I sometimes got chased home from Hyde Park High by gousters. I decided to be conciliatory. "I get what you're saying. I'm not looking to make trouble."

And I immediately regretted saying it, as if I was somehow agreeing with his intention to block any Negro who might want to work as a caddy.

But seven months later, just as the winter snow was melting away, my mind was again focused on making decent money at an outdoor summer job. So I called Eddie, to follow up about getting a caddying job at the South Shore Country Club.

He welcomed my inquiry with enthusiasm. "Your timing couldn't be better, Jeff. I've been made assistant caddying director, which means I can recommend guys as caddies. I also help make the assignments for which caddies work with which members at the club. Right now, they're definitely hiring."

So I went over to the huge club, whose entrance had the look of an army base, with watchtowers on either side of a grandiose black iron gate. Along the top, in case any Jews or Negroes might forget, it said in bold brass lettering, "South Shore Country Club. For Members Only."

I went to the back of the six-story clubhouse, where the food deliveries were made and the trash taken away, and filled out a one-page employment form. There was a space for the name of the person who recommended you, so I filled in Eddie's name. Two days later, Eddie telephoned my house, and told me I had been hired. He sounded excited, as if he had been able to put his influence to work on my behalf. "You'll do great, I know," he told me. "And hopefully you'll make yourself some serious money as well."

But when I told my parents about the "serious money," they were dubious. "I don't like going where I'm not wanted," my father said, yet again.

"I'll just give it a try," I said. "Eddie says I can make good money there."

"Maybe for a while," Dad countered. "But I am telling you, nothing good will come of it. If they hate Jews, they will find a way to make your life miserable. In the end, whatever you make won't be worth it."

16

I was definitely not sorry to see our softball game end, and not just because the hot sand and cooling Rainbow Beach waters beckoned.

My team of Hyde Park High kids had been soundly beaten by Eddie's team of South Shore High kids. And because we were playing for a nickel a run, thanks to Lee being a wise guy and insisting we play for money, the adventure cost me thirty-five cents of my $1 lawn-mowing earnings.

But it was Eddie's blustery racial taunts, and the approving nods from several of his friends, that wouldn't leave my mind.

He had warned at the start of the game that he had to leave promptly at noon to get to his caddying job at the South Shore Country Club.

"I hate to take off like that. But I know some of you guys will be around to welcome the darkies." He looked at the other nine teens gathered around for signs of approval. Guys on our team were all shifting their weight uncomfortably, fidgeting with their belts and t-shirts, as they looked off in other directions.

On Eddie's team, though, a couple guys were nodding in seeming approval. One of those nodding most eagerly was Drew Boggs, a friend of Eddie's I knew from having played a few softball games with him. A slender kid with a mop of unruly black hair and good hands who excelled at shortstop, he seemed more subdued than Eddie. At one of the games, I had seen him doing a quick pencil sketch of a group of trees and approached him between innings. In our brief but amiable discussion, I learned he preferred painting country scenes, while I was more inclined to draw portraits.

Eddie appeared not to notice the reactions of others. "Yeah, I'll have to miss the party. Who knows, though, maybe they'll wise up and decide this isn't the best place for them to hang out."

I could feel a slight churn in my stomach. Not because of anything unpleasant that might unfold later in the afternoon—I'd be long gone— but because Eddie had assumed a significant role in my life.

The next day, Sunday, was supposed to be my first day of work. What was creating the pit in my stomach wasn't nervousness about beginning life as a caddy. It was my sudden realization that Eddie's racism during our walk to Comiskey Park wasn't just a one-time thing. And here I'd become dependent on him for my summer job and extra cash.

The one encouraging development in the whole Rainbow Beach softball game fiasco came around the fourth inning, when Nate told me he'd heard about a Saturday evening get-together of kids from Hyde Park High and the Lab School, a private high school run by the University of Chicago over in the Hyde Park neighborhood, several miles to the north of South Shore. The get-togethers had apparently just launched in the last couple weeks and one would be going on this evening.

"I don't know," I said. "The last thing I want to do is run into Booker."

Nate was ready for me. "I doubt that will happen. This is going to be in University of Chicago territory. Not Booker's kind of place."

I shook my head. "We don't really know our way around there too well, you know, escape routes and all that." I ignored the fact I used to live near the UC when I was four and five-years-old.

Nate didn't care about my fears about being in racially unfamiliar territory at night. "What are we gonna do, spend another Saturday night hanging around at my house, talking about how there's nothin' for us to do, and how we're too good for the girls at Hyde Park High and South Shore High?"

Nate was right. We didn't have a lot of socializing opportunities. There was a youth group at our synagogue, but most of the kids who participated were from South Shore High School. They were used to hanging out with each other, so us Hyde Park High kids were afterthoughts to them. At the end of a social, a dozen or fifteen of them were off to someone's house to hang out or to a pizza place, while the remaining four or five of us were on our own.

17

Nate, Lee, and I approached the beach area carrying our sneakers and following Evie Weiss through the dense crowd of beachgoers, quick-stepping on the scorching sand toward the wool blanket she shared with two other girls.

I had spotted Evie along the sidelines as our game ended. I knew her from temple Sunday school classes, though mainly as a target during my pea shooting days a few years back. My friends and I would buy plastic straws that were a bit larger than soda straws, and small brown envelopes filled with dried peas. We'd put a few peas in our mouths and blow them out through the straws perhaps twenty feet or twenty-five feet where they might sting another kid's arm or neck.

In spite of such teasing, Evie and I bonded a year or two later, in my first year of high school, at an unlikely series of events put on by the local YMCA on 71st Street. It had the strange name of "Fortnightly"— apparently because the gathering of girls and boys for a couple hours occurred every other Saturday afternoon late one winter.

Somehow the Y convinced dozens of parents in our neighborhood that it was important to pay some money to have a competent adult teach their kids good manners with the opposite sex. It was nothing a group of self-conscious young teens would ever have agreed to independently, but in a big room one Saturday afternoon in early March, about sixty boys and girls—all white, the boys with their hair combed and wearing dress shirts and slacks, the girls in white blouses, dark skirts, and shiny black patent leather shoes—gathered together, subdued and shifting awkwardly.

The woman in charge, Miss Vickers, was a slender kindly looking, high-energy woman with closely cropped black hair who clearly knew what she was doing. She was about my mother's age, firm, yet good humored. "I know, some of you aren't glad to be here," she said in a gentle way, letting her words hang there a few moments as everyone relaxed slightly.

I had come with Nate, and was immediately relieved to see a number of other kids I knew from the neighborhood. Miss Vickers instructed the boys on how to politely ask girls to dance—"May I have this dance?" She limited our choices and the awkwardness that would result by instructing each boy to ask the first girl to his right to dance.

That girl for me was Evie. It was a relief for both of us that we recognized each other from Sunday school, even if we had said barely a dozen words to each other over the several years we were together each Sunday.

Miss Vickers then instructed us in the box step—"Boys, you want to lead your partner, with your movement and with your hand around her waist, and be careful not to step on her toes. Girls, follow along with how your partner is leading." Then, "Boys, escort the girl back to where you made your dance request and thank her for dancing with you."

Evie wasn't especially pretty, with short brown curly hair that had an oily unkempt look, and a nose a little too large for her pasty-skin face. She also had a mild case of acne and was a little chunky. But she also had large blossoming breasts pushing against her blouse and she was immediately friendly. "Did your parents make you come to this?" she asked when we began doing the box step.

I nodded my head and put on my pained-look face.

"Yeah, mine, too," she allowed. Feeling her boobs as we bumped each other awkwardly doing the box step definitely helped keep me focused on the dancing. Or, let's put it this way, it replaced one source of painful embarrassment with another more pleasant source.

After those initial few dances, we shifted partners. But Evie and I became sort of the "go-to" partner for the other as the weeks passed, as we were introduced to the fox trot, cha cha and jitter bugging.

I never had the desire of going beyond being a friend of mutual convenience with Evie because of her bossy and talkative persona, though I had to admit the thought of unbuttoning her blouse while we danced crossed my mind more than once.

So, on this Saturday afternoon at Rainbow Beach, Evie was once again my go-to girl, holding the tantalizing possibility of being useful for that Saturday night's arrangements.

Nate must have really wanted to go to this Saturday night thing, because he shot down pretty much every concern I came up with during the softball game. When I expressed worries about going to Hyde Park after dark, he made the case that it was probably safer than South Shore.

I realized he was probably right. Hyde Park, the neighborhood, was mostly white, but it had a significant minority of Negroes. Most everyone in Hyde Park who wasn't a student seemed to work for either the University of Chicago or its huge Lying-In Hospital. Though it was surrounded by tough Negro areas of Drexel to the north, Englewood to the west and Woodlawn to the south, it always managed to remain an island of racial stability.

As Nate and I continued our assessment of the Hyde Park party option while sitting on the green wooden bench along the first-base line during our softball game, we speculated we'd be best off arriving with girls...white girls, that is. Or, if not safer, at least more comfortable socially. We had little idea what we would encounter at the event, which was taking place at a student hangout, a coffeehouse known as the Medici—whether it would be mostly guys or perhaps, more uncertain and potentially provocative, heavy on Negro girls. We definitely didn't want it to appear we had come to the social because we were on the prowl to meet Negro girls.

As we tip-toed through the sand behind Evie, Nate whispered to me, with a sly smile: "Hey, maybe Evie and a friend might want to come with us to that thing in Hyde Park tonight. Maybe have some fun afterwards."

"You're reading my mind." I gave him a knowing look. "It's just difficult to imagine they would leave their South Shore island and go with us to the jungles of Hyde Park."

56

"Can't hurt to ask. All they can do is say no."

The beach was wall-to-wall people, mostly listening to their transistor radios, building castles with their kids, and playing Frisbee. Since Eddie's talk about darkies invading the beach, I found myself hyper aware of Rainbow Beach's all-white makeup.

I tried to imagine the reactions of these seemingly ordinary people if a handful of Negroes plopped down nearby onto blankets, turned on transistor radios to enjoy rock music, built sand castles with their kids or tossed around a Frisbee or two. I wished my fears were just idle fantasizing, but they weren't.

In the summer of 1960, the newspapers had been full of news about a "wade-in" at Rainbow Beach. A group of maybe thirty or forty Negroes, most of them in their twenties and thirties, had gathered quietly at the beach one July afternoon. They hung out in a small group together near the water, some of them in swim suits, some in street clothes. At first they were just there, a kind of curious oddity that people stared at, but after an hour or two, they were surrounded by hundreds of white teenage boys and young men, who began shouting, "We don't want you here!" and "Go to your own beach!"

It was when the Negroes started to pack up to leave that it got ugly. Rocks started flying and a few of the Negroes were hit in the head and bloodied. Fortunately, an onlooker got to a pay phone and called the cops because out of nowhere, a group of maybe a dozen police arrived and escorted the terrified Negroes off the beach.

I heard talk of a few more wade-ins later that summer, and during the summer after that, but I was never there when they happened. That was fine with me. Whenever I went to Rainbow Beach, things seemed pretty normal, like on this day, with an all-white crowd of kids and grownups sitting around on blankets and towels listening to rock-and-roll music on transistor radios and batting around beach balls or splashing in the refreshing Lake Michigan water.

It was easy to let go of the nightmare scenario, so pleasantly ordinary and summery was the scene before me. I focused instead on Evie and two of her friends, sitting on a big blanket she had led Nate and me to.

I recognized the two friends from our temple as South Shore High School students. They seemed to barely take notice of Nate, Lee and me as their attention remained on applying large handfuls of baby oil to their arms and shoulders to maximize the sun's tanning and burning.

When I realized that one of the girls was Robin, I knew right away that Nate's idea of recruiting these girls to accompany us to Hyde Park didn't stand good odds. Robin was a pretty, slender, dark-haired girl who didn't care much for my sketching talent.

It was at a Temple social, where the boys sat on one side of the social hall awkwardly teasing and shoving each other to avoid looking over to the other side of the big room where the girls sat quietly, chatting with each other and pretending the boys didn't exist. The rock music that played on the portable record player seemed appropriately silly and nonsensical— "Cathy's Clown," "Itsy Bitsy Yellow Polka Dot Bikini," and "Alley Oop," ("He don't eat nothin' but a bear cat stew…Alley Oop, oop, oop, oop, oop").

I was drawn to Robin, sitting at the end of the row, by her striking good looks—her dark straight hair just brushing her shoulders and brown sparkling eyes and somewhat above-the-knees skirt. So I quietly did a little sketch of her face. Accentuating her eyes and smile and the thickness of her hair, I thought to make her look more glamorous and mature.

Later in the evening, when everyone had loosened up enough that some of the boys were dancing with girls, I approached Robin and showed her the sketch, secretly hoping she would love it and we'd start dancing and it would be the start of a wonderful relationship.

As she looked at it, I could see the smile on her small mouth fade, replaced by a puckering of the lips that ushered in a frown and a look bordering on confusion. "This is stupid," she said at last. "It doesn't look like me at all." Then she lifted her brown eyes from the drawing to look hard at me. "Are you making fun of me?"

Suddenly I was the one who was confused. "No, definitely not," I stammered. "I just like to do drawings of different people. I'm not real good, as you noticed. I'm sorry if you thought I was trying to make you look bad."

She handed the drawing back to me, turned and walked away. Forget that pick-up gimmick, I thought to myself. No, it felt worse than that. I wanted to kick myself for even putting myself out there where Robin could so easily shoot me down, make me feel foolish.

I didn't know if she was ignoring me this moment at the beach because she didn't remember me, or because she was embarrassed to see me again up close.

"Anyone want to go down to the water?" Evie interrupted.

"Sure, let's go," I responded. No one else made a move to join us, so we walked down together. Since it was May, the water was still pretty cold, icy on the toes. The bulk of the swimmers were little kids very close to shore.

I broke the awkward silence. "Hey, guess what? Nate is our party explorer, and he just heard this morning about a fun party in Hyde Park." Without waiting for a reply, I added, "It'll be mostly smart kids from Hyde Park High School." "Smart kids" was code for white Jewish kids, as Valerie had correctly inferred. Such code had developed, I surmised, as our schools and neighborhoods changed racially, to spare us the discomfort of having to make blatantly racist distinctions. To further reassure her, I explained that I would drive, and Nate would come as well.

"I wouldn't mind going," she said. "It might be fun. But I don't think my parents would allow it. They'd be afraid about me going into Hyde Park. Maybe if Robin or Jessica came along my parents would be okay, but I doubt they'd want to go."

I knew it was useless to press her. South Shore High School kids were generally down on Hyde Park High—after all, many were at South Shore specifically to avoid having to attend Hyde Park, and spend any time in the Hyde Park and Woodlawn neighborhoods mixing it up with Negroes.

"Okay, well, I'm going to try to swim." I had this sudden urge to show off to her and the other girls. So I steeled myself and sprinted into the water until it got nearly waist high, and I was forced to plop in, stomach first.

On the shore, Evie watched and laughed as I screamed about how cold it was.

When we arrived back to the blanket where Nate and Lee were sitting with Robin and Jessica, it was clear we were interrupting a conversation. "Get this," Robin said to Evie. "Nate wants us all to go to a social in Hyde Park. Isn't that a scream? He said he'll protect us if we are attacked…or maybe he'll get some of those University of Chicago intellectuals to protect us."

"I didn't say anything about protecting anyone," Nate interrupted. "I said we won't get attacked, because Hyde Park is okay. It's not Woodlawn or Drexel."

"Hyde Park, Woodlawn, Drexel, they're all the same to my parents," Robin replied. "They won't let me go anywhere near Hyde Park or the University of Chicago."

Evie didn't say anything, but her answer was pretty obvious in the silence that enveloped our group on the blanket.

As I sat on the edge of the wool blanket, wondering if there was anything I could say to ward off the rejection taking place, and looking at Nate for possible clues, I saw a horrified expression take over his face. "Look out..." he began. WHAP! Something hard slammed the side of my head, and for a few seconds bright stars and lights replaced the images of people in front of me. I felt a touch light-headed.

When my vision returned a few seconds later, Nate was staring at me, starting to get up. "I'm pretty sure that was Tommy Sullivan. He hit you with a book or a board." Lee was scanning the crowd, his right hand on his forehead serving as a visor against the sun.

I looked around, and damned if I didn't see a familiar figure maybe fifty or seventy-five yards away, hopscotching among the beach crowd, avoiding the bodies, onto the sidewalk at the beach's entrance. Even in the scampering, I could discern his pigeon-toed gait. Yes, it had to be Tommy. Unfortunately, he was far enough away, and I was still unsteady enough that I decided against trying to chase him down.

"Bastard," I muttered.

Nate nodded. "Jesus, Rainbow Beach is getting to be more dangerous than Hyde Park," he murmured, just loud enough for the girls to hear. They pretended not to hear.

In any case, it was just going to be Nate and I going into Hyde Park that evening, since Lee insisted on staying home and working on some wood-working project. All I needed to do was convince Dad to allow me to take his Chevrolet Bel Air to Hyde Park.

18

Dad turned out to be much more casual about handing me the keys to his precious Chevy than I had reason to expect. It was strange, completely at odds with his usual hesitancy and suspicion. Maybe he was secretly proud he had a son who was grown up enough to drive and go out socializing. Whatever the reason, I wasn't about to question it.

Indeed, I was the one who was a little hesitant. I was still feeling slightly off-kilter from Tommy Sullivan's whack to my head. And though Hyde Park was the site of our first South Side apartment when I was four and five-years-old, and was only a few miles from our current South Shore apartment, I wasn't nearly as confident driving around there—versus South Shore.

Our destination this evening was the run-down coffee house just a few blocks from our old Hyde Park tenement. Even though it was on busy commercial 57th Street, it wasn't clearly marked. You had to walk through the dusty Green Door bookshop to even get to the Medici. The Green Door's tables were stacked with hardback and paperback books, which were in English, but seemed foreign nonetheless. They were nearly all books you wouldn't see at a regular bookstore. Books like *No Exit* by Jean Paul Sartre, *Politics Among Nations* by Hans Morgenthau, *The Metamorphosis* by Franz Kafka, even Karl Marx's *Communist Manifesto*, among many others.

And then there were the people hanging out in the bookstore. Several tweedy guys in rumpled short-sleeve white dress shirts, puffing on pipes emitting sweet-smelling tobacco smoke, whom I figured were University of Chicago professors. And young women with long straight black or blond hair who could have passed for folk singer Judy Collins, or Mary Travers of the folk group, Peter, Paul and Mary.

At the front of the store sat a skinny young man with long disheveled brown hair and wire glasses, elevated a couple of feet behind some book shelves; the cashier, I presumed. As I approached him to inquire if there were people in back, he brought his forefinger up to his pursed lips. "Shhhh." He pointed to a transistor radio. A sign next to the radio stated: "Support University of Chicago students marching for civil rights in Alabama." In front of the sign was a glass quart jar, stuffed half full with quarters and crumpled one dollar bills.

A man's voice came onto the radio. "And now from St. Luke's Baptist Church in Birmingham, Alabama, the Reverend Martin Luther King Jr."

There was some static, and then a deep voice intruded, speaking slowly.

"Never in the history of this nation have so many people been arrested, for the cause of freedom and human dignity. You know there are approximately twenty-five-hundred people in jail right now. Now let me say this. The thing that we are challenged to do is to keep this movement moving. There is power in unity…"

I had heard about the protests by marchers in Alabama, and the police with dogs breaking them up, but I wasn't following the events closely. Despite all the Negro students at Hyde Park High, the events seemed distant from our day-to-day racial tensions. Martin Luther King Jr.'s voice could have been coming from another planet. But wherever it was coming from, it grabbed my attention as it rose in intensity:

"And don't worry about your children. They are going to be all right. Don't hold them back if they want to go to jail. For they are doing a job not only for themselves but for all of America and for all mankind."

His oratory was almost enough to distract me from my light headedness and the aching in my arms from squeezing Dad's Chevy into a tight space out on 57th Street. I didn't mind not having luxury add-ons like air conditioning or power brakes, but power steering sure would have been nice. Standard steering was tough when you had to keep adjusting the car's position to get into a space like I just did. But I didn't want there to be any excuse for someone denting us. I put a dent in the car the first week after I got my license a year earlier by clipping a light pole at a curb and it took me three months to convince Dad to give me another shot with it.

Nate interrupted my daydreaming with a poke to the shoulder. He was jerking his head toward a dimly lit back room that smelled vaguely of stale coffee and tea. It held maybe eight or ten wooden tables of varying sizes with wobbly benches. About a dozen teenagers sat in clusters of three and four at a table.

I decided to be bold and lead Nate to a table with Paul Badger, a tan-skinned handsome and highly popular six-foot Ivy Leaguer, and Robert Clark, one of his Ivy Leaguer friends, a few inches shorter and nearly as handsome, a little darker skinned, who wore black horn-rimmed glasses. I knew him vaguely from a couple of classes we shared.

Then there were a couple of tables with white boys and girls I didn't know at all and presumed to be from the university's Lab School.

But the energy in the room seemed to be concentrated at a table toward the back where four light-skinned Negro girls were joking and laughing. I couldn't hear the discussion but I immediately recognized Valerie as one of the girls.

She was dressed in a plain white blouse like she sometimes wore to school, but she had a more mature look to her. It took me a few moments to realize it was the dark red lipstick and perhaps even some kind of reddish something on her cheeks. When she got up briefly to show something from her purse to a friend opposite her at the table, I also noticed she had dispensed with the usual school bobby sox in exchange for nylons, which showed off the pleasing curves of her calves.

I exhaled. Her presence was a pleasant surprise. It was also now a huge relief that Evie decided not to come along…until I saw Valerie leave the table to welcome Tyrone Lamond at the entrance to the Medici. There was no hugging or hand-holding, but they stood very close to each other, he bending his neck and upper back to get to her height. They spoke quietly, knowingly.

After a few minutes, the conversation seemed to become more animated, and argumentative. I got up and pretended to be walking toward another table, closer to where the couple was standing.

Tyrone wore the sneering angry look that had become his fallback expression years back in grade school after the Tommy-Sullivan-patrol-boy run-in. "What you doin' hanging out with all these white kids?" I heard him ask. "There's a party over at the Boys Club where it's all our kind."

I heard Valerie's voice. "It's Rangers, ain't it?" When Tyrone stood silent, I heard her again: "I'd just as soon stay here."

"Suit yourself," he nearly snarled, his lips curled in anger, as he turned and walked out of the Medici, leaving Valerie looking after him, speechless.

Tyrone's presence made some sense in the context of my having seen him and Valerie talking in school. Perhaps their relationship, however serious it was, might now be in trouble?

Valerie turned quietly away from the doorway, and with head lowered strode slowly back to the table with her friends. She was clearly rattled, because she said nothing to her three friends.

The energy emanating from that table just moments earlier had dissipated.

Paul and Robert seemed relaxed about Nate and me sharing their table. They directed us to a metal cooler in a corner stocked with carbonated drinks like Coke and orange soda. "Who brought it?" I asked. Paul pointed to a slender kid with fresh combed blond hair wearing a white dress shirt and sleeveless gray sweater at a table across the room. "He's a Lab School student," Paul said.

"Nice of him to do that," I said.

Paul nodded and smiled. "I think they're trying to be sociable to the poor kids at Hyde Park High. Maybe it's a project in one of their sociology classes." He smirked at Robert who smiled knowingly. Neither Nate nor I said anything, but the unexpected turn of the discussion had me sitting more forward on my seat. Even though the conversation was between Paul and Robert, the fact that they had it in front of us seemed at least a tacit inclusion of us two white guys in race-sensitive matters.

The voice of Rev. King couldn't be heard back here, because another transistor radio was playing music. Not Bobby Darin or Frankie Valli and the Four Seasons that I was used to, but rather Negro singers and jazz I had no familiarity with.

I decided to use the opening Paul and Robert had provided by inquiring where Robert lived. "We just moved to South Shore," he said.

Strange as it may sound, I felt as if I was heading into no-man's land, since I had never spoken in any kind of detail with a Negro student about his or her living situation.

"What made you move?" I asked, the words seeming to stick in my throat as they came out.

Robert looked at me a little more closely, as if he was also sensing the shift into foreign territory. "Woodlawn was getting seriously overcrowded. Six of us in my family were getting on each other's nerves in a one-bedroom apartment."

I could feel more intense nervousness invade my stomach and chest as it dawned on me that he might start quizzing me about where I lived and why. But something kept me at it, some kind of nearly morbid curiosity. I sensed I was going to hear something quite apart from the talk by my parents and other white adults about huge Negro families moving into our neighborhood, and the implied assumption that Negroes always had big families and liked living in crowded apartments.

I pushed on. "So you came to South Shore to get a bigger place?"

"Yeah, my parents wanted my brother and me to have our own rooms finally. I was fine with that. I'm only sixteen, but it sure would be nice to have some privacy."

Robert wasn't done. "There was more and more crime in Woodlawn. The new gang that started up, the Blackstone Rangers. They tried to recruit Marcus, my younger brother. Told him he had to beat up another kid if he wanted to join."

"Where in South Shore did you go?" I asked.

"We've got a really nice three-bedroom on Ridgeland," he said.

It was as if outside forces had taken over my side of the conversation. "Where on Ridgeland?"

"6830."

"Really? We lived in that building. Which floor are you on?"

"The third floor."

"Gee, you have our old apartment. Which is your room?"

"The back one, that looks out over the porch."

"That's too much. You have my old room."

Robert smiled at the irony. I moved back on my seat, expecting him to begin questioning me about why we had left that nice apartment. About where we had gone. And how the new place was working out. How candid should I be? Should I implicate my parents for their racism?

But neither of us said anything further. We had inadvertently stumbled deeper into foreign territory than either intended. Even though we went to school together and shared classes together and occasionally ate lunch and reviewed homework assignments together, whites and Negroes, even Ivy Leaguers, just didn't share feelings and experiences about race. Just as Tyrone Lamond and I never again spoke about his rejection as a patrol boy years earlier.

Then it occurred to me that Robert didn't question me for the same reason Tyrone hadn't questioned me when he was denied the patrol-boy belt: He knew the answer, and didn't need to experience additional hurt from hearing a white boy spell it out, or even worse, hearing me pretend there was no racial animosity.

Still, I was relieved to not be put on the spot. What would I have said to Robert? That my parents and their white friends and neighbors blamed families like Robert's for destroying our South Shore neighborhood? That our biggest fear in our new apartment a mile or so to the east of the Ridgeland Avenue place was that that our new neighborhood would similarly become all-Negro?

The awkward silence that followed was testimony to all the awkward feelings our little exchange brought up. I was aware that I didn't feel any of the resentment I'm sure Mom and Dad would have felt if they had been with me at the Medici to learn that Robert's family had moved into our old place. Maybe that was because I knew and liked Robert and thought it was neat that he had my old bedroom. To them, he would have been just another invading Negro.

Heck, it was difficult enough stuff for Nate, Lee, and me to discuss among ourselves, probably because we could match names and faces of Negroes to the turmoil so feared by our parents. So, we rarely had deep discussions about the racial problems around us, except to complain about being bullied by gousters.

19

Fortunately, a new distraction sprang up a few feet away from our table at the Medici. Valerie was dancing a jitterbug with one of the girls she had been sitting with. The sad distracted-looking Valerie watching Tyrone exit the Medici was replaced by the upbeat and smiling Valerie of earlier in the evening.

I asked one of the white girls, Beth Tollins, to dance. Beth was a friendly geeky small girl with straight brown hair and a bad case of acne, who sat behind me in nearly all the classes we were in together. Our friendship began and ended with our pre-class and after-class comparison of notes, until this meeting at the Medici. Fortunately, she was as awkward as I was dancing jitterbug, and we laughed with relief as the song ended.

As I was returning to my table, Valerie was headed in the opposite direction, toward me. She stopped as I approached her, and looked directly at me, a look of mock amazement on her face. "Hey, when are you going to show me that sneaky drawing you did of me in study hall?"

She was staring with large inquiring brown eyes, and I detected the beginnings of a smirk forming at the corners of her mouth. A far cry from the bored look after study hall the other day.

I was caught off guard that she even remembered the drawing. As it turned out, I'd been carrying it around since the study hall, folded in my back pocket. While I would have loved to show it to her, I didn't want to risk taking it out there and have her react badly or, even worse, possibly show it to everyone else hanging out in that back room at the Medici, poking fun at it and me.

I decided to take some risk. "I'll show it to you after you dance with me."

That sort-of smirk had now blossomed into a slight smile. She said nothing, presumably analyzing the situation in her mind. I stood there in the silence, my heart suddenly pounding for what seemed like forever, but was probably only fifteen or twenty seconds.

"Okay," she said finally. One of her arms moved up toward her shoulder and the other stretched out in invitation for me to come forward. A radio ad for a check-cashing store was ending and a slowly-sung song I'd never heard before was playing on what I presumed to be the Negro radio station.

Fortunately for my dancing ability, the song was slow enough to accommodate my awkward box step.

A deep man's voice was singing: "Try me...try me...your love will always be true..."

I was trying, trying, to avoid stepping on Valerie's toes...and to remember the instruction for the box step I learned at Fortnightly.

"Who taught you to dance like that?" Valerie asked mockingly after a few more steps, one of which had me landing on her right foot. Fortunately, she kept her voice down.

I noticed with relief that three other couples continued dancing—two were whites with whites, and one was Negro with Negro—and they seemed not to have heard Valerie's mocking question.

"I learned it in a program at the Y called Fortnightly," I said tentatively.

"Fortnightly?" I didn't even have to look—I could feel the smirk.

"Yeah, it's a program my parents signed me up for where a bunch of boys and girls get together on Saturday afternoons and learn to dance...and be polite to each other," I said, immediately regretting bringing up the last part, about being polite.

"So that's how white kids learn to dance?" I wasn't sure it was a question or a sarcastic observation.

"Where did you learn to dance?"

"Don't you know?" she said, halting our dancing momentarily to step back and look directly at me. "We're born knowing how to dance. We've got rhythm." She laughed.

I didn't say anything and we resumed dancing in silence. We were just close enough that I could hear her gentle breathing, and feel her breasts lightly against my chest. There was a slight smell of a sweet perfume or cologne I'd never smelled before. It was pleasing, not overpoweringly sweet like some of what the white girls wore at synagogue socials. I felt myself relaxing.

I made another effort at conversation as the song faded into conclusion, "I need you…"

"Who sings that?" I asked. "I'm not sure I've heard it before."

"Why, that's James Brown," she said. "He's all over." She didn't add that he was all over Negro stations, not white stations.

There was a pause as the James Brown song faded away.

Suddenly, a new song came on, one I knew, clearly not from the Negro radio station. The slow melody of "I Only Have Eyes for You" by The Flamingos.

"Looks like those Lab School guys got hold of the radio," I joked.

She was silent as we danced slowly, holding each other a bit closer.

I closed my eyes and felt genuine relief when I thought about how differently the evening might have gone had Evie accepted my Rainbow Beach invitation to come along.

It didn't take much of a stretch to realize how out of place she would have felt and that I wouldn't have even had a conversation with Valerie to boot.

Much better to enjoy the slow melody and romantic lyrics.

The moon may be high
But I can't see a thing in the sky
I only have eyes for you

Nate was dancing with one of the Lab School girls, a pretty blond in a tight white blouse that accentuated her large bust. Robert was dancing with one of Valerie's friends.

Valerie and I were the only interracial couple. But in this place, the back room of a Hyde Park coffeehouse, it felt nice and natural as we drew not even a glance.

The gentle song ended and was replaced by the jarring voice of the radio disc jockey, Dick Biondi, who announced Dee Dee Sharp singing "Do the Bird." Suddenly Valerie was standing, shaking and flexing her chest and mid-section in and out, moving her arms up and down in rhythm to the silly music. She looked something like she had as a cheerleader, coordinated and animated. She was quickly joined by the other girls.

"Come on baby, shake it more and more…twist and fly…do the bird with me…"

I tried to imitate her but it was a poor imitation. Thankfully, she ignored my gyrations and called over the music, asking me what I thought of our geometry teacher, Mr. Olive. He was one of several Negro teachers we had at Hyde Park High.

"He seems pretty good, given that it's math," I responded in a loud voice, trying to be sure she heard me. "I'm not good in math, but I can understand what he's doing."

Valerie nodded, continuing her dancing.

"He sometimes seems a little spacey," I added.

She smiled. "Yeah, he's probably high as a kite."

"What do you mean?" I asked. I really didn't know what she was referring to.

"He's probably smoking weed," she explained.

I must have looked as surprised as I felt because she stared at me. "You don't know about smoking weed?"

I didn't. Nate, Lee, and I had partaken of whiskey and bourbon, snuck from one or another of our parents' liquor cabinets, when we had an apartment or house to ourselves on a Saturday evening. But marijuana was a complete unknown, not even something we aspired to. I had read, probably in a *Time* or *Life* magazine article, about how some of the great Negro jazz musicians smoked marijuana, but that was kind of abstract. I kept getting the feeling that Valerie knew things I had no idea about.

"Can you give me a ride home when this is over?" she asked.

It immediately occurred to me that she arrived at the Medici expecting Tyrone to drive her home, and now had to find another option. I decided to leave the Tyrone issue for another time. "Sure," I said quickly. "I have a car here."

"I know. I saw you working like a crazy man to park it in front of the Tropical Hut when I was coming in here." The smirk. "I think some of the people inside the restaurant were having fun watching you work the steering wheel so hard. I don't know how they could see you, with all the rotisserie chickens turning in the window—but I could tell people were staring."

The song ended, and as if by common understanding, we each drifted toward the tables with the friends we came with. I was relieved. Maybe I was a little tired of feeling self-conscious, and more to the point, fearful that my naiveté would at some point turn her off. I didn't know about James Brown; I was a clumsy dancer; I didn't know about weed. Fortunately, my afternoon lightheadedness from Tommy Sullivan's whack had pretty much worn away.

My immediate problem was what to do with Nate. At our table, I asked him how he'd feel about fending for himself to get back to South Shore. His eyebrows rose noticeably when I told him I was giving Valerie a ride.

"Sure, I'll take the IC, or get a lift with someone here," he said. "Don't worry." The IC was the Illinois Central commuter train that ran through both Hyde Park and South Shore.

I looked directly at him, and lowered my voice. "By the way, good idea of yours to come here."

"I think so," he said, and grinned back at me.

20

The gathering seemed to spontaneously break up after a couple more songs. Valerie must have prepped her two friends, since they walked out of the Medici together without a glance at her.

Fortunately, 57th Street was quiet, because I was suddenly very self-conscious about walking out the door of a commercial establishment and onto a public street on a Saturday night with a pretty Negro girl, just the two of us.

I opened the passenger-side door of the blue Chevy for Valerie like I'd seen guys do in the movies and she slid in. I got in, and inquired where she lived.

"Isn't it a little early?" she asked. She was right, it was only about ten. "I don't want to get home too early and have to talk to my parents."

The nervousness I felt about leaving the Medici with a Negro girl followed me into the car. I hadn't ever been together with a girl alone in the car at night with time to kill. But I was persuaded not to press the point about taking her home, and took a major leap further into the unknown. "Hey, you want to go see the German sub? And I can show you the drawing."

Everyone, white and Negro, knew about the long gray hulk of metal that was a World War II German U-505 submarine parked along the side of the vast Museum of Science and Industry, right off Lake Michigan near Jackson Park. Kids from all over Chicago went there on school field trips from the time they were in third or fourth grade.

After trekking through a make-believe farm complete with real hatching baby chicks and then taking a bumpy elevator down into a dark mock coal mine, they were led through the sub's cramped quarters. There they were told how the German sailors spent weeks cooped up in the tight quarters while the sub searched out American and British ships to sink. Everything was just as it was then for the poor sailors, including the blue-and-white checked sheets on the bunks.

Everyone also knew that the vast parking lot outside the museum was the main South Side make-out spot. And sure enough, on this warm, late-spring evening, there were about fifteen or twenty cars scattered around the lot. In almost every one, the profiles of two people were visible, usually in the driver and middle seat, or else the middle and passenger seat. In two or three cars, only one person was visible, at least for a time.

I rolled my window down a bit, and Valerie did the same, to allow the refreshing lake breeze in. The huge ornate edifice we faced, with its marble columns and green dome, looked like it belonged in Washington DC.

I turned on the dome light inside the car, pulled out my drawing, slowly unfolded it, and handed it over to Valerie without a word. She studied it silently for a few moments. I could see her dark eyes darting up and down. I feared another rejection a la Robin at the youth-group dance. At least there weren't other people around to watch me being humiliated.

Then she began folding up the drawing, interrupting my worst-case scenarios. "Aren't you even going to kiss me?"

I hoped she didn't see the look of shock I must have had all over my face as I slid over on the car bench to the middle of the front seat, and leaned over to kiss her gently on the lips. They were soft and cool. I pulled back, expecting to see her eyes closed in rapture. Instead, she looked at me with that smirk. "You kiss like in the movies." She paused, taking in my bewilderment. "Haven't you ever heard of French kissing?"

I could feel my face flushing hot, despite the pleasant cool lake breeze flowing through the car. She put her arms around my neck, pulled me toward her, and the next thing I knew, we were kissing for real.

Her tongue was twitching around in my mouth, and mine in hers.

Her lips were noticeably warmer.

I realized as I put my hand on her neck, that her hair felt coarser than it looked. I wanted to ask her if she had it straightened, but decided that would have to wait for another time.

I placed a hand on a breast and she gently removed it.

I pulled back, and she had that smirk on her face. "You better watch out, white boy. I'll get Booker after you."

Then a little less smirky: "You just think us colored girls are easier, don't you? That's why you like me."

I let out a sigh. "No, I liked you the first time I saw you during the summer at Riverview." She had a puzzled look on her face.

"Do you remember seeing a white guy throwing up outside the Rotor?"

"That was you? Yuck!"

"You remember Vinnie and his friend?"

"How'd you know about that?"

"We were behind you, Nate, Lee, and I. We saw you tell those guys where to get off."

"I was so mad," she started. "But it was scary. Made me realize we probably shouldn't have even gone to Riverview. Tanya and I were just bored, I guess."

"You ever wonder why those guys didn't come after you?"

Valerie stared at me. This was fun. "After you and Tanya walked off, those two were passing around a bottle of booze with their friends, talking about how they were going to go after you two. I challenged Vinnie to play the African Dip, for money. He took the bait, and I beat him. He wouldn't pay up, but it took enough time that he and his friends kind of forgot about you and Tanya."

Valerie smiled, in a sexy kind of way, and we began kissing again. This time she just gave a low moan when I put my hand on her breast.

The way things were going seemed almost too good to be true, especially after all the frustrating pursuit. Maybe that's why my mind made a detour, and began raising new doubts.

Had she learned all she knew about marijuana and French kissing from Tyrone Lamond? How serious were they? Had they broken up permanently, or just had a little spat in the scene at the Medici? What did Tyrone's reference to "the Rangers" mean? All questions that would be best not asked till a more opportune time—later, I concluded.

21

I could tell it was getting late because there were fewer and fewer cars in the lot. We took a break from kissing, and just held each other together in a hug. I could feel her quick heartbeat and short breaths, and I was sure she could feel mine.

I decided to pop the biggest question that had been bothering me, the one about the fight. "Why did Booker put that knife away when you told him to? Did you and he have something going on?"

"No, I don't know him well," she said softly in my ear. "But he's been around my family for a long time. His family has gone through some hard times. His mom and dad bought a house years ago from a white real estate guy. Just as they were about to finish paying it off after ten years or so, and become owners, the real estate guy said they had done something wrong, had missed a payment or something."

She tried to explain the details, but it was difficult for me to understand, since I was totally unaware of such housing legalities. She told me Booker's parents hired some do-gooder white lawyer who spent two or three years suing the guy who sold them the building. The lawyer tried hard, but all the judges turned him down, said a contract is a contract. Just for good measure, the judges made Booker's parents pay $750 in court costs and penalties. That was just adding insult to the injury of losing the house they had paid $25,000 or $30,000 for.

"Booker's dad took up drinking after that, and from what I understand, drank himself to death two or three years ago. For a while, near the end, his dad was the janitor of our apartment building. Then, his mother got on welfare, just trying to make her money last till the first of the month, when she got her check. For a few years, Booker was friends with my older brother, Derrick. They run around in different circles now. So I've known him pretty much since I was a little girl. Both Derrick and I have been trying to talk Booker out of dropping out of school. He's fed up with his classes and all.

"But the fight? I really don't know why he listened to me. The only thing I can think is that Negro boys are mostly raised by their mommas, so when Booker heard a familiar woman's voice telling him to do something, he did it."

"Besides," she added, pushing back a foot or so to gaze directly at me, the smirk bigger than ever. "If Booker cut you all up, we wouldn't have been able to come out here and make out like this, would we?"

I could only nod, and smile at the irony. She was probably right about Booker's reaction to her knife command. I felt bad learning about his family's sad story, and that he wanted to drop out of school. Now I realized why he missed so much time in grade school, what with having a drunk father.

Her expression had turned serious. "Okay, so I have a question for you. Why did you make me look so light in your drawing? I look almost like a white girl with a tan."

Hmmm, she would question me on that. I had wrestled, somewhere just barely in my consciousness, about how dark to shade her. I had opted to go easy, sensing that lighter was more desired and desirable. But how to say that, without knowing the "right" answer?

"I guess I didn't want to make you look too dark," I started. She continued staring at me. No smirk. No grin. This was a big deal. "I thought you might be insulted."

"So, you think I'd rather look more like a white girl than a Negro girl?"

"I'm not really sure," I stammered. "I didn't think about it a whole lot. I just wanted something you might like enough to want to talk to me. I'm not really much of an artist."

"You're not too bad, white boy." The smirk was back. I felt like I had passed some kind of test.

I tried to take control of the conversation. "One more thing for you," I said. "Are you an Ivy Leaguer or a gouster? You act and talk like an Ivy Leaguer. But when you hang out with guys like Booker, I'm thinking maybe you're a gouster." I wanted to mention Tyrone, but something told me that should wait as well.

"What do you think, white boy?"

Now it was my chance to be the wise guy. "Maybe I'll just call you 'gouster girl.' You call me 'white boy' and I call you 'gouster girl.' How's that?"

"Shee-it, white boy. Gonna hit you upside yo head and kick yo white ass all the way to 63rd Street, you call me a gousta one mo time." She smiled slightly, as if she was impressed with her own cleverness.

I certainly was.

She had an answer for everything. I was half tempted to ask her if she and her Ivy League friends engaged in gouster talk when they were alone, outside white company—but I had my answer, in a way that made me feel good, like I was part of a special club.

Given an opportunity to change the discussion topic, I took it. "Why didn't you want to get home while your parents were up?"

"You sure are dense, white boy. Did it ever occur to you I wanted to be with you? Now, doesn't that make you feel like some kind of big ass?" The smirk. I had to laugh.

"Oh, yeah, and my father hates whites. He would give me some kind of whipping if he knew I was out with a white boy, making out in his father's car."

Gulp. "You probably wouldn't want to bring me over quite yet for an introduction, then, would you?" I deadpanned.

Valerie smiled at my effort at humor.

I resisted the temptation to empathize by telling her my father would give it to me as well for using his prized Chevy to drive a Negro girl around. Somehow, it was as if her father's racism was more understandable than my father's racism. So I stuck with the subject at hand.

"What got your dad so pissed off at whites? Or, let me put it this way, I know it could have been a lot of things. But was there something in particular that made him so angry?"

Valerie leaned back against the car seat and stared straight ahead. The smirk was gone. She spoke in a lower more serious tone of voice I hadn't heard before. "My daddy used to like whites. His job was out in the steel mills in Gary with lots of white guys. Since he got paid as much as the white guys, he got it into his head that we could also live with whites. Imagine that kind of crazy thinking." She paused, as if she was wondering for the umpteenth time about such ridiculous thinking. "So when I was a little girl, he tried to buy a house in Cicero. He did it together with another guy he knew from the steel mills, who also had a family."

She paused again, perhaps to let me imagine how bad the rest of the story was going to be. Everyone knew about Cicero, a suburb bordering the West Side of Chicago, and its periodic race riots.

"No bank would give them a loan, because they didn't loan to Negroes. But a white real estate guy offered to sell them each a house direct, under contract. So Daddy and this other guy put payments down on these two cute little houses about a block apart, and we moved in. About a week after we moved in, this mob of white people marched past our houses shouting stuff like, 'Niggers, move out!' and 'Go back where you come from!' Daddy tried to tell Mom it would all blow over, not to worry. Was he ever wrong.

"A few days after that, someone threw a firebomb in our living room window. Daddy and Momma got me, James, and Derrick out of the house, and the fire department put the fire out before it got past the living room. While we were standing outside, a bunch of neighbors began gathering out in the street, and they were all staring at us, like we were some kind of freaks. They were talking soft with each other, but loud enough so we could hear. They were saying we had just come here to make trouble, and we should go back where we came from."

I felt myself cringe in shame as she told the story. It was like a world of horrors she was describing, from not being able to buy a house like white people, to being taunted and firebombed.

I had read in the paper about firebombings in white neighborhoods around Chicago, where homes bought by Negroes were attacked. But this was the first time I had been able to put a face and name with it. "That must have been so scary," was all I could think to say.

She nodded. "It was awful. I still have nightmares about it. I can hear the glass shattering when the firebomb was tossed in. Even today, I can't stand the smell of gasoline or lighter fluid or even charcoal fires."

"Did the police arrest the people who did it?" I asked.

"They supposedly investigated, but no one in the neighborhood would give them any information—they didn't want to wind up like us, I suppose. The cops told us they had an idea of who did it, but they could never prove anything without witnesses."

"So what did you do?"

"The man who sold us the house said Daddy would have to pay for the repairs if he wanted to move back in. Daddy would have done it, to try to save the $5,000 down payment, but Momma said there was no way she was staying there with little kids. The wife of Daddy's friend was the same. So we all moved back to Woodlawn."

"And your family lost $5,000 you couldn't afford to lose."

She nodded.

"And your dad never cared much for whites after that."

"No, he never did. He started going to lectures given by Elijah Muhammad, and got more and more involved with the Nation of Islam. They got him a job doing maintenance on their temple."

Now I knew for sure I didn't want to talk about the basis of my family's racism. My family had experienced nothing even close to what her family went through.

"Who is Elijah Muhammad and what is Nation of Islam?" I asked. I hadn't heard or read about any of that.

"Elijah Muhammad preaches that the white man is the devil, and that Negroes should live separately from whites," Valerie said, without emotion. "His followers are Muslims, like in the Middle East."

Pause. "You probably should take me home."

Not the most upbeat ending to the evening, though I was grateful she didn't mock my ignorance about Elijah Muhammad or Nation of Islam. I was also grateful she felt she could be so candid about the racial prejudice her family experienced. But, selfishly, I was probably most grateful she didn't get around to asking me about how my family would have reacted if her family had moved to our block in South Shore instead of Cicero. I knew there wouldn't have been firebombs—that hadn't happened in South Shore. But I did know there would have been lots of hard stares, maybe even some name calling. Could I have told her that?

Or maybe, like Tyrone and Robert, she already knew the answer, and didn't need to experience the added hurt of hearing it spelled out from a white boy.

We rode in silence to the edge of Woodlawn, on 60th Street and Kimbark at the modern glass-and-steel University of Chicago Law School campus. She insisted on getting out there and walking the few blocks into Woodlawn to her apartment. There were no hugs or kisses. But I felt good...no, great, about Valerie.

22

The South Shore Country Club may as well have been a secret military base for all I knew about it. It was a mile or less from our apartment, but all I had ever seen in years of riding my bicycle past was what appeared to be a very lush golf course, occupying prime real estate hugging Lake Michigan, from 67th to 71st Streets.

The golfers I saw through the chain link fence were all white men, nattily dressed, some even in knickers, golfing on the greenest grass anywhere in the area. Certainly greener and more carefully manicured than the nearby Jackson Park public golf course where I sometimes played with friends, decked out in t-shirt and Bermuda shorts.

The club's "restricted" nature was the stuff of endless gossip and speculation in our heavily Jewish neighborhood. Here was this fancy club, situated on some of the most desirable land in the city, and it completely rejected the many Jews in the neighborhood that nearly surrounded the place. At least some of those people were well-to-do professionals and merchants, who could have afforded its very high membership fees.

I sometimes found myself wondering if the white non-Jewish members personally hated Jews, and that was why they kept the place "restricted." What was it they so detested about Jews?

I gave barely a passing thought to the fact that the club also barred

Negroes. I guess in a city where Negroes and whites lived such separate lives, that particular aspect of the club's bias didn't strike me as unusual, and worthy of anywhere near the same analysis that friends and I gave to the Jewish bias.

Until I walked into the club the next morning for my first day of caddying, following my adventuresome Saturday evening with Valerie, I had no inkling just how opulent the place was. It was another warm and hazy humid day, and I arrived at 8:00 a.m., just as the golfing traffic was picking up.

The opulence didn't apply to the places "the help" hung out. The caddy room at the back of the main clubhouse was a drab place, with peeling paint and dented wood on the counter that separated caddies from a supply room of golf clubs and bags. Standing behind the counter, Eddie greeted me like a long-lost cousin.

"Hey, sorry to take your money in the game yesterday, but business is business." He smiled. "You at least have some fun last night?"

"Just hung out with a few friends," I said casually. It didn't seem like the time to tell him about the Medici and Valerie, if ever there might be such a time.

Eddie made like he didn't hear me. His mind was on the business at hand. "Let's get you making some serious money."

I should have been raring to go, but his remark about money brought me back to an unpleasant reality. Dad had given me another dressing down earlier in the morning as I was getting ready to leave our apartment for my new job. "You're really going to go work for those Jew haters?"

I had used Eddie's logic. "I need to make some real money, Dad. I want to have money to help pay for college."

"There must be other jobs around where you can make money. I could ask at Goldblatt's if there is something for you in the stock room."

"Dad, I made a commitment to take this job. I need to follow through."

"You don't owe those Jew haters anything!" He hesitated. "Your mother and I came here to get away from Jew haters."

He caught me off guard. He rarely made reference to his and Mom's escape from Germany just before the Holocaust. It was as if it was a forbidden topic.

I ended the conversation. "Gotta run." I was out the door. I felt a heaviness in my chest. I never felt I could respond to his very occasional Holocaust references, either with a question or an intelligent response, because I knew so little about what had happened. I knew lots of people had died in concentration camps. But no one, including my parents, seemed to want to provide details about our family's specific experiences, so I just stopped asking questions. My mind stayed focused on my own little world and its risks: If Dad was this unhappy about my new job, imagine how he'd feel if he knew about Valerie being a passenger in his car.

Eddie was true to his word, at least about getting me work. I was assigned to carry the bulky golf bag of Jack Cunningham, a short balding overweight man who looked to be in his forties. His brown knickers and fedora hat made him look like a character out of the 1800s. He barely acknowledged me as he clip-clopped in his spiked golf shoes along with two friends. I followed them out to the first tee. I was feeling jealous of the other caddy in our group, a muscular dark-haired guy who looked to be in his twenties, because he'd been assigned to carry the friends' two bags. I'd make $2 for one bag and he'd make $4 for the two. That was before what could potentially be generous tips.

I felt a tad better when I handed Jack his driver and his first shot arced prettily to within sight of the green about 170 yards away. Much neater than the shots of his friends, one of whom sliced his shot into some trees, and the other hooked his into a sand trap to the left of the green.

"Eight iron, Mr. Cunningham?" I asked as we approached the ball, cradled conveniently in some short grass. He nodded and grunted.

Even though I only had one bag, I anticipated this could still turn into some decent money, as Jack addressed the ball. Maybe be done with the scheduled nine holes in an hour-and-a-half. Two dollars the club was paying me, and if Jack was pleased, maybe another three or four dollars in tips could have me making possibly six dollars for less than two hours of work. I would have loved returning home to let Dad know my financial instincts were correct, and therefore justified me working for Jew haters.

Jack quickly put the kibosh on my fantasy by topping the chip shot, rolling the ball a few feet, just a foot off the green. "Gimme the putter," he ordered. He rushed the putt and the ball ran past the metal flag in the hole, nearly as far to the other side of the green as where he hit from.

Three putts later, Jack was sweating profusely and swearing.

It didn't get much better on the second, third, or fourth holes. On the fifth hole, I could sense he was questioning my club selection advice. When I offered him a number-four wood club for his second fairway shot after slicing into a clump of weeds, he glared at me sternly. "Nah, gimme a five-iron," he barked. He dug a deep divot as the ball skirted perhaps twenty-five feet in front of him.

"Jesus Christ!" he exclaimed. "This is unreal." Finally, he connected with a six-iron, and the ball soared beautifully, only to plop into a tiny pond in front of, and to the left of, the green.

The ball might have been gone, but Jack remained stuck in follow-through, both hands holding the club over his left shoulder, staring in disbelief. I bit my lip to keep from laughing. I tried to put Eddie's face into my mind, reminding me sternly to not laugh, or even smile, no matter how ridiculously a member's game deteriorated.

Jack's game improved a bit on the last four holes, but he was still at fifty-four for the nine holes while his friends were in the high forties. Moreover, they were ribbing him for his poor play and talking about having steaks for lunch—apparently the loser had to buy lunch.

Instead of an hour-and-a-half, the nine holes took two-and-a-half hours. Without looking directly at me, Jack handed me a single dollar bill as a tip and clopped off with his clubs. The other caddy was happily pocketing a five-dollar bill and three singles—eight dollars. I had made a total of three dollars for the two-and-a-half hours, and this other guy had made twelve dollars.

The tip differential stung. It wasn't as if the other guys played a lot better than Jack. Yet they generously rewarded the other caddy. Did Jack know I was Jewish and somehow blame me for his bad game?

23

I tried to wipe such negative thoughts from my mind as I returned to the caddy room, where Eddie asked how it went. "It started great," I told him. "But Jack's game was off, and it got worse as the round went on. I had to try very hard to take your advice and keep from laughing. He wasn't the greatest tipper, either."

Eddie looked perplexed. "Sometimes you get a dud. We'll see if we can do better by you this afternoon. You have a few minutes right now?"

He came around the counter and motioned outside. "It's been crazy this morning, but we have a little break now, and Stan, the manager, has an eye on things. I'll give you a quick tour. This place is amazing. I hear Jack Harshman is going to be playing golf here Monday after pitching today for the Sox. We'll get you back to the caddy room pronto and get you started making some serious money, for real this time."

Eddie seemed genuinely proud of the clay tennis courts down the access road from the clubhouse. "Watch how the ball stirs up a little cloud of dust when the serve hits," he directed me. I had never before seen clay courts, my tennis confined to paved public courts, so that little cloud of dust was impressive. The players were elegantly dressed in white collared pull-over sport shirts and white shorts.

Next he showed me a huge expanse of closely cropped grass, almost like an extended golf green, dotted with small black balls being rolled by men in white dress shirts and white slacks. "It's lawn bowling," said Eddie. "I don't understand it, but I guess all that matters is that those guys get it."

He pointed ahead of us. Out of a cavernous indoor riding arena further down the access road came a line of about twenty horses being ridden by men and women, and a few teenagers and children, in formal riding gear of dark suit-like jackets and tight pants. "There is some serious horse competition here," Eddie told me. "And there's a group of special Spanish horses sponsored by Jackie Kennedy that's going to start here next week."

We made our way back toward the golf clubhouse along the lake-front promenade with the tan-sand beach on our left and what Eddie identified as "the beach house," a low building with striped awnings over changing rooms on our right. The beach had a small playground at one end; at the other, some eight or ten men in khaki jackets were lined up holding rifles and shooting at clay disks being mechanically thrown into the air over the water—"skeet shooting," as Eddie referred to it. "Just like at Rainbow Beach," I joked to Eddie. He smiled and nodded.

The beach was much smaller than Rainbow Beach, but unlike Rainbow, wasn't very crowded. A few dozen club members in swim suits lounged on fancy orange-and-green striped canvas-and-wood reclining beach chairs, some of them sipping at ice drinks.

To their left, they could easily see the rapidly growing crowd of Negroes surging onto the 63rd Street Beach less than a mile to the north. And to their right, to the south, Rainbow Beach was visible as well—a sea of white bodies filling up much of the expanse.

There was one last amazing sight as we returned to the clubhouse in its lower level: a fully equipped "rec room" with three or four long shuffleboard lanes and a half dozen billiards tables covered in bright green felt. I'd only had a couple opportunities to play pool, at George's house, in his family's "den." I enjoyed it, but I didn't see George that often outside of school.

Out in the deserted hallway, Eddie stopped, and turned toward me, speaking in a low voice. "This is top secret, but the word is this place is in big trouble. The membership is dropping quickly."

"Gee, it seems so luxurious," I replied. "Lots of people would love to spend time here."

"Yeah, but they won't open the place to Jews. There's a big argument going on between board members about letting Jews join up, but the old-time big wigs are dead set against it. I don't get it, because there are a lot of Jews with a lot of money in South Shore who would join up in an instant. But these old timers hate Jews too much." Eddie shrugged his shoulders.

Eddie's inside information about the resistance to allowing Jews as members resurrected the heaviness I felt when I left home that morning. There was no denying that many of the members were *truly* the Jew haters Dad anticipated.

24

Back at the caddy room, Eddie had another assignment for me—Slim Jim Sullivan. As in the morning round, I carried Jim's bag, while a more experienced caddy carried the bags of Jim's two friends. Where Jack was short and fat, Jim was tall and lanky. He also seemed more laid back than Jack, and even sort of friendly. But his game wasn't much better.

His relaxed manner came under stress as he hit slices and hooks and landed in sand traps he couldn't easily exit.

Unlike Jack, who had at the very start of our time together politely inquired into where I went to school, Jim was completely impersonal. Yet as we walked from shot to shot and hole to hole, I sensed something familiar about the man. I couldn't put my finger on what it was. I was sure I had never before met him.

It wasn't till we approached the dreaded fifth hole, with its strategically placed pond, that I realized, with each step he took, that his toes pointed inward. What was his last name again? I pulled the small hand-written assignment slip from my pocket. "Jim Sullivan." As we approached the tee area, I studied his face, and saw more clearly in Jim's mouth and eyes the resemblance to patrol boy kingpin Tommy Sullivan.

With the dreaded fifth-hole pond nearly in front of us, I felt around in my right pocket for the golf ball I had found sitting in very shallow water on the edge of the pond after Jack's misfire that morning. Jim was engrossed in conversation with his two friends when I carefully set the water-logged ball onto the fairway grass, in place of the new Titleist ball Jim had put on his tee at the start of the hole.

I was prepared to plead extreme carelessness if he noticed the funny ball, but he didn't. He hit it full with a nice relaxed swing, but instead of it soaring high over the pond as it should have, it made a low arc, plopping directly into the middle of the pond. Jim never swore, but after that final indignity, he went completely silent. Unlike with Jack, I felt a bit of smug satisfaction when Jim handed me a one dollar bill for a tip, without looking directly at me, or even mumbling a thank-you.

No, my act of retribution, tiny as it was, felt like sort of poetic justice, retribution for the head whack Tommy had given me the previous day, and payback for his son's penny-tossing on the bus a few days before that. Neither action would make any Jewish history book, but at least I had fought back against active Jew haters.

Yet my sense of satisfaction was fleeting, quickly replaced by a deeper pit in my gut than I had ever before known. Surrounding that pit was a sense of loneliness and isolation that came from spending a day on this foreign planet of a place they called a country club.

25

As I walked from the ninth hole along the service road back to the clubhouse, I tried to ignore the people in their tennis whites, as well as the low booms of skeet guns shooting at clay disks along the beach. Instead, I tried to construct a conversation in my mind with Eddie in which I inquired about how I could be assigned to carry two members' golf bags and thereby double my earnings. I felt a strong need to return home that evening with more than just dumb excuses about why the South Shore Country Club wasn't a pot of gold for this Jewish caddy.

My internal rehearsal was interrupted by a loud shouting voice. It was Eddie's boss, Stan. I heard him shouting well before I entered the caddy's room. "Don't come over here anymore, ya hear me! We don't got no work for you guys. Just follow the cop out at the entrance. He'll make sure you get out of this area without getting your asses kicked."

As I approached the caddy room, two Negro teens were coming out. Uh-oh. I recognized them. There was Robert Clark, along with Paul Badger, my tablemates from the previous evening. They were nicely dressed in dark slacks and light-colored short-sleeve sport shirts, but their expressions were a combination of bewilderment, embarrassment, and anger. I stopped immediately and bent down to tie my shoe, so I was positioned away from them, and they couldn't identify me.

What stuck in my mind was Paul's look of confusion, and pain.

It was so at odds with the charismatic and cool classmate I knew, and sometimes envied. I had especially envied him about six months earlier, when we were both involved in a class election. Nate had had this bright idea that we'd run for class office. Nate would be president, and I would be treasurer.

I let his enthusiasm and visions of grandeur overcome my inclination to lie low and be unobtrusive.

So we made big cardboard signs with our names, and planned short speeches to the 400 or so members of our class gathered in the darkened auditorium. Nate spoke about the importance of "opening a dialog" with administrators over how our class schedules were put together. I proposed that we have a way to set aside a small amount of funds for unusual educational outings for members of the class who were interested. It had all felt lame when we were planning and rehearsing a couple days before, but Nate remained enthusiastic.

We were met with polite applause from the sixty or seventy white students in our class, along with a few guffaws and hoots from the gousters.

"Go sit down, stupid honkies!" called one.

Next it was Paul's turn, and he walked coolly onto the stage. He was fully dressed for the occasion in dark slacks, starched white shirt and olive green V-neck sweater. He carried no signs or index cards with speaking points like Nate and me. He showed not the slightest sign of nervousness. Quite the opposite. He looked so relaxed it was almost as if he was doing everyone a favor by ambling up onto the stage.

"Y'all lookin' good!" he beamed, emphasizing the "good." "Y'all feelin' good?" A deafening roar of approval rose up in the auditorium. I didn't know Paul well, but in the past, I had heard some of the gousters mutter "Oreo" when he walked by—black on the outside and white on the inside. But when push came to shove, as in this election, gousters and Ivy Leaguers would unite against the common white enemy.

Nate and I looked at each other in bewilderment. It was obvious we were done for, even before Paul introduced his running mate, our old friend from elementary school, Tyrone Lamond.

As embarrassed as I was by the class election trouncing, I admired Paul. He never rubbed it in, never said much of anything. Now, the sight of Paul being abused by the country club caddy supervisor felt wrong in so many ways.

The only good news was that the confrontation was over quickly, with no one being physically hurt. But when I entered the caddy room, I could tell Eddie was still agitated, because he was immersed in a monolog directed at no one in particular, since Stan was preoccupied arranging golf clubs in another part of the room. "Fucking darkies think they can walk in here and be caddies. There's no way that's going to happen. They don't get it that they could be killed just coming over here if some of my friends see them. They should know they're not wanted over here. Why can't they just stay in their own neighborhoods?"

It was as if he was genuinely puzzled about why Negroes would even consider coming to a white area, knowing that many of the whites didn't want them there. After all, he wouldn't go to a Negro area knowing he wasn't wanted. It seemed pretty obvious to me that the Negroes were coming to where the jobs were, and he would do the same if the situation were reversed, if the jobs were in Negro neighborhoods. But that definitely wasn't what he wanted to hear at that moment.

I took about five minutes to go to the bathroom and wash up from my earlier caddying assignment. Then I decided to take a chance and approach Eddie. I wouldn't argue with him, just appeal to his sense of decency.

"Hey, Eddie, isn't there a way you might be able to try those two guys out if some other guys don't show up? I've seen them playing in Jackson Park, and they're good golfers. I'll bet they'd work hard to be good caddies."

Eddie glared at me. I probably should have let him calm down some more before bringing up such a sensitive subject. Or maybe not ever brought it up.

At least he didn't go off on another rant. Instead, he came up close to me and looked me directly in the eye: "You just do your job, and I'll do mine," he said softly, pausing before his final dig. "From the looks of your tips, you've got a ways to go on your job." There would be no more caddying opportunities this day.

While bicycling home, I concocted a story for Dad about how my first day was spent in training, and that my big opportunity would come the next weekend. Fortunately, he accepted my story without comment.

26

Saturday night couldn't come quickly enough for me. On Monday morning, I was walking through the crowded halls at Parkview humming "I Only Have Eyes for You." It wasn't until Tuesday that I saw Valerie in geometry. Mr. Olive was getting ready to go over the most recent homework assignment. I caught Valerie's eye just as we were taking our seats, and she gave me a wink and a smile. I smiled back.

As the class ended, she walked out with a friend, and disappeared into the throng of students changing classes, without waiting for me. I had hung back, hoping she would hang back as well, and we could have a few minutes to greet each other, hopefully chat casually in the wake of the intense Saturday evening experience.

I didn't want to be negative and read too much into seemingly small events, but it did feel as if she was avoiding me. Indeed, that wink and smile represented the beginning and end of our contact that day, and nearly the rest of the week.

Yet a part of me was relieved. As wrapped up as I had been in romantic fantasy about Valerie, I also felt a nagging fear about the unfamiliar turf I'd been walking on since I entered the Medici Saturday evening.

Supposing Valerie had snuggled up to me after geometry class, and we had walked along the echoing hallway during the change in classes holding hands. Or even just been engrossed in deep conversation. How would that have gone over, especially with the gousters?

Maybe Valerie had similar uncomfortable concerns, and anticipated the potentially serious consequences more quickly than I had.

Even with Nate and Lee, I sensed some discomfort about the previous Saturday evening's events, and they didn't even know the full story, or so I thought. At lunch on Tuesday, Nate brought it all up. Fortunately, he waited until a few other classmates left the table, so it was just the three of us.

"Aren't you even going to ask me how I got home Saturday?" Nate asked, with just the hint of a grin.

I had completely forgotten about casting him adrift, what with the events with Valerie and then the South Shore Country Club fiasco on Sunday. "Jeez, I'm really sorry..." I began.

He put his right hand up, as if to halt my apologies. "All's well that ends well. You saw that girl I was dancing with?"

"Yeah, the nice-looking blond from the Lab School, the one with the tits. What was she doing dancing with you?"

Nate ignored my dig. "Dancing wasn't all we did," he proclaimed, victoriously, the grin now wider. "Turns out she had a car there, and she offered me a ride home. But first we stopped at the museum parking lot, to see the sub...I never realized how fast those Lab School girls are. I thought they were just a bunch of stuck up UC intellectuals. Carolyn couldn't get enough."

Nate paused for effect, looking at Lee, who was listening intently, and then at me. He was clearly relishing the moment. "And guess whose car we saw in the museum parking lot?"

I could feel my face burning as I blushed. Nate wasn't going to let it go.

"It sure didn't look like you and Valerie were discussing the Kennedy administration's new policy toward Latin America."

He glanced at Lee. "Those two were all over each other. I mean, all over."

I tried to challenge Nate. "If you were so busy, how could you tell what we were doing?"

"We were parked right in back of you," he replied. "Carolyn kept wondering why I was looking over my shoulder, when she had her blouse half unbuttoned."

"Don't worry," Nate added. "I didn't tell her what was going on. I figured you would want as few people as possible to know what you two are up to."

I nodded. "Yeah, you're right."

"I mean, I don't think you want word getting to Booker and his friends that you are riding around Hyde Park and Woodlawn, and making out with Valerie. I don't know why, but I have a feeling it wouldn't go over real well."

I nodded again. "Thanks for not saying anything."

"I won't say anything, for sure," Nate said. Then he hesitated. "There is one thing I'd appreciate, though."

Once again, Nate seemed to be relishing the moment.

I was pretty sure his request would have something to do with study material for one of our classes. Our competition for grades that started in grade school had continued unabated.

Now, ending our junior year, we were practically in a tie for number ten in our class. We teased each other about what a big difference there is between ten and eleven, but behind the jokes was a lot of seriousness. Each of us wanted to be able to claim on college applications the next fall that we were in the top ten of our class.

"I'd like your notes from AP English, just for a couple days. I want to see if I'm missing anything."

He had me over a barrel, and he knew it. I generally took more complete notes than Nate, and ordinarily we didn't share notes for any class.

"Sure Nate, no problem," I said, in as relaxed a tone as I could muster, through nearly clenched teeth.

Nate smiled. "I know Lee won't say anything, either. But you can be sure that at some point, word is going to get out. You can't keep something like that a secret for too long around here."

In my high over Valerie, I had obviously neglected to think carefully enough about the longer-term ramifications. And I appreciated more clearly Valerie's desire to not be openly demonstrative or affectionate in school.

I was glad when Lee shifted the conversation. "So, when are you having another one of these Hyde Park get-togethers at the Medici? It sounds like a not-too-bad time."

I couldn't recall the exact reason Lee hadn't come with us the previous Saturday, except that there was some model car or airplane project he was working on. He could be like that, occasionally detached from what Nate and I were doing. Maybe because he wasn't in all our classes—he had difficulties with math and science, so he took those with many gousters in regular classes.

"Okay," I said. "Same deal this Saturday as last Saturday. I should be able to drive there, if my dad is okay with it, but you may be on your own getting home."

27

The week dragged along, except for social studies class on Wednesday afternoon with Mr. White. Normally, his classes were borderline boring. Ivy Leaguers and whites alike would sit holding their heads, even occasionally dozing off, as he droned on.

Here was Mr. White, a dark-skinned Negro who looked to be in his forties and clearly had a lot of factual knowledge, making American history uninteresting, even the amazing events around the Civil War and slavery. Part of it had to do with his tendency to stick to the history texts, which emphasized dates and events over drama and irony. I couldn't help but wonder if he had an ulterior motive—that he feared possibly stirring up racial unrest in our classes, with dramatic accounts of the sale and abuse of slaves and the refusal of the U.S. Supreme Court and the Congress to put a lid on the abusive treatment of Negroes.

As our class neared the end of the school year, and our history lessons moved into the twentieth century, with its continuing repression of Negroes, I frequently found myself wondering during those classes how the Ivy Leaguer Negro students, along with Mr. White, felt about what we were learning. It certainly seemed natural that they should be suspicious of whites at best, and resentful and pissed at worst.

But Mr. White rarely went in the direction of making the connection between our tense racial situation on Chicago's South Side during the spring of 1963, and the exploding Civil Rights movement in the South, with its marches and defiance by Negroes of Jim Crow laws and segregated schools, restaurants, and even Greyhound buses.

It wasn't until that week's Wednesday class, when Mr. White seemed a changed man. Normally dressed in a wrinkled gray suit, with his expanding belly overhanging belted slacks, this day his suit looked pressed and seemed to fit him better. His eyes sparkled and the front of his balding head nearly glistened.

"Someone asked me after the last class about my own history, where I was born and how I wound up in Chicago. So I want to tell you about it, since it relates to the new material we'll be studying, about the Civil Rights Movement," he began.

"I was born in Alabama. I knew I wanted to leave Alabama from the time I was about eight months old." He paused for effect and many snickered at his not-so-subtle humor. "The Chicago *Defender* newspaper used to send the paper around the South. We'd read about life in Chicago's Negro community, and we realized it had to be better than the lives we were leading."

He paused again, taking in the rapt class of Negro and white students. "We arrived in Chicago in August of 1919, about a month after Chicago's race riot. That riot started when a South Side Negro boy was swimming, and by accident wound up near a white beach. He was beaten so badly he died."

I gulped to myself, wondering if that might have happened at Rainbow Beach. It probably didn't, but it certainly could have.

"But even with all of that, my parents felt safer on the South Side of

Chicago than they ever felt in Alabama. We had everything in the Bronzeville area, a kind of parallel society. We had our own movie theaters and food stores and banks and tailors and movers. So our money stayed in the community.

"My father worked in the steel mills south of Chicago," Mr. White continued. "He made good money there, enough to provide for his family."

"So what was the problem?" one of the Ivy Leaguer students interrupted.

"The problem was we couldn't live where we wanted," Mr. White replied. "There was something in the real estate and banking business known as 'restrictive covenants,' where the whites agreed among themselves not to sell houses and buildings to Negroes. That made my dad pretty angry—he could work at the steel mill with white workers, but he couldn't move his family to live with them."

This was sounding like the story of Valerie's dad.

"I guess it made me angry, too, because in 1943, right after these big race riots in Detroit, I received a draft letter. It said, 'Uncle Sam wants you.' I sent the letter back and wrote, 'I don't have an Uncle Sam.'" More snickers.

"Well, my mother didn't appreciate what I did. It was World War II, and she said I'd get in big trouble if I didn't cooperate. So I got drafted, and fought as part of a Negro unit in Europe, and was part of the D-Day invasion."

Another Ivy Leaguer interrupted: "You ever think that things here are as bad as they are in the South? We can't get jobs here. We can't live in other neighborhoods. We can't go to the beaches we want. The police are mostly white, and they treat us like we are all criminals."

Mr. White wasn't about to equate Chicago with the South. "People sometimes ask me if I ever go back to the South to visit relatives. I tell them the only way I go back to the South is when a relative dies and I go to the funeral. And then, I get out of there as fast as I can."

He paused again, and looked past us, as if he was looking out a window. "Except I was down South this past weekend. I had been hearing about this preacher, Dr. Martin Luther King Jr., and I liked what he was saying about equality and nonviolence. So this past weekend, I went down to Montgomery. I had the honor of meeting him and helping in the marches he has been organizing there."

Wow! So Mr. White must have been down there during the speech I heard Dr. King give over the radio in the Medici. That really brought the whole thing home.

The bell ending the class rang just then, and I realized the time had flown by.

I felt as if a whole new world was opening before my eyes. At Thursday's geometry class, I caught Valerie's eye just before Mr. Olive called us to order. I mouthed the words "Medici, Saturday" to her. She smiled back, nodding slightly.

28

I was nervous as I arrived early Saturday morning for caddy duty at the South Shore Country Club. I had no idea what to expect, given the chewing out from Eddie about my Negro school friends who wanted to be caddies. Would he yell at me in front of the other caddies? Send me on my way? Would I have to admit to Dad that, yes, he was right about how the country club was no place for Jews?

So what did I find, but a smiling Eddie. "I'm going to pretend I didn't hear what you said about those darkies who wanted to work here," he told me, as if he was doing me a big favor. "I haven't said anything to Stan. I've asked him to assign you some easier members to work with today. Hopefully, you'll make a little more money." He paused, turning serious, and almost fatherly. "I'd really like to see this work out for you, Jeff."

He was true to his word. The day kept getting better as I made more and more money. The first member was cordial, and handed me a $3 tip as we parted.

Then, I got my first two-bagger, carrying the bags of two golfers. It was definitely hard work, especially in the heat. The fact that they were good golfers made things easier, but what especially caught my interest had nothing to do with golf, but rather what they had to say about investing in real estate in Negro neighborhoods.

The two men seemed to be longtime friends who hadn't seen each other in some time, one a stock broker and the other a doctor of some type. The stock broker, a tall blonde-haired, handsome fellow with a deep tan, was informing the doctor, a much smaller man with graying black hair and a receding hairline who appeared to be at least ten years older, and was busy chain smoking, about an "investment syndicate" that paid "amazing rates, double what you'll get from any other real estate syndicates."

The reason the broker's syndicate paid so well? "These are apartment buildings in colored areas, sold on contract," the broker explained on the third hole's putting green.

When the doctor wondered, somewhere just before the dreaded fifth hole, with its little pond, about whether such an investment was safe, since "colored people are usually down and out financially," the broker reassured him. "These are safer than syndicates in white areas."

I was curious to hear the broker's explanation. The doctor's concern would have been my dad's concern, I was sure.

The broker hesitated, for emphasis. "You'd be amazed how much cash a lot of these colored people have. I don't know where they get it, but they put down big down payments, often ten or fifteen grand. And then they make their monthly payments like clockwork. They know the rules, that if they miss a single payment, they'll be hauled into court, and lose the property. It's not like a bank mortgage, where you get a few months leeway to get back on track, or can even sometimes renegotiate terms."

"You mean the judges don't just let them off, the way they do if the colored rob you?" the doctor asked, sincerely amazed.

"Absolutely not," the broker said, just before setting up for a chip shot onto the sixth green. "A contract is a contract. The judges are tough on that."

I half expected them to end their discussion, and agree to continue it in private later on, when I wasn't around. But they just continued as if I wasn't there.

"So what happens if they stop paying on their contracts and the judge says they have violated the contract?"

"That's the beautiful thing," said the broker, continuing the conversation on the green, as the pair lined up their putts. "The syndicate gets the property back, and can sell it on contract, again. There are plenty of colored buyers out there who can't wait to own real estate. They can't get bank mortgages, so they come to us, and we sell the property again, with another big down payment. I've even seen syndicate heads, and we don't endorse this, make up problems as the Negroes come to the end of the contract, to keep them from taking ownership. That's why these syndicates pay double what the ones in white areas pay. Because our syndicates get higher prices for the apartment buildings, higher interest rates on the loans, higher down payments, and then they can be easily re-sold when buyers can't keep up."

The broker's explanation of buyers forfeiting their properties sounded like what Valerie had explained about Booker's family, how it had lost its home just before taking ownership. And how Booker's dad had been driven to drink himself to death.

By the seventh hole, the doctor was telling the broker he was ready to put up "twenty-five K" for five shares in the syndicate.

I was beginning to understand how business gets conducted on the golf course.

This round of golf was a big win for everyone present. The broker and doctor each handed me a $5 tip. Along with the $4 from the club, that made a total of $14 dollars, for two hours' work. And with the $5 earlier in the day, a total of $19. One last golfer also parted cheerfully, with a $5 tip. Now I was looking at $26 in earnings for the day. Together with $5 in lawn mower earnings the previous two days, I now had $31 in my pocket, more than I had ever carried before.

It had begun dawning on me as the money accumulated that I might want to take Valerie out for a burger or a shake after the dance at the Medici. That would help show her I was serious about wanting to continue going out with her.

Just as important, I finally had something to brag to Dad about, to justify my working for the Jew haters.

29

As pleased as I was with my earnings, I couldn't rid myself of the discomfort that lingered afterwards from the broker-doctor dealings. I was going to have a quick supper with Mom, Dad, and Emily before heading off to the Medici.

Mom made one of her most popular meals, a breakfast-served-as-dinner dish she used to have as a child growing up in Germany, which she called "Jagerfrühstück." It was eggs mixed together with sliced potatoes and pieces of salami, all fried up piping hot.

It was fortunate everyone loved the dinner, because there was all-too-familiar bad news as we sat around the small Formica kitchen table. Our palatial six-unit apartment building, which was all white when we moved in three years earlier, now had three Negro families, Mom told us. They had all moved in within the last couple months.

Maybe because I was so distracted with school, I hadn't noticed much difference in the building, though there did seem to be more Negroes, adults and children, on the block and around the neighborhood.

Emily piped up that her class at the O'Keefe elementary school a couple blocks away was now half Negro. "But they're mostly nice kids," she said.

No matter to Dad. "It's like Ridgeland all over again," he moaned, supporting his balding head in his right hand, as if he had just heard terrible news.

"I didn't even see them move in," he offered, as if possibly, by some chance, Mom might be mistaken.

"Of course you didn't," she said. "They come either while you are at work, or while you are sleeping at night. I saw one family move into the Landers' place on the second floor a couple weeks ago, during the day."

"Where did the Landers go?" Dad asked.

"They went to the North Side. They had talked about moving further south, but when push came to shove, they decided they didn't want to keep running. So they just left the South Side altogether. In the end, they didn't even say they were leaving. One afternoon I came home from work, and they were gone."

I didn't know if Mom was restraining herself, or just didn't remember the bad argument she and Dad had three years earlier, before moving over to Clyde Avenue, when she predicted this turn of events. Whatever the case, she didn't offer an "I told you so" exclamation point to her bad news.

"They're going to drive us out sooner than we expected," Dad said glumly. "I thought we might get eight or ten years here, but the way it's going, we may not even be able to last through Jeffrey graduating next year."

I tried to change the subject with Dad to my productive day. "Guess what? I had my best day ever today, over at the South Shore Country Club. Twenty-six big ones!"

That snapped Dad out of his funk. "You're earning as much as your old man," he said, with true amazement in his voice. "Maybe I ought to go over there and try carrying golf bags around for the goyim. It's probably easier than chasing after schvartze kids stealing leather jackets from Goldblatt's."

I decided to ask Dad about the investment syndicates, since he was always talking with Mom about how his stock market investments were doing. "My broker has tried to sell me those," he said when I recounted the conversation between the blonde broker and chain-smoking doctor at the country club. "He doesn't bring it up any more. I told him, first of all, I don't have ten or fifteen thousand to put on a single investment. Second, I don't feel like those syndicates are very liquid."

"Liquid?"

"If I want to sell the investment quickly, because I need the money for some reason, I can't be sure I can get rid of my shares in a syndicate. With my shares of U.S. Steel or AT&T, I can just call the broker, and they'll be sold immediately. I may not get all my money back, if the stock's price has gone down, but I'll be able to sell at some fairly decent price right away."

He wasn't done, though. "There's another reason I wouldn't invest in those syndicates." He paused, and made eye contact with me. I waited for his version of a punch line. "I would never invest in those schvartze areas. The whites are running away. The schvartze are too poor, and they're robbing and killing each other. My guess is that in ten or twenty years, the South Side will be a wasteland, and all these white property owners will be begging people to take their buildings. The doctors and lawyers can afford to throw their money away. I can't. I work too hard for my money."

Financial lesson over. Dad seemed relaxed as he handed over the car keys to me. He looked me over with a look of mock amazement. I was wearing my best khaki slacks, and a freshly ironed baby blue short sleeve buttoned sport shirt. "You look like a regular gosh-darnit!" Some slang he had heard to describe someone all dolled up for a good time. "Have fun. Don't spend all your money in one place."

I nodded, calmly. I felt relieved I still had his confidence, but it hung by the slenderest of threads, any of which could easily snap at any time.

30

Lee wasn't the only newcomer to the Saturday evening scene at the Medici. Word must have gotten around that the previous Saturday was fun, because the crowd had nearly doubled in size, from fifteen to about twenty-five. The new kids seemed to be from both Hyde Park High and the Lab School.

I was a little concerned because Valerie wasn't there when I arrived with Nate and Lee. She was one of the last to arrive, about twenty minutes after me. She was wearing a short-sleeve dark blue dress with a big blue and white collar that appeared almost like something the Navy might have issued. It was definitely not trendy, but on her it looked smashing.

She arrived with her friend, Tanya, who had been with her at Riverview but hadn't been present the previous week. Tanya was also in the geometry class I shared with Valerie, and also cute and vivacious, though a little taller and big-boned. The two of them were fun to watch, animated in their conversation and giggling.

I interrupted them to ask Valerie to dance, to the Four Seasons singing "Walk Like a Man." I was feeling brave enough to walk like a man, and try shaking opposite her. Her face turned immediately serious as we stood and strutted. "I almost didn't make it here. Daddy wasn't in a good mood. He wanted all kinds of details about where I was going, how I was getting there, who was going to be there, and when I was coming home."

"Was he upset because you got home late last week?" I asked.

"No, I think he's upset because of the new gang in Woodlawn, the Blackstone Rangers. They've been recruiting kids on our block. I think Daddy is upset because Booker might be joining. Booker is also talking more seriously about dropping out of school."

"What does that have to do with you?" I inquired. I avoided expressing the relief I felt that Booker might disappear from the Hyde Park High scene, and not be around to settle old scores.

"I think Daddy is more worried about Derrick, my older brother, that he could get sucked into the gang thing. He hangs out at the Boys Club a lot, and the Rangers hang out there, too."

I remembered back to what I heard Tyrone talking about when he argued with Valerie at the last Medici get-together, about the "Rangers" and the Boys Club.

Now it was making sense. Still, I decided to react naively. "What's so bad about the gang?" I asked.

She stopped stepping to the music, and stared at me. "You don't know about gangs, do you," she asked, more as a statement than a question.

"There's another gang over in Englewood, The Devil's Disciples. These gangs sell heroin to make money, and then fight each other about who controls what territory. But the part that scares him the most is you have to prove yourself to get into the gang, like by going out and beating up a member of another gang, or maybe even going out and robbing a white person."

"You mean Booker could have been fighting with me to prove himself to the Blackstone Rangers?" I asked.

"Probably not then. Next time you fight, it could be about that. Hopefully there won't be a next time."

Her reference to "next time" got my heart pumping more quickly, and butterflies flapping in my stomach. Our gym class had moved into our school's ancient swimming pool, where Booker and other gousters were less threatening, since they had generally never learned to swim, unlike the whites. So I had relegated Booker to the back of my mind, in favor of more immediate threats, like Tommy Sullivan.

A new song was playing, a slow one, "Out of My Mind." We didn't even bother to assume a formal dance position, as she placed both hands on my shoulders, and I held her around the waist, as Johnny Tollitson intoned, "Going out of my mind, over you…"

No conversation, just holding each other a little tighter.

I saw Nate dancing with the blond Lab School girl the same way.

I wished I could feel as comfortable as everyone else looked, as if I danced like this all the time, when it really was only the second evening in my life of such fun for me, and with a Negro girl to top it off.

A tad comforting, I saw Valerie's friend, Tanya, dancing with a white guy whom I assumed was from the Lab School.

We took a break. Someone had brought in a few piping hot cheese and sausage pizzas.

The music came back on, and it seemed to have switched to a Negro radio station, because the songs stopped being familiar to me. But they were big hits to Valerie and Tanya. One with a quick rhythm and a deep male voice sounded sort of familiar. "Please don't go. I wanna be your lover man!" Then the refrain, "Please! Please! Please!"

Valerie was singing along softly. She clearly knew all the words, even if I couldn't make them all out.

"That's James Brown again. I love that man. I saw him when he was in Chicago last year. Derrick took me, and James did all these dances."

Good timing on the dances, because the next song was "The Watusi." "That's the Vibrations," Valerie pointed out. "They're singing the real 'Watusi.' Some other group sings the 'Wah-Watusi' and does a bad imitation of the Vibrations."

As The Vibrations in their song found fault with other dances like The Twist ("Never, never do you get yourself kissed, 'cause you're always dancin' far apart"), The Fly and Mashed Potato, Valerie stopped and did little impressions of each dance. "I learned all that from James Brown," she said glancing sideways at me as she and Tanya danced.

A couple more male Negro singers came on as she and Tanya jitterbugged. Then finally, a women's group, which seemed to be telling a soulful story.

Lover of mine
Gone to a faraway land
Serving your country
On some faraway sand
But you should get no name
Remember that your heart belongs to me
I'm sending you a picture
To carry with you all the time

I cut between Valerie and Tanya, held Valerie around the waist.

"That's this new group out of Dee-troit," she said, sounding sincerely excited. "They're called the Soo-premes. They started as the Primettes, and then changed their name a couple years ago. This is their first song as the Soo-premes, 'Your Heart Belongs to Me.'"

I hadn't heard of the Supremes any more than I had heard of any of the other singers she named earlier.

"How do you know all this stuff about these singers?"

"This is stuff we hear around the house, and on the streets," she said. "I cheat a little, I read some of the fan magazines, and *Ebony* magazine."

At first, I was feeling uncomfortable again, as if Valerie maybe thought I was dumb, or very uncool. But as I watched her become ever more animated in her descriptions, I realized she enjoyed sharing all this information with me, that she had pride in the talented singers she was telling me about. I was learning about a different world; I relaxed.

After a while, I felt this urgency to demonstrate I wasn't totally ignorant of music. "When are we going to hear 'The Lion Sleeps Tonight'?" I inquired.

Valerie stepped back and smiled sympathetically. "You won't hear it on this station."

I must have looked very puzzled.

"It's sung by a bunch of white guys, the Tokens, trying to sound like gouster girls," she said, with a hint of contempt.

The song certainly had had me convinced. It must have even had some Negroes convinced, because sometimes I'd hear it sung in the halls of Hyde Park High.

Then the music stopped and we stood there. But Valerie wasn't done. "You also won't ever hear, 'I'm Dreaming of a White Christmas.'"

"Why not?" I asked, sensing in advance there was a racial slant.

"It's a racist song. That's why we don't ever sing it in school."

I played the words slowly in my mind. "I'm…dreaming…of…a…white Christmas…" Wow. I had no idea about that, either.

"Okay, I get it. But you don't think Bing Crosby, or whoever started singing it, thought they were singing a racist song, do you?" I was truly mystified.

She just looked at me and raised her eyebrows, with a slight hint of a smile. As if she really believed it, but wasn't about to debate it.

But I was curious about her reference to 'gouster girls.' "It sounds like you don't care too much for gouster girls, like you're above them or something."

"I'm not above them. The big difference between us is that our families have more money than the gousters' families."

"You sure seem smarter than most of them," I offered.

"Some of them are pretty smart. Ivy Leaguers just care more about school. I think maybe because our parents care, we care. Booker is smart, but he doesn't always act smart. Maybe because his father is off drinking a lot. He thinks he can just goof off. Some of my good friends are gousters. Or sort of gousters. Like Tanya. You probably don't even realize it, but she used to be a gouster. But a few of us got after her and she got more serious about school, and now she's an Ivy Leaguer.

"Once they get to high school, it is hard for gousters to change. They get stuck in these remedial classes with the worst teachers, and no one cares—even the teachers don't care. If they do care, like that girl who told me about your drawing after our study, they can't earn better than a B or C, no matter how well they score in tests."

"How is that?" I asked. "If they get 100, shouldn't they get an A?"

"You'd think so. But these are slower classes, supposedly, so the kids aren't allowed to get the full credit like in a regular or accelerated class."

It dawned on me that the kids were mostly stuck in those classes, no matter how hard they worked. "So, there is no way to advance?" I asked.

"No way. Well, I suppose there is one way. The teachers tell them that if they do well, they can move up, into a regular class. But I've only heard of one girl who ever did. I think everyone stops caring, stops working very hard."

I couldn't believe the track system could be so heartless and hopeless. But before I could mount an argument, Tanya returned from dancing. I used the interruption to get back to hugging and holding.

The white music from WLS had come on. I am feeling as I hold her that all we have done is talked about race and grades and music. I need to make this more fun, more romantic. "I've been thinking about you all week," I say softly into her ear. "How much I liked being with you last week. Then going over to the sub."

She didn't say anything, but I could feel her holding me more tightly. I was relieved she wasn't laughing at me. So I kept going. "You're the prettiest girl I have ever been with."

Now she pushed back. "Prettier than those girls at...what did you call those dance lessons?

"Fortnightly."

"Yeah, prettier than the girls there?"

I laughed. "Yes, prettier than the girls there."

I was glad she had not mentioned their race.

I was tempted to use the opening she created to inquire about her relationship with Tyrone. But something told me not to mess with the good vibes I had going, that my question could wait till another day.

31

Then Valerie wanted to leave. Dad's car was parked a few blocks down 57th Street. We walked by the Ray School, which I attended for first and second grade, when we lived in that Hyde Park tenement building. I told Valerie about the time I was in first grade and decided during a recess to leave school and walk home, and how teachers mounted a brief search for me.

She was telling me some story about her misbehaving in early grade school as we walked past a small Chinese restaurant with a neon "Chop Suey" sign, when who should pop out but Eddie, in conversation with two laughing friends.

Our eyes locked, and his smile vanished when he caught sight of Valerie. "Hey, Eddie. How ya doin'?" I said, trying to appear casual, even as my voice felt shaky. "Since when do you come to Hyde Park for chop suey?"

"My friends here say this is the best Chinese food around," he said, nodding his head toward the two other guys. I recognized one of them, Drew Boggs, from our softball games. I had never seen the third guy, who appeared to be at least Eddie's age, and maybe a little older, based on his big belly.

Eddie was clearly thrown off by the surprise of the scene in front of him. His eyes darted back and forth, from Valerie to me to Valerie. Should I introduce Valerie? He didn't introduce his friends, and something inside me said it was probably a conversation that would only add to the tension we were both feeling.

Eddie's look of confusion was replaced after a few moments with a kind of forced smile. "See ya tomorrow, Eddie," I said to conclude the conversation.

I was hoping the conversation looked casual enough to Valerie that she wouldn't think a lot about it. In the car, I told her about my latest surprise. "I did another drawing of you. It's a little more interesting than the other one. Want to go over to the museum and take a look?"

I had been trying a portrait of her with the smirk. I figured she'd either love it or hate it—there wouldn't be anything in between.

But her mind was in the place I hoped it wouldn't be. "Who is Eddie?"

I decided to play it straight. "Eddie is kind of a friend, someone I know from playing softball. He helped me get a job as a caddie at the South Shore Country Club. I started last week. I've just worked there a couple times."

"So you were ashamed to introduce your Negro friend to him?" Her tone was more accusatory, and she was staring at me.

"It's kind of complicated," I started.

She was staring at me, no hint of a smile.

"You see, the country club won't allow Jews or Negroes as members. They call it being restricted. But it allows Jews to be caddies. Eddie is Jewish, but he hates Negroes."

"I bet that's the place Robert and Paul went to apply for jobs last week," she said. "They practically got tarred and feathered and run out on a stick, from what I heard."

"That's the place. I saw Robert and Paul just as they were leaving, or being ordered out. They didn't see me. But after they left, I asked Eddie if there was a way the club could try them out as caddies, since I had seen them play golf. Eddie basically told me to mind my own business. I thought I was done for. When I came back for work today, he said he was going to give me another chance. Crazy, but I had a really good day, earned some decent money. But after tonight, well, I expect when I show up tomorrow, I'll be told to get lost."

"So hanging out with Gouster Girl may have cost you a good job," she remarked, still staring at me. Then she was shaking her head, "You white boys sure do have some strange ways of doing things."

I started the car and headed east along 57th Street, toward the museum. "Hey, let's not go to the museum," she said. "I have a better idea, someplace where there aren't so many curious eyes."

I nodded, relieved that my explanation about Eddie and the South Shore Country Club seemed to have rung true.

I decided against telling her about how Nate and his new Lab School friend had parked in back of us in the museum parking lot the previous week.

"You ever been to La Rabida?" she asked.

I knew it was a hospital somewhere in Jackson Park, but I had no recollection of having been there. Her voice turned deep, seductive. "It's more private than the museum parking lot."

32

Valerie was right. La Rabida was a ways south of the museum, down some winding roads in the vast park, and when we arrived at the deserted parking lot, I had this feeling of being out in the country. You could hear crickets and the only light came from some lamps mounted on the main building maybe 100 yards away. We were the only car in a much smaller lot than at the Museum of Science and Industry. I made a mental note to ask her how she knew about this place. Had she been here with other guys? With Tyrone?

I moved over into the middle of the bench seat, and put my arm around her. I sensed she wanted reassurance. "Gouster Girl, you're much more important than some stupid job," I said. I went to kiss her.

She pulled back. "Wait, what about that new drawing you were bragging about?"

In my eagerness to resume where we left off the previous week, I had forgotten about the drawing. I pulled it out, unfolded it, and watched her reaction. I felt as if I'd gotten the skin tone more accurate, and to her liking. I saw the hint of a smile begin on her pensive face. She folded the drawing and tucked it into a small leather purse she had been carrying.

"You're getting there, white boy." She was smiling more broadly. We began kissing and hugging and groping about.

I mentally noted a car's headlights in my peripheral vision out the rear window, and assumed another couple had arrived for the same purpose as us. I had a hand on her inside thigh, under the blue dress. It felt smooth, cool. As she moved her legs apart, all the while caressing my hair, and tickling my ear, it was as if I had turned into one giant nerve ending.

Then the flashlight shined in on us on the driver's side.

We each stiffened, and immediately pushed back from the other. She shifted her weight to pull her dress down. I could see through the window that the flashlight was being held by a man in a police uniform. I rolled down the window and shielded my eyes, noticing that the man holding the flashlight had moved it slightly so we could see out more easily.

"Police," he said. "You know, you're trespassing. This is a private lot. Let me have your license and registration." I wanted to provide a casual, even humorous, response to the cop, that my friend and I had just stopped to chat, and would be on our way. But something in his tone, and the lack of a "please" in his order to hand over the license and registration, and the fact that he was wearing his police visor, told me he wasn't looking for an explanation or conversation of any type. When I reached silently over to the glove compartment for the registration, I noticed Valerie was staring straight ahead, her face stony.

As I dug my wallet out of my back pocket to retrieve my license, my mind was racing, because I realized at that moment I never followed Dad's suggestion when I obtained my driver's license four months earlier. "If you're ever stopped by the police for anything, like speeding, or going through a stop sign, I don't care what it is, and they ask you for your driver's license, make sure there's a ten or twenty dollar bill clipped to the license."

"What's that for?" I had asked, knowing the answer in advance.

"Nine times out of ten, what they'll do is go back to their car, and when they return, they'll tell you they're letting you off this time, but don't do the same thing again. The money will be gone."

"And what about the one time it doesn't work?" I asked.

"They'll just give you the license back and say you need to think about what you did, and what you are going to do to make it better. You attach another five or ten dollars to the license and hand it back. That's all."

Of course, I knew why I failed to attach $20 to my license: I didn't have $20. I assumed once I began earning some money, I'd take the precaution. But I'd only just that Saturday earned enough that I could feel comfortable taking the precaution. And it looked at this point as if it might be too late.

Instead, I had to deal with a tough question: How do you tell a cop you want to offer him a bribe? Having a twenty dollar bill attached to the license saved having to come up with any preamble. Everything was right on the table, including the actual payment. I rapidly developed a plan in my mind. If I could tell from his language or gestures that the cop and his partner wanted money, I would apologize for having screwed up, and ask if there was something I could do to make the whole thing better.

Valerie and I sat for a few minutes in silence after the cop returned to his car. It occurred to me that her presence could complicate the situation, make it something more than a trespassing problem. I didn't want to create anxiety for her, though I was sure similar thoughts were shooting through her mind. I decided to break the silence. "What are you thinking?"

She responded immediately, in a flat voice. "You know, they're going to say I'm a prostitute you picked up. They'll threaten to arrest both of us, unless you pay them enough money."

"Wow. I sure hope you're wrong." I couldn't have begun to imagine such a horrible turn of events. Then I saw the officer in my rearview mirror walking toward our car. "Here he comes," I whispered.

I rolled down the window. "You want to step out of the car?" It was phrased as a question, but was really an order. I rolled up the window, opened the door, and stepped out into the mild spring evening.

"Follow me," said the officer. I walked slowly behind him, toward the sky-blue-and-white police cruiser. For some reason, I noted the words, "Protect and Defend" in black under the Chicago Police logo. He stopped in front of the back door on the driver's side, and turned toward me. He was about my height, bordering on heavyset, with black greased hair combed back under his visor. I looked for a name on the badge on the left front pocket of his blue shirt, but couldn't make anything out in the dark. "You want to tell me where you picked the girl up?" he asked matter-of-factly. "Over on 63rd Street?"

"I didn't pick her up. She's a friend." I tried to be matter-of-fact as well, not get emotional.

He ignored me. "So, you have her by the hour? Maybe you want to share her with me and my partner. Then you can go on your way without any problems."

I was thrown by the fact he wasn't asking for money, and I couldn't think of what to say in response. After some moments of agonizing silence, at least for me, I said, "I told you, she's a friend, from school. We were just over in Hyde Park with some friends."

Once again, no acknowledgment of my explanation, no follow-up, like inquiring into where we had been in Hyde Park. For what sort of event.

"You know, this could get serious. The girl could be charged with soliciting for prostitution. If she's under sixteen, you could be charged with statutory rape. And if you keep saying I'm lying, there could also be a charge of resisting arrest."

I could feel panic spreading through my body. My legs were shaking. This situation was deteriorating beyond anything I could have imagined.

Just then, the front window on the cop car's driver side rolled down, and the officer at the wheel said, "Jimmy, wanna get in for a minute?"

"Stay right here," Jimmy ordered. In the meantime, he went around to the passenger side of the car and climbed in.

I wanted to go back to my car and tell Valerie that it was all going to take a little longer, but I dared not move and risk irritating these guys further. I stood there, basking in the dim yellow light created by a swarm of lightning bugs.

Three or four minutes later, the front driver's window rolled down again. "Jeff, wanna climb into the back seat here?"

I couldn't decide whether the fact that one of my inquisitors was now addressing me by my first name was a good sign or a bad one. As I climbed in, Jimmy was just finishing up on the police radio. The car had a stale smell, and the seat felt soft and worn, as if a lot of different people in various stages of hot water had sat where I was sitting. The driver turned around. He looked to be a little older than Jimmy. He wasn't wearing a hat, and his hair was thinning and gray. He looked even chunkier than Jimmy, though it was hard to be sure without seeing him stand up.

"So, Jeff, I see from the registration that the owner of your car is Kurt Stark. Is he the same Kurt who works at Goldblatt's?"

"Yes, sir, that's the same guy, he's my father," I said, feeling a slight sense of relief course through my body.

Dad often complained at the end of especially tough days about the problems he had with shoplifting gousters. The cops never came in a timely way in my father's experience, until he was able to convince his superiors to supply the necessary cash to pay weekly bribes similar to what other downtown merchants shelled out to keep the cops hanging around their stores and occasionally nabbing shoplifters.

Sitting in the back seat of the cop car, I realized that, to these cops, I was no longer some anonymous white kid making it with a slutty Negro girl. I had some status, tenuous as it might be. Clearly, in checking my license and Dad's registration with headquarters, someone Dad had paid off must have alerted these guys to the connection.

"The fellows downtown say your dad works with them to catch shoplifters."

I nodded my head yes, all the while marveling at driver cop's strange way of describing Dad's relationship to the police. But I remained silent, because it seemed clear I was edging closer to learning the terms of a deal, and likely a financial arrangement that didn't include a girl-sharing component. I just hoped there was some way I could afford to make it happen and get the hell out of here.

"Your dad is a good guy, Jeff, so we're going to try to help you out here," Driver said. "I'm sure you appreciate you could be in a heap of trouble. Trespassing. Soliciting for prostitution. Statutory rape. Resisting arrest. Could be hundreds or even thousands of dollars in fines. Maybe even some jail time. I'm sure your dad wouldn't be happy to know you're using his car to shuttle colored prostitutes around."

I resolved to resist the temptation to contradict him and explain, yet again, what really was going on. No, I needed to focus entirely on taking advantage of the slight show of good will. "Thank you, sir, for your offer to help. Just tell me what I need to do to make things right."

"We won't be looking for the hundreds of dollars you'd have to pay the court, but rather something that would help us do our job," the driver cop said. "Something like a hundred dollars so we can feel that justice has been served."

I very nearly laughed about the "justice being served" statement. I continued on negotiation mode, and hoped my voice wasn't shaking and betraying the nervousness I felt about whether I was going to be able to make a deal happen. "I wish I had a hundred dollars, sir, because what you are saying sounds very reasonable. But I don't have that much."

"How much do you have, Jeff?"

"All I've got is thirty dollars," I said. "You're welcome to look through my pants and wallet."

"I believe you, Jeff," Driver said, sounding soothing, almost sympathetic. "Okay, so we'll help you out here, this once, because everyone likes your dad. Just place the thirty on the back seat when you leave. We'll call it even."

Whew! Now, should I press my luck? As I was taking the bills out of my pocket, I decided to toss the dice. I made a final plea: "If there's any way you could keep my dad from hearing about this, I'd really appreciate it."

I half expected a fatherly, "No problem, Jeff." But instead, Driver's face hardened, and he glared at me. "The thirty bucks only covers your crimes. If you want help on the other stuff, it's going to cost you more. Since you don't have more, you get what you pay for. Now take your little colored whore and get the hell out of here."

I exited the cop car, and walked quickly back to my car. Valerie was sitting in the same position, with the same stone-faced look on her face as when I left. I started the car without a word, and quickly exited La Rabida. No sign of the police car following us.

33

We drove in silence through Jackson Park. I pulled into the Museum of Science and Industry parking lot, stopping along a far edge, away from the couples necking. I took a deep breath and looked over at Valerie. "Well, that was fun. Protect and defend. Isn't that their motto?"

I hoped she didn't detect in my voice the new anxiety I felt over whether the encounter with the cops we just escaped would have turned her against all whites, including me.

Valerie's stern face was noticeably more relaxed. She turned toward me. "So, was I right about what they were up to?"

"You were so right. How did you know?" I was relieved that she was still talking to me as before, as the friend, the guy she was necking with before the police escapade.

"The cops are always hassling us. The guys more than the girls. My brother told me about how a friend of his was out with a girl, and they were both dressed to the hilt, and they were pulled over, and the guy was accused of being the girl's pimp. He was handcuffed and beaten up and kept overnight at the police station. So I figured, a Negro girl out with a white guy, in an isolated place, they're naturally going to assume I'm a whore."

I could only listen in amazement before letting her in on my experience, or at least some of it. "At first, it seemed like they were going to throw the book at me. They talked about trespassing and prostitution and how it could be hundreds or even thousands of dollars in fines." I left out the bit about the statutory rape, and about the cops wanting to be serviced by Valerie.

"Nothing else?" she asked, her eyebrows raised slightly.

I could tell from her expression that she probably heard more. "You heard the other stuff, about statutory rape and them wanting their turn with you?"

She nodded.

I looked down to avoid her penetrating gaze. "I guess I was trying to protect you from hearing that stuff, from learning how demented these guys are, these guys who are supposed to protect us."

"I'm a big girl," she said. "I hear much worse stuff around the neighborhood. So how did you talk them down?"

"I caught a break. Somebody downtown who was checking out my driver's license and car registration over the radio knew my dad from Goldblatt's. My dad pays the cops to keep an eye on things, help catch shoplifters. I could tell things were turning my way when the driver started calling me 'Jeff' and being polite. They wanted a hundred dollars."

"A hundred dollars! What did you do?"

"Well, I didn't have a hundred. I mean, what kids go around with a hundred dollars? But I did have thirty. I told them it was all I had, and they took it."

"Where do you go carrying thirty dollars around?" she asked, smiling again. "You fixing to spend that on me?"

My face relaxed as well. "I had some ideas earlier about going out for burgers or a shake. You definitely had me where you wanted me, right before those guys showed up," I joked. "That thirty dollars was everything I earned today at that racist country club."

"I'm sorry about the money," she said softly, the smile now gone. She sounded sincere.

"I'm just glad I had it," I interjected. "I hate to think of how things might have turned out if I hadn't." I had only begun to think about the awful possibilities with the cops at La Rabida had I only been able to offer them $1.25 in lawn mower earnings.

"I can tell you how it could have turned out." Valerie was looking straight ahead. "About a year ago, I was sitting in Tyrone's car in front of a currency exchange when some cops ordered him out of the car. Said he fit the description of someone who had robbed the currency exchange. He denied it, and that just got them pissed. They pushed him up against the car, searched him, took him off in cuffs. Didn't even give him the chance to pay them off, just charged him with resisting arrest, a felony. His parents had to hire some white lawyer to keep him from getting sent to jail for six months or a year. When he finally went up in front of a judge, the lawyer got it reduced to a misdemeanor, and the judge let him off with a twenty-five dollar fine. But now his parents have to pay off the lawyer bills, and he can't apply to college with a criminal record, so they're going to have to pay more to try to get the crime off his record."

I felt badly for Tyrone. He definitely didn't deserve that.

"It sure does help to be white, and have a white person's job and connections with the cops," Valerie sighed, as she looked back at me.

I hadn't thought of it that way, but, of course, she was right. I nodded in agreement, relieved yet again that she wasn't turning her back on me as a white. As outraged as she might have been about the blatant discrimination, there was also a degree of cynical acceptance about the order of life around her.

"Bet you didn't realize what you were getting yourself into hanging out with a colored girl." The smirk was back. So was the seductive tone in her voice.

I slid over on the bench seat and gave her a long deep kiss.

When we paused, I decided to break a piece of likely bad news to her. "This may be our last time driving around in this car."

"Why do you say that?"

"Those cops are going to tell my dad about all this. And that will be the end of the car for me for a long time."

"You think he's not going to like it that you've been driving a colored girl around in his precious Chevrolet?" She had a look of mock amazement.

I could feel myself blushing.

I had presented the dilemma entirely from a white point of view.

"Because if you were driving a white girl around, and you paid the cops to get out of a ticket, he wouldn't care, would he?"

I tried to defend my father. "He'll be pissed because I'm in trouble with the cops. He's a law-abiding citizen."

"Yeah, that's why he pays off the cops at Goldblatt's," she retorted. "And then those cops hassle me and my friends when we try to shop there; just assume because we're colored we must be shoplifters."

I continued in defense mode. "My dad wouldn't be bothering girls like you and your friends. He's after the gousters who are stealing leather jackets and knit shirts."

"Ask him about it sometime," Valerie retorted. "You don't think I'm making it up, do you?" Her voice was becoming more agitated.

I tried for a comeback with a shift. "Maybe your father wants to let your white boyfriend drive his daughter around in his car."

She was silent for a few moments. "We don't have a car," she said softly.

Nice going, Jeff, I thought to myself. Talk about letting the air out of that balloon.

I wanted to avoid giving the impression anything was terribly wrong. "Well, I guess that leaves the El," I said casually. "I'm probably going downtown next week to check on a possible job. A few guys I know are selling shoes at a store on State Street after school. They've been telling me to apply, that they're hiring. Maybe we can ride down there together, spend some time downtown."

"You mean they're hiring white boys, right?"

I tried some humor. "Why do you always have to correct me? I haven't been there yet, but yeah, you're probably right."

"That might work, going together," she said. "I have an interview Tuesday for a part-time job at *Ebony* magazine. Helping them on a Negro music column."

"*Ebony* magazine! That's great," I said. "Very classy magazine. I'll bet they aren't hiring too many white boys, though."

The smirk.

"By the way," she said. "If things turn out the way you expect tomorrow at the country club, come on over to the Point. I've been hanging out there on weekends lately. It's a lot nicer than the colored beach on 63rd Street."

"The Point," I repeated. "I haven't been over there in years, since I was a little kid, and we lived in Hyde Park. Yeah, I'll bet it's an improvement on Rainbow Beach."

34

Fortunately, by the time I arrived back home, everyone was asleep, and I didn't have to answer any questions about my evening. I was still rattled enough by the police encounter that Mom, in particular, might have sensed something amiss.

My relief at not encountering Mom or Dad didn't translate into calmness once I crawled into bed. Instead of falling quickly asleep like I usually did, I tossed and turned for what seemed like several hours, before finally descending into a dream realm, where things were more vivid than I could ever recall.

I was riding easily on my well-broken-in red JC Higgins bike. It was a model sold by Sears Roebuck, a far cry from the nearly new blue Schwinn Nate was riding to my left. His straight blond hair and roundish face, and especially his pug nose, always made him look decidedly non-Jewish, even though he was Jewish and his family fairly observant.

On my right was red-headed Lee, who was riding some kind of beat up hand-me-down, presumably from an older sibling. Always the teaser, he interrupted Nate's introspective silence: "You aren't worried we can't outrun a few gousters, are you Nate?"

I'm not sure how we could be riding three abreast on busy 71st Street, but I guess that's the beauty of dreams. It felt like it was a year or two previous, because Nate and Lee each looked younger, showed no signs of whiskers.

We were passing the huge Woolworth's five-and-dime and then the Peter Pan Restaurant, a hamburger joint and meeting spot on the corner of 71st Street and Jeffery, the commercial nerve center of South Shore. I loved Peter Pan's burgers, especially with fries and a thick chocolate milk shake.

Like I said, everything was so sparkling and clear. We rode past the

Fanny Farmer candy store, where one or another of us occasionally splurged for a small box of nougat chocolates for our moms on their birthdays. And then the grandiose Jeffery Theatre, where Nate and I sometimes hid in the balcony and shot broken paper clips onto unsuspecting adults sitting below. Past the Rosenberg Drug Store, site of my first paying job, working after school for several months, at sixty cents an hour, unpacking boxes of aspirin and antacids, and mixing fizzy cherry Cokes and chocolate phosphates for customers young and old. And past the South Shore YMCA, the gathering place for my wrestling and dance classes.

We left the busy thoroughfare, taking a right onto Constance Avenue, laughing as we each took a turn riding no-hands on this quiet side street of South Shore's Highlands section, with its cozy well-maintained single-family brick homes and tidy lawns. Then past Parkside, my old elementary school on 69th Street, and its expansive gravel schoolyard.

Past streets lined with handsome three-story dark red and brown brick apartment buildings on Ridgeland, where I had lived while at Parkside.

Next we were passing the Jackson Park Theatre on Stony Island Avenue, the scene of many a horror show and twenty-five-cartoon special marathons for Columbus Day and Lincoln's birthday. And nearly next door, a favorite hangout: the deli on 67th Street, where Mom often sent me to pick up a small sliced rye bread without seeds plus a half gallon of milk.

There was shared nervousness as we headed north on Stony Island, past the popular spanking new McDonald's drive-in on 65th Street, one of the first of its kind in the country, with its bargain fifteen-cent hamburgers, ten-cent hot crispy fries, and twenty-cent shakes. "For forty-five cents, you can eat like a king," I often reminded Nate and Lee.

And past the start of the El at 63rd Street, a depressing gargantuan steel and wood structure that launched the squeaky elevated trains on their journey from this southeast corner of the city through Woodlawn and Englewood, and past the all-Negro high-rise projects near Comiskey Park, the home of the White Sox, and underneath downtown.

At 60th Street, we turned our bikes west into Woodlawn, and suddenly beer bottles littered the unkempt curbside grass. Lanky Negro girls, maybe ten or eleven-years-old, wearing faded white cotton dresses, played flawless double Dutch with long jump ropes. The girls' stiff little braids barely moved as they stepped effortlessly like skilled tap dancers over the two ropes circling quickly under and over them.

Skinny Negro men in dirty sleeveless white t-shirts sat on stoops, heads on forearms resting on knees. A few teen boys pitched pennies, looking nearly like statues as they completed a toss, standing on one foot, arm extended, watching the flight of their coin on its journey toward the crack between two sidewalk blocks and possible victory for a few cents extra change.

What were we doing in this off-limits neighborhood? Maybe Nate had heard about a neat park and playground in a white area just beyond the slums we were attempting to navigate.

The weather was crisp and cool on this day, but as we rode west and north, the air reeked ever more of the putrid smell of animal manure and blood and guts. It must have been cattle slaughtering time over at the stockyards on south 30th Street.

Or maybe the foul smell was coming from my gut, the smell of panic as the chase began. "Honkies!" cried a husky voice somewhere in the distance. Were we still in Woodlawn, or in neighboring Englewood? Not that it mattered—they were equally unfriendly to white strangers.

"Git those white boys!" a second higher-pitched teen voice shouted from somewhere closer, to the side or in back of us. Lee peeled off to the left and Nate to the right, presumably hoping to confuse our pursuers by heading in different directions.

Little by little, the pursuers were gaining on me. There were four or five of them, bundles of endless energy in white or tan t-shirts, probably my age or a little older.

Up ahead, at the end of the block I was on, I saw a police car. Relief! Except, as I drew closer, I realized the two uniformed officers standing next to the car were Jimmy and Driver of the previous evening's shakedown with Valerie. They wore slight smiles, and each was giving me the middle finger. Where the heck were Lee and Nate?

I couldn't be sure if my pursuers saw the police abandoning me, but it didn't really matter. I had no choice but to keep riding, and not have to go face-to-face with them in this alien territory.

Egging me on were their breathless words to each other. "Wait till I git that white muthafucka," said one. Another: "Gonna kick his white ass!"

Then, seemingly out of nowhere, in my periphery to the right, I caught sight of a light-skinned Negro girl with a bouffant-style hairdo, riding a bicycle on the sidewalk. She was riding slowly, apparently alone and seemingly oblivious to the chase scene drawing nearer to her. Just as I was about to pass her on the left, I noticed her motioning. At least I thought she was motioning. Her right arm was moving slowly, from her right ear and straightening and then back toward her right ear. She clearly didn't want to stand out to my pursuers.

A side street just ahead…I slammed my brakes, skidded, and turned sharply to the right onto a narrow shaded street. I passed in front of her in a flash, and saw that she was about my age, dressed in red pedal pushers and a white t-shirt. She was staring straight ahead, smiling slightly, as I cut in front of her. She didn't look familiar, but she definitely had a kind face.

My pursuers missed the turn, giving me a few moments reprieve from the tension of their pursuit. Just a short block ahead was another busy street. Finally, a traffic light was with me, and I barreled across. I looked back to see my pursuers heading toward the same light, but slowing down.

A playground beckoned on the other side of the street, along with the unmistakable sights of Nate and Lee sitting on a park bench, their bicycles on the ground nearby. Around them, playing peacefully on swings and teeter-totters, were other white kids I didn't know. The important thing at that moment was that they were all white. I had made it to Western Avenue, and into white West Englewood. When I looked back, I could see the backs of my pursuers riding slowly away from Western Avenue. There was no way they would continue chasing me into a white neighborhood.

I was so out of breath, I could barely speak as I approached my friends. "What took you so long?" Nate asked. He was smiling, calm, in a lounging position.

I wanted to punch him. Yet underneath my rage, I knew I probably would have behaved the same as he did in splitting off.

"How'd you manage to lose those gousters?" Lee inquired.

I was still too out of breath to say more than a few words at a time. "A girl motioned me down a side street," I panted.

"Why did she help you?" Lee asked. "She could have gotten in big trouble with the gousters on your tail."

I nodded. "You're right. I don't know. I sure wish I could thank her." The dream ended without anyone being thanked, and I woke up.

35

I was still trying to make sense of the dream while riding over to the South Shore Country Club the next morning. The sight of the cops giving me the finger rattled me the most because it reinforced my nervousness that they would tattle to Dad. I presumed the Negro girl helping rescue me was Valerie, even if she didn't look familiar. I sensed the dream was projecting tough times ahead.

The lush scene at the country club quickly brought me back to reality. The sun had just broken through low-hanging clouds over Lake Michigan, turning the water from dark gray to resplendent blue. On the maintenance road, workers were leading a dozen miniature ponies, decked out in blue, pink and yellow ribbons from horse trailers into a corral, presumably for a children's birthday party. Wished I was going there rather than the caddy room.

I walked in to the usual collection of a half-dozen guys hanging around waiting for caddying assignments. Behind the counter, Eddie looked over a schedule of tee times and a list of caddies. He had some serious sunburn on his forehead and nose that I hadn't noticed the previous night, probably because he was wearing a baseball cap then. When I approached him to say hello and let him know I had arrived, he barely moved his sunburned head from the sheets of paper he was focused on.

"Looks like we have more guys than we need today," he said into the papers.

My heart was racing, my mouth dry. "Is it okay if I hang around for a while, see if things pick up enough that you might need me?" I asked.

"Nah, the schedule is set, and I can see we won't be needing you. You can just take off. Enjoy the day. Looks like it's going to clear up." Eddie paused. "Maybe take your girlfriend to the beach. I didn't catch her name."

I stood there for a few moments, wondering if I should make believe I didn't hear the last thing he said about my girlfriend, and inquire if there might be work the following weekend. For a fleeting moment, I wanted to say, "Her name is Valerie." As if that might make Eddie shift.

But I sensed that pretty much anything I said would be demeaning myself, leaving him another opportunity to stick his racist needle in deeper. Without a word, I turned and left the building, my brief career as a golf caddy over.

Or just about over. As I exited the clubhouse building and turned to walk toward the imposing country club gate, I heard a husky voice behind me. "Hey Jewboy. Who let you in here?"

I knew even before I finished looking over my shoulder that the voice belonged to Tommy Sullivan.

He was standing along the side of the clubhouse, maybe fifteen feet away from me, decked out in tennis whites, his arms folded across his chest, and glaring at me. He appeared skinnier and more gangling than I remembered him from the bus a few weeks earlier.

I wasn't about to give him the satisfaction of learning how ignobly my caddying career had just ended. Indeed, something in me wanted to confront him, finish up what I hadn't felt free to do on the bus a few weeks back, or at Rainbow Beach the previous weekend.

Something inside also told me not to rush, but rather to try humoring him, get him worked up so he'd do something stupid. "Hi, Tommy. Big news. They want me to join up here. Become the first Jewish member."

He took my effort at humor seriously. "Bullshit! I heard you were a caddy. My father told me what a terrible job you did."

"Maybe your dad is just a crappy golfer. He couldn't get the ball over the water hole on the fifth hole if he threw it over."

Now Tommy was walking quickly toward me, his arms unfolded, his feet pointing in at the conclusion of each step.

He kept coming, his arms moving outward to shove me in the chest. Except I shifted my body to the left at the last moment, and with my left hand pushed him toward my extended right foot. This was another move I had learned in wrestling class at the Y, with the proviso that it wasn't always a legal move in a match.

Tommy tried to stop, but couldn't quite pull up, and he went into a nearly slow-motion fall toward the ground, not unlike what had happened on the bus a few weeks earlier. I heard a soft but unmistakable crack as his hands tried to break the fall, and then a sharp exhale and muffled cry as he grabbed his right wrist. "Shit!"

Then he was sitting on the ground, holding his wrist against his chest, his face grimacing tightly. "You're going to pay for this, Jewboy!"

His mention of "pay" triggered my response. I dug into my pants pocket, and picked out two pennies. I threw them toward him.

"Here's my payment, Tommy. You left these on the bus a few weeks ago."

He looked absently at the pennies in the sand and gravel next to him, and seemed to grab his wrist even harder against his chest, exhaling a slow moan.

Then I walked the few yards out through the imposing country club gate with its "For Members Only" gold-lettered reminder just under the club name overhanging the gate. Standing outside, the satisfaction I felt in injuring Tommy quickly dissipated, and I felt tears welling up. I wanted to cry, but damned if I was going to be seen mourning outside the racist and anti-Semitic South Shore Country Club. I should have known better than to expect things could somehow work out well in this place.

I had a vision of Valerie, staring at me. "Now you know how we feel when we go for jobs," she was saying.

Somehow, that made me feel better, less alone in my outrage and humiliation over losing my job. I walked over to Mitchell's, an ice cream and candy hangout with red leather booths nearly across the street from the country club entrance, and ordered a chocolate chip ice cream cone. Mitchell's had the best chocolate chip ice cream anywhere, and I decided I was entitled to the pleasure, even if it cost fifteen cents and even if I had to savor it alone.

I knew I should check if my lawn mowing jobs were still available to begin replenishing the cash I paid out to the cops the previous evening. That would be the responsible thing to do. But as I finished devouring the ice cream and sugar cone, I had this strong urge to take a bicycle ride, somewhere, anywhere, outside the hate that had become South Shore.

36

I rode my bicycle over to Nate's house, where he was just finishing up an enforced piano practice session, and was glad for any excuse to get out of the house.

"Aren't you supposed to be caddying?" he asked as we rode down his street, Cregier. I told him they had too many caddies this day and I came out on the short end of the draw. I didn't mention Valerie and Eddie, or my run-in with the police the night before. I didn't want to take any chances on the encounter with the cops going public, not so long as there was still the possibility the cops would neglect to tell Dad about it.

Nor did I mention Tommy, though I wanted very much to brag about tripping and injuring the Jew hater. But, of course, that would lead back to events of the previous evening. Fortunately, Nate didn't quiz me.

I felt almost sneaky not saying anything. We shared so much of what was going on in our lives, and the previous evening's events were a big deal, no matter how you looked at it. Maybe some other time, after things settled down some, I told myself.

We rode the few blocks over to Lee's house, only to find him buried in the basement, in the middle of this crazy project he'd had going of building his own airplane. He'd completed the fuselage, most of it a reclamation from an old 1930s plane that had been junked. It wasn't that large, but looked positively huge in the confined space of the basement. In another section of the downstairs area, he was working on a wing out of balsa wood. "I've got to be here till the glue finishes drying in a couple hours," he said, by way of explanation as to why he couldn't ride with us.

"Just remember, when this is done, we'll fly over all those gouster areas and give them the finger from way up high," he said, motioning toward the fuselage. We nodded, not believing a real plane that actually flew would emerge from all his effort.

Then, he turned to look directly at Nate and me. "I also have to get this plane built because we may be leaving before too long. My parents are talking about selling the house."

Nate and I just nodded. There was no need to question him, express surprise. We understood.

As Nate and I rode along Stony Island, the western border of South Shore, I realized it had been at least a year since I had been back to this area of South Shore, where we had lived in the Ridgeland Avenue apartment Robert's family took over. It looked much different from my recollections, and from my dream of the previous night.

The two glitzy movie theaters I attended as a young boy, the Stony

Island on 69th Street and the larger and more ornate Jackson Park on 67th Street, were boarded up, their marquees absent of any lettering and the hundreds of light bulbs underneath, which turned night into garish day, burned out or missing. I could make out the lettering on a dirty empty storefront adjoining the Jackson Park Theatre: "Karmelkorn."

The pharmacy between the two theaters, where friends and I purchased our pea shooters and paper envelopes of dried peas for shooting, was gone, as was the deli on the corner of 67th Street, where my parents sent me on weeknights for the bread and milk. So was the barbershop, just round the corner from the deli, on 67th Street, where the Filipino barber, Karl, cut my hair and used a straight razor to get my sideburns just right.

The good news was that the peace doves were with us for this ride as we headed into Woodlawn and through Washington Park into Englewood—probably because it was Sunday morning, and the neighborhood toughs were still asleep. We could hear soothing melodic voices coming from a storefront Baptist church on East Garfield Boulevard, singing what sounded like a Negro spiritual song. True to my dream, some young Negro girls were showing off their double Dutch skills, and a few down-and-out men in sleeveless white shirts were lounging on apartment entrance steps.

There was one close call when we stopped at an Englewood gas station to buy a cold drink. It had one of those huge steel soda coolers where, after you paid your dime and made your selection from among orange, cherry, grape, or Coke, you reached into icy water to pull your soda out of the metal holder that held them in place at their necks. My fingers were numb after just a few seconds of immersion in the gray water, but my grape soda was so icy cold and thirst quenching, it was worth the frozen-hand plunge.

Unfortunately, we spotted three gousters riding on tiny two-wheelers approaching the station and instinctively decided to scram, chugging our sodas before quickly and quietly re-boarding our bikes and heading off in a different direction before they took notice of us. I tried unsuccessfully to suppress a series of burps from too quickly gulping down the soda.

There was another scare in the early afternoon, as we headed back east, toward Hyde Park. We were chased by three or four gousters, also on tiny bikes. They shouted at us to "stay outta our areas, crazy honkies." We rode quickly, but without panic as we were close enough to Hyde Park that we knew they wouldn't leave their neighborhoods for the unknown, and sure enough, they ended the chase at Cottage Grove Avenue.

Except for those brief scares, we had a pleasant ride in the heat of a ninety-degree day, and a nice reminder of how welcoming leafy Hyde Park Boulevard could be. As we approached the Point, at 57th Street and the lakefront, it was noticeably cooler from a lakefront breeze. We rode through the underpass beneath the Outer Drive, shouting and hooting for the echo effect, just like we did as little kids.

37

I hadn't been to the Point at least since I started high school three years earlier, and maybe longer. Mom and Dad used to take Emily and me there quite often when we were little and lived in the Hyde Park tenement. They had friends who hung out there, and Emily and I would play with their kids, riding tricycles around and playing catch with tennis balls, while Dad hung out with other men listening to White Sox games on the radio. Later, when I learned to swim, I'd join friends plunging into the refreshing water off the huge white limestone rocks that line the shore. Swimming there wasn't for the faint of heart, or for very little kids, so it was rarely too crowded, even on the hottest days.

Once we moved to South Shore, I had taken to hanging out more at Rainbow Beach on weekends. I had forgotten just how spectacularly beautiful the Point was, especially on a clear warm day like this Sunday: a compact park of softball fields and shade trees of varying sizes ringed by picnic areas; the huge jetty of flat limestone rocks for sunbathing; the skyscrapers of downtown seven or eight miles to the north. To the south were the two big public beaches—the 63rd Street beach barely a mile away, all brown, and Rainbow Beach a couple miles further on, all white. Probably because of its location in the University of Chicago territory of Hyde Park, it was a racial oasis—neither whites nor Negroes declared ownership, so all seemed welcome.

I spotted Valerie within minutes of our ride around the Point. On one of the sidewalks, she, Tanya, and two friends I didn't know were jumping double Dutch. Not the rapid intense style I was accustomed to seeing when riding through Negro neighborhoods, but more relaxed, and playful.

I signaled Nate to pull off the sidewalk, so we could sit on a park bench and watch from a hundred yards off. Sometimes the girls speeded up the rope so the jumper had to show serious jump roping ability, and other times they slapped it around, laughing when they missed a step and got tangled up.

If it wasn't for her shapely body in a yellow two-piece swimsuit, Valerie could have been a silly twelve-year-old passing the time. I enjoyed watching this other side of Valerie, while unwrapping the well-worn wax paper from a peanut butter and jelly sandwich on rye bread that Mom made early that morning, assuming I'd have it for lunch at the South Shore Country Club. The paper was probably recycled from one of Dad's lunches—she seemed to make that wax paper last forever. Whatever the paper, the sandwich sure tasted delicious sitting outside in the warm sun.

After a little while, Valerie and friends shifted their play. She was chasing one of them around the field for possession of something I couldn't quite make out. I poked Nate and we headed onto the field.

Valerie caught sight of me and her face brightened. "Hey, Jeff, catch this." She stopped and with a flick of her right wrist, let a red Frisbee fly. It curved away, and then toward me, and I caught it easily. Everyone had spread out and I flipped it about twenty yards to Nate who tossed it to Tanya. As the Frisbee made its way around, I realized it was the first time Valerie had called me by my real name, instead of "white boy."

After about fifteen minutes, Valerie took sole possession of the Frisbee and asked in a loud voice, "Anyone up for a swim?"

I signaled that I'd like that, as did Nate and Tanya. Nate and I fortunately wore swim trunks under our Bermuda shorts, and before long, we all had made our way gingerly off the huge flat rocks into the icily-cold Lake Michigan water. I was impressed with Valerie's strong crawl and elegant breaststroke.

"Good idea about the swim," I said when I caught up to her. "That was the perfect time. By the way, where did you learn to swim like that?"

She looked at me with the smirk, while treading water and pushing wet hair out away from her eyes and forehead. She knew where I was coming from.

"When I was seven or eight, and my dad still had this idea of living together with whites, he enrolled Derrick and me in a Hyde Park day camp with a lot of whites. Swim instruction was one of their big things, so we learned to swim."

"They did a good job. You're like a mermaid."

"Yeah, I don't do too bad for a colored girl, do I," she said breathlessly, more as a statement than a question, then ducking under water for a long series of breaststrokes.

As we neared the rocks to climb out, I grabbed Valerie's ankle from behind. She quickly flipped over and began splashing me. More splashing as we gained tentative footing on some smooth, submerged rocks by the shoreline, and Nate and Tanya joined in.

Before long, we were all sitting breathless on the giant white rocks, just soaking in the sun and warmth and fun. It helped turn the South Shore Country Club disaster of the morning into more of a distant bad dream.

I tried to simply appreciate the sun's warmth and the refreshing tingling on my skin left over from the frigid water. After a few minutes, I became aware that I hadn't been thinking for some length of time about real or anticipated racial problems, and that not thinking about those things was a huge relief. Screwy.

Valerie broke the silence as if she had been reading my mind. "I love it here. Sometimes, when I'm upset about something, I'll come here and just sit and look out over the water, and whatever it is that upset me won't seem as bad." She paused. "Hey, you ever been in that castle up there?"

She was referring to the field house set back from the rocky shore, which housed bathrooms and an indoor activity center for day camps on rainy days. The structure resembled a small castle because it was made of stone and featured a round turret at its center that rose fifty to one hundred feet above the rest of the one-story structure. I had only vague memories of having been inside and those memories were of a cool dark damp place.

On this warm day, the cool interior was a welcome respite from the intensity of the sun. Still in our swimsuits, we wandered into a large open area with a smooth, cold stone floor.

A fantasy floated through my mind of asking Valerie if she'd like to be "pinned." It was a custom at South Shore High School, when a guy and girl began to "go steady." I didn't actually know any couples that were "pinned," but as I understood it, the guy bought some kind of jewelry, pin or bracelet to give to his girlfriend, to then ask her to go steady.

The fantasy didn't last too long before I dismissed it. No, Valerie would probably be hysterical laughing after she put me through the discomfort of explaining what it was all about. Another crazy "white boy" idea.

She interrupted my thought process. "So you're not caddying. Is there a message there?"

"Yeah, a real clear message, as in 'you're fired.' Eddie didn't put it that way. He just said there wouldn't be work for me today and I shouldn't even hang around on the off chance the work flow might improve."

"So Eddie didn't like me," Valerie said dryly.

"No, he didn't. In fact, he said now that there wasn't work for me, I could spend time with you, so that was definitely his problem. But don't take it personally. He doesn't like anyone with dark skin."

I'm not sure why, except maybe I wanted to brag to Valerie that I didn't always need her around during a fight, I decided to share the Tommy episode. "I did make a spectacular exit from the country club."

She was staring at me with a puzzled look. It was at that point I realized how complicated it would be to explain beyond what I told her the previous evening, how some whites hate other whites because of their religion.

I tried to keep it simple. "There was a white kid there who's the son of a member, and the kid hates Jews. He came after me just as I was leaving, called me 'Jewboy.' Then he started a fight, and I threw him down. I think he might have broken his wrist, because he didn't get up to come after me."

She looked impressed. "Kick his ass! Way to go! You don't need to take that shit!"

Then she looked pensive. "A white boy coming after you because you're Jewish sounds a little like gousters coming after Ivy Leaguers. Calling us Uncle Toms or Oreos."

"It's worse than that," I said. "It's more like the whites coming after your family and setting your house on fire in Cicero."

"You mean whites can hate each other as much as they hate us?"

"I guess that's one way of putting it, yeah." Despite the discouraging tenor of our discussion, I was feeling uplifted, even a little aroused, that I had impressed her with my fighting ability.

We continued walking gingerly through the spacious main floor of the building and into the round castle in the center, which seemed to be comprised of storage rooms and offices. I tried a door, and it opened into a barebones office with a metal desk and chair. No one was inside, presumably because it was Sunday. We tentatively walked in. After Valerie had fully entered, I gently closed the door and approached her, as if we were about to dance. We embraced and I could feel her bare shoulders and stomach against my skin. Then a long deep kiss that ended with my hands on her rear end, with each of us pushing hard against the other.

"Very clever, white boy," she said breathlessly as we ended the kiss. "Very clever."

Hmmm, where did we go from here?

Valerie made the decision easy. "I have to get back to my family and friends barbecuing dinner," she said softly. "This place is good to know about. We'll have to come back again."

"So that's your family sitting out there, grilling?" I inquired. I was curious, because the assemblage of perhaps a dozen Negro men and women in addition to Valerie's two friends didn't have the look of a family sort of thing—it was missing the familiarity and comfort with each other that families have. There was little laughing or jousting.

"Not entirely. Some of them are family friends. There's some political discussions going on. I can tell you more about it when we go downtown next week."

I took the hint. "Tuesday? Maybe meet over at the El after seventh period?"

She nodded her agreement. I told her to go on ahead, till I could calm things down under my swim trunks enough to return to a more public setting.

38

I returned home in the late afternoon, just in time for Sunday dinner. This was always our most special meal of the week, something luxurious or unusual, like a sirloin steak or a small roast beef, topped off with homemade cake or pudding for dessert. This day it was fresh beef tongue, one of my favorites.

Dad usually made an admiring comment about Mom's cooking creations, but not today. He was preoccupied by something much more important to him.

In my imagination, I hadn't calculated that Dad would have already heard about my previous evening's run-in with the police. I assumed nothing would happen until the workweek started, and maybe by then, hope against hope, the two cops I encountered would have moved on to more important matters like arresting real criminals, and dropping our La Rabida episode. I obviously didn't take into account the presence of telephones.

We were just about to dig in to Mom's beautiful meal when he launched his attack. "So, were you ever going to tell me about how you were using my car to drive a schvartze girl around last night?" He was staring at me with his most serious expression, bushy eyebrows furrowed.

"Not now, Kurt. Let the boy enjoy his meal."

Dad barely averted his gaze from me. "No, it has to be dealt with, Hilde."

My heart rate quickened and I took a deep breath. "Everything turned out okay, so I didn't think I needed to say anything. You heard from your police friends?"

"Heard from my police friends?" Dad said loudly. "They were wondering what kind of a family I have. They say you were parked at La Rabida, in a very isolated area, and they were worried you were with a prostitute. They were going to arrest her, and you."

"Yeah, I'm sure they were real concerned about your family, Dad. She's a girl I go to school with, we're just friends. We are in the same math class. She's a very nice girl, and a smart girl." I knew he valued smart. Except tonight. He clearly didn't value anything positive I had to say.

"I don't care if she's the reincarnation of Albert Einstein. She's nothing but trouble for you, and for all of us."

I tried to make our activity sound normal. "Kids go up to La Rabida all the time and park," I said. "It's not a big deal."

"Not a big deal?! Not a big deal?!" He was practically shouting. He paused, as if he was trying to collect himself, and his voice returned more to the normal range. "I thought you had better judgment than that, Jeffrey. I wouldn't have given you the keys to my car if I realized you had lost your senses and were chauffeuring schvartze girls around."

I decided to try the social justice tack. "Dad, I don't think you should be critical just because my friend is Negro. What if I was with a white girl and got stopped by the police. Would that be so bad?"

Not a good direction. Now Mom piped up. "Don't you see all the problems we have with the Negroes? They are destroying our neighborhoods. Bringing in crime. They took over our building on Ridgeland. Now half of this building is schvartze. Your father is afraid to come home from work each night. He's already been threatened a few times on his walk home from the bus. Big schvartze boys looking for money. He doesn't know if they are carrying guns or what. We'll be lucky if we can stay here through next year when you graduate."

Jeez. Mom wasn't supposed to out-and-out take his side. She usually stood up for me when Dad went on the attack. Yeah, sometimes it made me feel like I was a momma's boy, but he could be pretty tough, like when he refused to pay for me to go to overnight camp with Nate and other friends, said he never went to camp and I should earn the money myself. Mom realized that was impractical, since I was only twelve. Out of sight, Mom convinced him to back down. I had a great time, and was always grateful for her intervention.

On this Sunday, I felt like I had no choice but to aggressively defend myself, since no one was going to help me. "Maybe it wouldn't be so bad if the cops weren't stopping them all the time when they're just driving around minding their own business. Those cops who came after Valerie and me had it in their minds she was a prostitute just because she is a Negro. If she had been driving around with other Negroes, I'm sure they would have been arrested. They let us off because I was white and had some money. That's not right, it's not fair."

The mention of money got Dad's attention. "How much did you have to pay them?"

I wasn't sure I should tell him, it would just aggravate him more when he learned of the substantial payment I made. But I couldn't figure out how to put him off, or change the subject. After a few moments of silence, he asked again. "What did you have to give them, fifteen dollars?"

"No, thirty."

"Thirty! That's highway robbery!"

"Yeah, literally," I agreed.

"Those guys knew you were afraid, and took advantage of you."

"Well, they started out saying they wanted a hundred bucks, or they were going to charge me with all kinds of terrible crimes, with huge fines. So I thought I got a good deal."

I was hoping Dad was beginning to see the blatant injustice of what had occurred, but he wasn't. He shifted to blaming Valerie.

"That schvartze girl is costing you a lot. But that's what happens with them. They're destroying the shopping downtown, too. The police can't keep up with all the shoplifters and robbers. That's why we have to pay the cops extra, to keep an eye on our store. But if the police can't stop them, and Goldblatt's can't stay in business, then I won't have a job. We're trying to save money to buy a house in Skokie or Lincolnwood. We can't do that if I don't have a job."

I decided to try one last tack, a desperation argument I knew ran the risk of completely alienating him. "Isn't that what the Nazis said about the Jews, that the Jews were destroying all the good things about Germany?"

He stared at me in disbelief for a moment, his eyes suggesting confusion. But just for a moment. He had an answer. "The Jews weren't doing anything. We were scapegoats. But the schvartze are making our lives impossible here. I see it with my own eyes."

There clearly wasn't much more for me to say. There was no way I was going to promise to stop seeing Valerie. I had just hoped the cops wouldn't be so efficient about tattling on me, and this discussion would be delayed for a few days, or even weeks. I remained silent, munching on the beef tongue and baked potato, which now were cold, and felt dry and tasteless in my mouth.

When Dad saw I had nothing more to say, he piped up again.

"I don't want you picking up schvartze girls in my car, understand? Don't even ask to use the car if that's what you are going to be doing."

I resisted the temptation to tell him what he could do with his car and his money, and to storm out of the apartment. Something told me that was more of a dead end than where I was at that moment.

I had enough to figure out as it was. It wasn't going to be easy dating Valerie going forward. Outside of the car, there weren't many places for a white boy and a Negro girl to hang out.

39

The next morning at school, my mind was wrapped up in trying to figure out what I should say to Valerie about my dad and the car. Despite having clued her in to the likely bad reaction from Dad, I sensed that mulling over a theoretical possibility and actually having it happen were two different things.

While she might not be surprised that the cops followed through and told Dad, I sensed my own shame and embarrassment as I considered possible ways to tell her. I suppose I could have put it in the context of my parents feeling under siege, with each neighborhood turning Negro and us moving on. But it was difficult to imagine explaining that as a problem to someone whose family aspired to move into our neighborhood, someone whose family home in a white neighborhood had been firebombed. No Negroes ever did that to us, or to any white family we knew.

I was still contemplating my new dilemma while standing at my locker Monday morning, just before home room, sorting out which books I needed for which upcoming classes, when who should amble up and start a conversation but Booker Walsh. I had no idea what he might have on his mind, except I sensed it was nothing positive for me, especially given that our most recent encounter had been a fight.

The most positive thing I could come up with in my mind was that he wasn't immediately hostile or threatening. "Hey man, how you doin'? You have a good weekend?"

"Yeah, okay," I said, curtly, continuing my sorting, hoping he would move on.

This was a different Booker Walsh. He seemed somehow more relaxed, even more confident than I had seen him in recent weeks, when he'd appeared uncomfortable, possibly embarrassed, as a result of our fight. Maybe it had something to do with the fact he was wearing what looked to be a new Italian knit shirt, in a bright yellow, which gave him something of a sunny and cheerful appearance.

His niceties were way beyond anything he had extended my way before, so my radar was on high alert, trying to figure out what was really going on. Did he want to resume our fight? Threaten me? Did it have to do with Valerie?

"So, you go to the park with your family and enjoy the nice weather? Me, I went to a picnic."

What did he care about my family? I could feel butterflies beginning to flutter about in my stomach. I decided to try to steer the direction of the conversation away from me and toward him. "What's happening, Booker? I haven't seen you much lately."

He seemed to welcome my response. He broke into a smile, revealing front teeth widely spaced apart. "Sheeit," he snarled. "I been hearing a lot about you, white boy. I hear youz a big lady's man."

A pause. I didn't respond. My heart was moving up toward my throat.

"Yeah, I hear you been having yo'self some real good dessert, some chocolate pussy. How you like that chocolate pussy? Nice and sweet, I bet."

All I could think to do was to get away from Booker. "Hey, I gotta get going," I said.

"You means you don't wanna tell me how good that chocolate pussy tastes? How sweet it is?"

He watched me packing my books and notebooks together, ready to make my getaway. His expression grew serious, and he brought his face closer to mine. His voice softened so it was barely audible. "Valerie ain't doin' herself no favors makin' it with some hot-shit white boy. She know better. But sometimes our bitches don't know what theyz doin'. Theyz think if they make it with a honky they won't have to worry about money or nothin' like that. But it's up to you to set her straight, tell her you wuz just after that chocolate pussy, and go on yo' way."

He paused again, expectantly. I wanted so badly to change the subject or distract him somehow, get him off this whole sex thing, but I couldn't think of what to say. It was as if my mind was frozen in place. So I didn't say anything, and the silence became uncomfortable, till Booker resumed talking.

"I'm goin' to give you some advice, white boy. How would you feel if I was gettin' strawberry pussy from yo friend, or cousin, or sister? Youz wouldn't like it much, would you?"

Once again, he looked at me as if he was waiting for an answer.

My mind remained frozen. I definitely didn't want another hallway fight.

All I could think to do was just let him keep talking, and hope he didn't do anything crazy.

I guess he had his answer in my silence. "I know you wouldn't like it. None of yo white friends would like it. Yo mama wouldn't like it, either, her little girl makin' it with some brown-ass gouster."

He paused yet again, but this time to prepare for his concluding words. "So do yo-self a favor, and understand that from now on, youz allergic to chocolate pussy. You get my drift?"

He waited expectantly, presumably for a nod of my head. For a brief moment, I was tempted to give in to him, to end the torment. But I couldn't. My mind was unfreezing, at least a little, the ice of terror replaced by a feeling of warmth, of caring. Something told me I couldn't walk away from Valerie, not under Dad's threat to take the car away, not under the cops' threat to arrest me, or even under Booker's clear suggestion of bad things happening to me.

Not getting the nod he was seeking, Booker began to shake his head, drawing even closer to me, raising his voice slightly: "You think I'm messin' around, I know. Try feasting your eyes on this lil' baby." My eyes followed his downward glance, where in the palm of one hand, he flashed a chrome snub-nosed revolver.

I could feel my throat clench and my chest tighten. My breathing seemed to stop. Booker turned and resumed walking down the hall, as if nothing was amiss. In the few seconds it took me to lock my locker and turn into the hallway, my whole body had begun trembling. This was way beyond the push-button knife he had shown during our fight.

So, in a flash, my big concern shifted from what I was going to do for a car so I could meet Valerie, to what I was going to do to stay alive. Amazing how quickly priorities can shift.

My mind hop-scotched to Mom's warning last evening that it was impossible for a romance with a Negro girl to work out, because whites and Negroes couldn't get along. Her implicit suggestion was that I was in over my head trying to make such a romance work. Booker sure did make a strong case on her behalf.

My next two classes were a blur. I kept trying to figure out whether Booker was serious about killing me, or whether it was just a charade. I needed some feedback from somewhere outside my churning mind.

But whom could I consult?

Not Mom and Dad, for sure. They would have heart attacks if I told them a Negro student at Parkview flashed a gun and threatened to kill me. Yes, Dad had connections in the police department, but getting the cops on this would be more humiliating and distasteful than I could imagine, beginning with the "I told you so" from Mom and Dad, and continuing to the legitimizing of the police shakedown at La Rabida ("We knew she was no good, and her friends are even worse"). And that was all before even considering the fact that I'd be viewed as a snitch by all the gousters.

The thought flashed into my mind to ask Valerie for help, but I sensed that should only be a completely last resort. She helped me out of my earlier jam with Booker. That should have been the end of her involvement in protecting me, at least for a while.

I also thought about Lee. He was on my list of possible saviors during my fight with Booker, because he was in a couple of "regular" classes, and thus had gousters as classmates. Fortunately, he was alone at our cafeteria lunch table when I arrived. But how to explain my situation?

I decided to try a "what if" scenario. "Lee, let me try a situation out on you. Supposing when you came to school today, a gouster came up to you at your locker, and said he didn't like the fact that you were hanging out with a Negro girl from our school. In fact, he was so pissed off, he flashed a gun, and threatened to blow you away unless you stopped hanging out with the girl."

I could see Lee's green eyes widen underneath his unruly mop of red hair. "Wow! You wanna tell me who the bad gouster is?"

"Okay, but this is top secret, right?"

"Sure. I'm just wondering if I might be able to sweet-talk him some."

"It's Booker Walsh. I thought he had faded away, but it seems my going out with Valerie has really pissed him off."

"I could talk to him. If I did, he would at least know that you are talking about it, and that might scare him off from doing anything."

Such a potential solution, trying to intimidate Booker with information that I was sharing his threat with a white friend, struck me as very much of a long shot.

"Let me think about it," I told Lee. "For now, don't do anything. And remember, this is all completely private."

"Absolutely. I don't think you want to make Booker nervous, or more pissed than he already is."

40

Even on a normal day, taking the Elevated train, or El, from 63rd Street, a couple blocks from Hyde Park High, was a risky affair for whites. The risk was lowest on weekend mornings, like the Sunday morning Eddie and I traveled to Comiskey Park to see the White Sox play.

The risk went way up on weekday afternoons and evenings. And this particular Tuesday afternoon wasn't even a normal day. I was dressed in a white shirt and tie for my job interview at the shoe store, making me stand out as more white and obvious than usual. Walking with Valerie so soon after Booker's threat made me feel as if I was walking around with a big target on my back containing a mouth-watering invitation: "I'm a stupid white boy. Shoot me."

The stubbornness in me didn't want her to know how terrified I was, so I tried to act casual. She looked dynamite, showing a touch of red lipstick and blue eye shadow and dressed in a black pleated skirt, and long-sleeve white blouse, her shapely legs set off with stockings and dark loafers.

She was laughing about Mr. Olive's math class that we had just shared. "He sure was spacey today."

"Maybe that's why I didn't understand the homework assignment," I replied, knowing that the problem was more likely that I was continuing to be distracted by Booker's threat the previous day.

The sight of 63rd Street as we approached on Stony Island didn't do anything to calm my nerves. It was a dark place, with bars and liquor stores, currency exchanges and a pool room, made darker by the presence of the hulking El, which blocked out any sunlight to the street below.

On one brick wall I noticed some new graffiti in large thin white letters: "Blackstone Rangers Rule." There were lots of people milling about, with the biggest crowd outside the pool hall. They all seemed to be tough Negro teens or skinny alcoholic Negro men. There was no blending in with the crowd for a white guy like me.

As we were climbing the steep corrugated steel stairs of the El platform, I suggested to Valerie that we sit separately on the train, and she agreed without discussion. For once, she seemed a tad nervous, though I wasn't sure if it was about being with me or going to her new job.

As I sat on a pale blue plastic train bench facing out, I opened my sketch notebook and tried to look busy doing a rough sketch of Valerie from the side as she sat about twenty-five feet up from me, near the other end of the train car. She was reading a paperback, *To Kill a Mockingbird*. I was almost certain it wasn't assigned in any of our classes at Parkview, which meant she was reading it on her own. Going interracial all the way. I drew in a breath. It somehow didn't seem like great judgment for a young Negro girl to be sitting on a Chicago elevated train reading the story of a black man accused of raping a white woman.

My thoughts were interrupted at the second or third stop, still in Woodlawn. I noticed a group of four or five gousters enter our car from a neighboring one. I intentionally remained focused on my sketching, even when one of them was standing just to my side, his loose-fitting black pant leg and silver belt buckle in my peripheral vision.

"Hey, white boy." There was a long pause, and then I heard the fellow's voice louder, "I's talkin' to you, white boy."

I looked up. "Sorry, didn't know you were talking to me." I tried to appear casual, as if this was just a brief interruption that would quickly pass. I saw the lanky gouster standing over me, and got a glimpse of two of his friends who appeared to be watching his back, their eyes scanning either end of the subway car. I hoped they didn't notice me doing a double-take—one of the friends was Booker Walsh.

The only encouraging part of the scene before me, and it wasn't really all that encouraging, was that Booker was so intent on watching out for cops he hadn't seemed to take notice either of me or of Valerie.

Out of the corner of my eye, I saw another Negro fellow, slender and handsome, hanging back, as if he wasn't an official part of the threesome hovering around me, but monitoring its activities. He was set off also by his appearance—while the intimidators wore loose-fitting Italian knit shirts and baggy pants, he stood ramrod straight, dressed in a form-fitting, dark-brown, button-down shirt and tight black pants. Atop his head, slightly askew, was a maroon beret made from felt. The combination gave him a military bearing. He looked as if he was concentrating with deadly seriousness on the scene playing out in front of him.

"Don't play smart ass with me," the first gouster continued. "Now, I's looking for a few dollars. You better have somethin'."

I apologized, told him I didn't have anything, hoping against hope they would move on.

"You's bullshittin' me! You want to give me a few dollars, or you want me to go lookin' for it?"

As this exchange spiraled downward, I noticed Valerie had gotten up and was speaking hurriedly into the ear of the guy who was hanging back. He nodded slightly, then turned his head to look directly at Valerie. "This ain't yo' business. Don't go messin' with me again, bitch!"

In an instant, he moved forward. "Leave this honky," he brusquely ordered the three junior gousters. "We'll go to the next car." He gave me a quick non-smiling glance as he walked past—as if to say, "You are one lucky white dude."

Whatever he actually meant to communicate, I knew well that I was one very lucky white dude. But at what cost to Valerie? I returned to my sketching, and the remainder of the trip through the South Side projects and then into the subway under downtown proceeded uneventfully.

41

We exited to the hurried throngs of people and traffic at State and Madison. "What was the story with those guys on the El?" I asked Valerie as we made our way up the concrete steps into the fresh air.

"I don't know how to explain it, because I'm not sure exactly what was going on," Valerie said. She looked genuinely puzzled.

"You ever hear of Jeff Fort?" she asked.

I shook my head.

"Jeff used to be at Hyde Park High, till he dropped out or got thrown out a year or two ago. I'm not sure what the exact story was—it depends who you talk to. He became a hustler, like a lot of the gousters who drop out. Running drugs and stuff."

"So what was he doing on the train?"

"Jeff is a very smart gouster, the young guys look up to him. He hangs out at the Woodlawn Boys Club. He talks about how they have to get organized, to protect themselves from the police, and from gousters in other neighborhoods, and a lot of the gousters in Woodlawn feel he cares about them. The last few months, he's been organizing a gang, the Blackstone Rangers." Blackstone was a main street in Woodlawn.

"So was that a gang activity on the El?" I asked.

"I assume so. Remember at the Medici, I was telling you that to become a gang member, you have to prove yourself by doing some kind of crime? So I guess he was watching the guys who hassled you to see how well they did at getting money out of you. Booker and the other kid were keeping an eye out for cops."

"How do you know Fort?" I asked. "Through your brother?"

"Yeah, through my younger brother and Booker. Fort is around the neighborhood more and more, trying to recruit kids. I've never had a conversation with him, but he knows I'm related to my brother, James. The families try to fight him. But he's very smart. He'll do favors for people, like he did with you and me this afternoon. Then we owe him."

"What did you say to him?"

"I said you are a friend from school, you were going to work, and I'd appreciate it if they could leave you alone."

"And Booker was being sucked in?"

She just nodded her head.

I was beginning to understand the bleak picture she was painting. "So now he sees you as a possible enemy, interfering with his recruiting."

Valerie didn't say anything, but I could see her eyes had become teary. "It could be worse. Jeff Fort may be so pissed off, he decides to come after my whole family..." Her voice trailed off.

She had stopped looking directly at me, and spoke softly, her words coming out quickly. "I won't be able to meet after work, I need to get right home." We had talked about meeting up at a downtown burger place after work.

Another long pause. "I need time to think." With that, she headed east, toward Michigan Avenue and the *Ebony* satellite office.

My heart raced. Just like that, my relationship with Valerie seemed to have been put on ice, or maybe even gone up in smoke. On top of that, she may have put her family in danger. Or I may have been instrumental in putting her family in danger. All because she was trying to keep me from getting assaulted on the elevated.

It was 3:00 p.m. I needed to pull myself together for the upcoming job interview. I walked a couple blocks south on State Street to Maley's Shoe Store, a huge women's retail store. My interview was on the lower level "Budget" floor. The customers heading down the stairs seemed to be mostly Negro.

A friend at our synagogue, a South Shore High student, had tipped me off to the opening at Maley's. I asked to see Mr. Foster, who turned out to be a pale broad-shouldered man with a roundish face and jutting chin, dressed in a light gray suit and black tie, perhaps in his late twenties or early thirties. To me, he looked like another walking commercial for Brylcreem ("a little dab'll do ya"), with thick black hair, slicked back.

Fortunately, the interview was brief. After I told him how I made my connection to Maley's, he got right down to business. "I need guys who are willing to work hard and aren't afraid to sell," he said. When I told him I knew something about selling from spending time with my father at Goldblatt's, Foster seemed impressed.

"Okay, I'll give you a shot. You'll be paid a dollar an hour, plus what you make in selling extras. I'll tell you the same thing I tell all the new guys—there are three rules you have to follow if you're going to make it here. First, no looking up women's skirts. They don't want to buy shoes from perverts. Second, you have to push polish and PMs."

"PMs?"

"Didn't your dad teach you about that? PMs are for past models. Last year's shoes. You get an extra quarter for every pair of PMs you sell. Same for polish; you get a quarter for every bottle of patent leather polish you sell."

"And what's the third rule?" I asked.

Foster smiled. "No pocket pool while you're standing around waiting for customers."

I was about to ask what pocket pool was, but his leering smile pretty much explained it. I nodded in agreement.

He showed me the huge back room with its hundreds and hundreds of boxes of shoes arranged by size from floor to the nearly ten-foot-high ceiling. We also did a quick measurement of my right foot, so I could see how to use the metal foot sizer. A few minutes later I was waiting on my first customers, alternating with two other white teen sales guys. The activity actually seemed to take my mind off Valerie.

When a young heavyset Negro woman walked out without buying from me because the two styles she liked were too tight on her feet, Foster pulled me aside. "If a lady says the shoes are too tight, that doesn't mean they don't fit. Let her know that that's normal, that the shoes will stretch. And if it's late in the day, her feet may be a little swollen. Mr. Maley doesn't like it when people walk out empty-handed."

Over the next couple of hours, I took Foster's advice, and sure enough, sold a few pairs of shoes, including a PM. I was also successful in selling two of the small glass bottles of liquid black patent leather shoe polish next to the cash register. When it came time to leave at 8:00 p.m., Foster was smiling. "Good first day, Jeff. See you back on Thursday?"

42

Sitting on the IC train returning home, I felt at once empty and anxious. Empty about losing Valerie. Anxious—or maybe consumed is a better word—by Booker's threat. I still had no good ideas about whom to seek advice from, other than Lee. It was as if my mind was tangled into silly putty when I thought about ways to escape his threats.

That night, I had a rerun of my dream of a few days earlier about being chased by gousters on bicycles, except with a twist. Nate, Lee, and I were riding along 71st Street, and then from South Shore into Woodlawn and Englewood.

The chase started at about the same place, only this time I was unable to outrun my pursuers. They forced me off the street before I could cross into the white section of Englewood, and cornered me outside an abandoned brick house.

Surprise of surprises, the group's leader was Jeff Fort. I asked him if he knew Tyrone Lamond. Here in my dream, he didn't get angry as he had on the elevated, but rather smiled. "Sheeit, Tyrone is a good gouster. If you know Tyrone, you must be a good honky." Presto, I was released.

I woke up, and breathed a major sigh of relief. Not just because of my release in the dream, but because I might have discovered the makings of a solution with Booker.

As I dressed for school, though, my heart was pounding again. School was the last place I wanted to go. The weight of my secret was heavy, testimony to the desperation of the plan I had concocted.

I had no appetite, but forced myself to eat half a slice of the toast with butter and grape jelly Mom prepared. To her expression of concern, coupled with the back of her hand against my forehead to check for fever, I insisted I was okay, just a little worried about a geometry quiz.

The good news, I suppose, was that I got a chance to try my plan first thing. Booker appeared seemingly out of nowhere shortly after I arrived at my locker. He ambled slowly, in a kind of confident gouster walk, over to my locker, and got right down to business.

"So how's the ladies' man today?" The sarcasm was practically oozing from his lips as he stared through me. He didn't wait for an answer, perhaps remembering that our last discussion was pretty much a monolog on his part. He was wearing a subdued green knit shirt this time that seemed a tad more elegant than the one he wore last time.

"That chocolate pussy must be so good, you can't stay away. Is that it?" He let the question hang for a few moments, and continued. "I been wondering if maybe you didn't hear everything I said last time we talked. Or if I didn't make myself clear." He projected an air of cockiness that told me he hadn't the slightest expectation of encountering resistance.

It was time to again roll the dice, big time. "I heard you loud and clear, Leroy," I said, as forcefully as I could, even as I felt my voice trembling. "There was no way I could misunderstand."

I paused for effect and then said, "I was just wondering, do you know Jeff Fort?"

I watched Booker's face closely and saw a quizzical look begin to take hold. That was what I was hoping for, some hesitation. If he had immediately smiled and said he and Jeff Fort were tight, or something to that effect, I would have made an excuse about how I had heard about how important Jeff was becoming in Woodlawn, and then quickly shifted the direction of the discussion, though I'm not sure exactly how or where. Maybe told him I wasn't even going with Valerie anymore. But his hesitation indicated that what I saw on the elevated the day before was the reality—he was at the lowest rung of the Blackstone Rangers totem pole, just one of many teens trying to get Jeff Fort's attention and move up in the gang hierarchy.

So I continued on with Phase Two of my plan. "Does Jeff know you're giving me a hard time?" I hoped Leroy didn't see my knees shaking.

"How you know Jeff Fort?"

"Let's just say Jeff doesn't have any problems with me." I paused, and continued to monitor his expression. The quizzical look had changed slightly, to puzzled. I could tell he was trying to figure out in his mind just how much I knew, how serious I was.

I was feeling more emboldened. "I don't think Jeff likes it when other guys create problems where he doesn't have problems...you get my drift?"

Booker's cockiness had completely dissipated, kind of like during our fight on the stairwell weeks earlier. And the fact he didn't react to my hijacking of his own phrase about "my drift" made me feel as if I was nearing victory.

"Just stay outta my way, honky," he mumbled as he adjusted the collar on his shirt, and walked off.

I let out a sigh of relief, and headed to my first class, a heavy load now lifted from my shoulders and gut. An image of a tightrope walker flashed in my mind. Now I just had to hope Booker really didn't know Jeff Fort very well, and wouldn't start asking him questions about my relationship with Valerie.

My lightheartedness was short-lived, however. When I met Lee at lunch and told him I thought I had solved the Booker problem, he didn't smile. "I heard Sylvester Chase mumbling about you to some of his friends. Saying you are some kind of crazy honky for messing with their bitches and he thinks you're giving other white boys bad ideas."

Now an image of Davy Crockett at the Alamo, fighting off Mexican soldier after Mexican soldier, popped into my mind. It was discouraging, and scary, to think I might well have to figure out how to maneuver around yet another pissed off gouster. And another one after that, and then another...

43

Concentrating on classes was a big challenge the rest of Thursday. But I did have one moment of clear thinking, when I remembered Valerie's remark about how she liked to go to the area of large limestone rocks at the Point overlooking Lake Michigan to sort out tough problems.

I immediately decided to make a stop at the Point on my way into work after school. I called in to Maley's that I'd be a little late.

It was a coolish day, mostly overcast. I walked to the Point the same way I had ridden with Nate the previous Sunday, through the tunnel. Sure enough, I spotted a girl sitting on one of the rocks where we had lounged, with knees up, head cocked slightly to the right, and facing toward the lake. I could see she was wearing blue pedal pushers, the same sort Valerie wore that day at Riverview Park nearly a year earlier.

The closer I got, the more certain I was it was Valerie. I decided to be bold as I approached her from behind: "What are you thinking about Gouster Girl?"

The girl started, and turned quickly around. Fortunately, it was Valerie. Her eyes looked teary, her cheeks tear stained.

We stared at each other in silence. "Aren't you supposed to be working?"

"I'll be a little late. I had a hunch you might be here."

She shook her head, her voice breaking. "I don't know if I can do this any more. It's just too complicated. It was bad enough I was lying to Daddy. Now I'm messing with Jeff Fort and putting my whole family in danger."

I decided to take the blame. "That's my fault. I can't tell you not to stand up against Fort, except you don't seem like the kind of person who would just accept his threats, or any threats, without a fight."

She shrugged her shoulders. "I can stand up for myself, but I can't put members of my family in danger."

I decided to continue with my line of reasoning. "Can't your brothers decide for themselves what to do? If they decide not to join the Rangers, couldn't Booker or someone else you know help you?"

Then I decided to reverse myself on the latest Booker incident. "I stood up to Booker yesterday after he told me to stop dating you. Let him know I wouldn't listen to his threats."

"What did he say he'd do?"

I had gone this far. I decided to go all the way. "He showed me a revolver he was carrying."

"You see!" she exclaimed. "We're getting ourselves in too deep. We're going to get ourselves killed."

"I told him I didn't think Jeff Fort had a problem with anything I was doing, and he shouldn't either. He seemed kind of rattled when I said that, which told me he wasn't in deep with Fort."

Valerie didn't respond, so I continued my argument. "I think Fort is constantly recruiting kids. He knows he's not going to get every kid he wants to sign on. He also knows he can't go and shoot up every family that has a kid who won't join his gang."

Valerie remained silent. Then, a long sigh. "I guess that's why I liked you. The way you stood up to Booker reminded me of something I might have done, standing up to bullies, even when it's dangerous." She was speaking slowly, softly.

"I wasn't sure I liked the idea of being with a white boy. I still don't know that. Daddy says there's no way we can get along with whites because we have the same racial separation here they have in South Africa. They call it apartheid. Look at how our neighborhoods are separated, how you can be beaten up or killed for being in the wrong neighborhood."

"I don't know anything about apartheid except what I see on the news. I just know I liked you from the first time I saw you at Riverview and then being a cheerleader."

She seemed embarrassed. "Well, I liked the idea you were making drawings of me. It made me feel special. And a clever way to pick up girls." She smiled, took a breath, and wiped away tears.

This was definitely a more promising situation than two days ago. But I needed to get to work. Then she said, "Come by the Medici tomorrow evening, after dinner. I'll tell you more then."

44

What could Valerie have in mind for Friday evening? Something in her voice told me it wasn't about anything fun, like picking up where we left off after our previous get-together at the Medici, or in the castle at the Point. Was her family moving away, like so many others? It almost didn't matter. The fact that I was back in her good graces energized me for my shift at Maley's.

As luck would have it, my first shoe customer was a young petite dark-skinned Negro woman, probably in her twenties. She was dressed in a loose-fitting, beige summer dress that seemed to radiate the same joy as the woman. She was accompanied by an older heavy-set woman, who wore her hair in a bun and was dressed in darker, old-looking clothes, and appeared to be the younger woman's mother.

"My little baby is getting married in a few weeks," the older woman said, cracking a slight smile and nodding toward the younger girl. "We need a pair of wedding shoes. Something nice, in a white or beige or black, not too expensive."

I had already learned enough about the retail shoe business to know that the daughter was a prime candidate for a pair of PMs, because she no doubt wore a very small size, probably a four. As Mr. Foster explained to me, the smallest and largest shoe sizes experienced the most uneven sales. That left more PMs in those sizes at reduced prices than in the more popular sizes.

So I started by bringing out a couple pair of PMs in sizes and colors close to what the younger woman needed—one a narrow version of a size four in a brown and the other a narrow four and a half in black patent leather. I could tell from the grimace on the daughter's face that neither fit very comfortably.

She made believe they were tolerable, though, presumably for her mother's sake, since the PMs were up to twenty per cent cheaper than regular models. If I sold either one, I'd make an extra twenty-five cents, and if I sold polish to go with the black patent leather shoes, I'd earn yet another twenty five cents, or fifty cents total.

"I just need to wear them for one day," the daughter told her mother. "Either of these will be fine."

The mother wasn't buying the daughter's explanation. "It would be nice, Florence, if you could wear the shoes after your wedding as well, to nice occasions."

The mother looked at me, businesslike. "Do you have anything else that might fit her a little better?"

I brought out two current models in a regular size four, one in white cloth and the other a beige leather. I could tell immediately by the look of relief on the daughter's face that they fit perfectly. The current model shoes were $7.95, versus $6.50 for the PMs. The women debated back and forth, until finally I intervened.

"I think you definitely want to be comfortable on your wedding day," I said to the daughter. "You'll be standing a lot, and dancing."

They seemed relieved and accepted my advice. I felt especially good when the mother took out a small change purse, stuffed with crumbled bills, and carefully pulled out the right amount. This was clearly a big deal financially. It felt good to see the mother and daughter happy and satisfied, even if I wasn't making an extra twenty-five or fifty cents.

Almost immediately after they left, Mr. Foster pulled me aside. He had been listening in. "Why didn't you push one of the PMs? They would have bought it. We want to get rid of those first. We can always sell the current models."

"This was a big purchase," I explained. "I wanted the woman to be comfortable at her wedding."

Mr. Foster looked at me quizzically. "Our job is to sell shoes, not be friends. These people will buy what's cheapest and what you convince them to buy. Don't let me see you pulling that kind of crap again, or you're outta here."

For whatever reason, I didn't feel terribly threatened. I'd been though much worse in the last few days. It was almost like déjà vu. No matter how seemingly innocent my interactions with people, racial problems seemed to lurk.

As I walked up the stairs from the Maley's bargain basement at the end of my shift, feeling preoccupied with the threat of losing my second job in a week, I did a double-take at the store's nice upstairs main entrance. Just on his way out was none other than Tyrone, with Yoshana Bradley, thebeautiful Negro girl at Hyde Park High Nate had once tried to date, on his arm. They were both dressed to the hilt—he in a baby blue suit with white shirt, she in some kind of silvery cocktail dress—kind of like they were going to a prom, except it wasn't prom season.

For the first time since seventh grade, his angry scowl was nowhere to be seen. In fact, his handsome face seemed positively radiant, his eyes sparkling, as he laughed at something the glamorous Yoshana said to him. As he ended his laugh and looked back in front of him, his eyes caught mine.

"Hey Jeff, how ya doin'?" He sounded sincere, but obviously didn't want an answer. He was just being polite to a schoolmate in front of Yoshana. Then, just as he was nearly past me, he gave me a wink, and continued walking.

If he wanted me to feel jealous, he succeeded. Here he was with the most beautiful girl in our school, and he didn't have to worry about getting in trouble over her race. Lucky guy.

45

At the Medici Friday evening, I found Valerie in the back room, where we had previously danced and gotten to know each other. But on this evening, she wasn't with our high school friends, but rather with a group of maybe twenty Negroes who looked like they were college students or a little older. They weren't dancing, but rather sitting at the wooden tables drinking coffee or tea. The mood was serious, almost somber.

Valerie was one of the youngest people there, and when she saw me at the entrance to the room, she left her table to come greet me. She was dressed for summer in blue shorts and a white blouse, and no makeup on this evening. "Let's go outside," she whispered, and led me back toward the entrance to the bookstore.

"Who are those people?" I asked as we began walking along 57th Street, toward the chop suey place where we had bumped into Eddie.

"They're mostly friends of my older brother, Derrick. He's at the University of Illinois at Navy Pier but he has some friends at the University of Chicago who are members of a youth group that is part of the N double-A CP."

Fortunately, I knew that the NAACP was the National Association for the Advancement of Colored People, the largest Negro organization in the country pushing for equal rights. She explained that Derrick and his UC friends had decided to resurrect the "wade-in" protest at Rainbow Beach.

We stopped and sat down on a park bench at a small playground outside Ray School, and she gave me the Negro version of the wade-ins. It was a lot different from what Eddie described when we were playing softball at Rainbow Beach, and closer to what I read in the papers. The first wade-ins took place three years earlier, she said, in 1960, when a group of about thirty Negroes went to the beach, and sat around for an hour or so on blankets and towels, just like any other beach goers.

Suddenly, they found themselves surrounded by dozens of white toughs. There were some verbal taunts about why they were coming some place they weren't wanted, followed by a shower of rocks. One of the rocks hit the oldest person in the group, a woman in her fifties, who was the godmother of one of the wade-in leaders, on the side of her head. She was bleeding profusely and had to be rushed to the hospital. It took dozens of Chicago police to rescue the group.

"Did the woman recover okay?" I asked.

"No, she never recovered all the way. She still gets dizzy a lot and has to stay off her feet. She can't work."

The group held several more wade-ins during the rest of that summer, and the next summer as well. Each time, group members alerted police, who showed up to head off trouble.

But Negroes still didn't feel comfortable casually coming to Rainbow Beach. They didn't like that they had to depend on the presence of police to enjoy that most ordinary of summer-time activities of going to the beach. So the organizers had decided they needed to test whether it was safe for Negroes to go to Rainbow Beach on their own, not just in organized groups. The only way to do that was to go without alerting the police.

"Aren't you a little young to be participating in this sort of thing?" I asked Valerie. "Shouldn't you maybe leave this to the university students and adults?"

"I know what you're saying. But then I heard Mr. White talk about going down to Alabama to meet Dr. Martin Luther King and how even young kids are being arrested down there. I used to think Mr. White was an Uncle Tom, but now I feel like I should be doing what I can."

I took a deep breath. "You're very brave," I told her. It was all I could think to say.

"Will you be at Rainbow Beach Saturday?" she inquired. I had the feeling she was getting to the real point of our get-together.

"I'll definitely be there if I know when you all are planning your thing."

"We'll arrive about two," she said. "We want to be there when it's most crowded. Hopefully the bad white boys won't want to make trouble when there are a lot of mothers and young kids around."

She sounded to me like a veteran organizer. "How many of you will there be?" I inquired.

"I think about twenty or twenty-five of us."

I decided to ask her about something that was bothering me. "What about Booker, or Jeff Fort? Do they want to be part of your wade in?"

She looked surprised that I had raised the question, and hesitated. "Okay, this is totally secret," she said, looking at me expectantly. I nodded my agreement.

"Jeff Fort hears about everything that is going on in the neighborhood. So he must have heard about the plans for Saturday, and had one of his lieutenants ask about it. There was no way Derrick or any of the other people putting this together wanted the Rangers to be part of this. The absolute last thing they want is some kind of race riot. From what I heard, Fort took no for an answer, and didn't fight it. My guess is the Rangers have their hands full fighting the Devil's Disciples."

"It's definitely one less thing to worry about," I said. But I still wanted her to know I cared. "So how can I help, or can I help?" I asked, though I wasn't entirely sure I wanted to know the answer.

Valerie was prepared, as if she was hoping I'd ask. "We need two things. First, we need you to be ready to call the cops if things get too hot. Second, we need you to try to tone things down with the tough guys, the guys like Eddie."

I hesitated, and took a breath. "I can definitely be ready to call the police. But you really think I can calm Eddie and his friends down?"

"Yeah, just do kind of what I did with Booker during your fight, or with Jeff Fort on the El."

She said it matter-of-factly, but I detected a slight hint of you-owe-me in her tone. As in, "I was there for you, surely you can sweet-talk some white hotheads."

I thought back to the softball game at Rainbow Beach a few weeks earlier, and how revved up Eddie was when he thought there might be Negroes at the beach. And his reaction at the South Shore Country Club to my suggestion that he hire two Negro caddies.

But I didn't want to let on to my nervousness about trying to hold Eddie and his friends back from their hooligan tactics. If Valerie, a girl, could rescue me from the toughest gousters, including a gang leader, certainly I, a street-smart honky, should be able to deter a few white toughs from beating up on innocent Negro men and women.

Or so my mind was trying to convince my gut of at that moment in time, even as my gut was refusing to get the message.

I tried to show my bravado, while lightening things up. "Let's see what I can do. But only for Gouster Girl."

A smile took hold. And now the smirk. "Okay, white boy."

She was taking my humor as commitment, and our conversation shifted gears to less weighty issues. We compared notes about our classes and tests and college plans. She asked me where I wanted to go to college. I hadn't made any decisions, except that I was enamored of the idea of leaving home, and going to an East or West Coast campus. I told her I was thinking of applying to Boston University or the University of California at Berkeley.

She was quiet as I explained my dreams. "What about you? Any ideas?"

"I'll probably go to the University of Illinois at Navy Pier like Derrick."

"Would you live near there?" I asked.

"Live there? You've got to be kidding." She looked at me with wide eyes. "Who can afford to live at college when we can barely afford our apartment?"

"Maybe you can get some modeling assignments, like Yoshana," I offered. "That could bring in some serious money."

"How did you know about Yoshana modeling?" she asked, as if I had somehow learned a state secret.

I hesitated, not sure I should reveal that at the start of junior year, Nate got it into his head to ask Yoshana for a date. Lee and I were shocked. Yoshana looked like a model—slender, sharp nose, high forehead, and nearly straight shoulder-length hair—who held herself erect and tall and dressed in obviously expensive dresses and blouses. She was in our French class, and while all the boys, white or Negro, couldn't help but drool over her, she seemed aloof. Word had it that she was dating a Negro boy from another school.

Nate was brave enough to not only pursue Yoshana, but also to tell Lee and me about the unfortunate outcome. She said she was really busy for the next couple months doing modeling, and couldn't go out.

None of us was inclined to gossip about Nate. But I decided then and there sitting on a park bench on 57th Street, that Valerie was as unlikely to reveal our conversations as I was, if only because both of us had a stake in keeping them quiet. "Nate asked her out last fall, and she turned him down, said she was too busy doing modeling."

"You white boys really like Yoshana, don't you?"

"I think all the boys like looking at Yoshana," I responded.

She was not about to be distracted. "What other colored girls do you white boys like to rate?"

She had me off balance. "Hmm. I know some of my friends like Tanya a lot. And, of course, you."

"You're just saying that to be nice. I'm asking, because we sometimes talk about white boys we think are cute."

"Like who?" I asked, feeling tentative in my questioning, because I sensed I wasn't on anyone's lists of cutest white boys.

"Mel Graham is the cutest white guy." In addition to Mel, the swim team captain, she mentioned two other juniors I didn't know.

"So you guys sit around and rate white boys?"

"Yeah, you know how girls are when they're just sitting around, bored."

I didn't know before, but I did now. She looked at her watch. "Hey, I've got to get back to the Medici." She got up, bent over to give me a kiss on the lips, and was gone.

46

I saw Valerie only from afar at math class on Friday. "See you tomorrow," she mouthed at me just before class began. I smiled and nodded back, though I very much wished she was referring to seeing me at the Medici for socializing, and not the Rainbow Beach wade-in.

The next day, Saturday, I tried to make believe it was just another weekend day. I was back to mowing the two lawns, and while going back and forth along the expansive back yard of the second one, I decided I should tell Nate and Lee about the coming theatrics at Rainbow Beach.

I was hopeful they'd be open to getting involved, since I knew there was no way I could be trying to defuse the situation with Eddie and simultaneously running to call the police. Hopefully, they'd help out.

I bicycled by Nate's house and together with Lee, who was already there, we hung out in the expansive living room. Nate lived in the enclave of nice single-family homes in South Shore known as the Highlands. I always felt a little intimidated at Nate's place with its grand piano and one wall lined with books, most of them great works of history and literature. There was a big formal dining room adjoining as well. It was much fancier than our apartment, even our latest nice apartment. His father clearly did well as a dentist.

Nate and Lee were quickly engrossed in figuring out how we were going to get to and from the Medici that evening. Nate was bragging about his Lab School girlfriend, wondering aloud if tonight was the night "we go all the way."

I could almost feel the air hissing out of their collective balloons when I told them, "The Medici may be off tonight."

"Whaddaya mean?" Lee asked. "I go one time, and then it's all over?"

"If we're lucky, the social at the Medici will still happen," I told them, trying to maintain a positive front. "It's just difficult to imagine it happening, given this other event....You see, some of the Negroes who have been at the Medici are planning to participate in a wade-in at Rainbow Beach this afternoon."

"A wade-in?" Nate looked truly perplexed.

I told them what I knew about the wade-in at Rainbow Beach a few years back. How the presence of a small group of Negroes enraged some of the young whites enough that they threw rocks at and injured some of the Negroes. How the police had to escort the Negroes off the beach and out of the park. And how some of the Negroes were upset that they still couldn't go to that beach without Chicago police guarding them.

I recalled for them how a few weeks ago at our softball-game-for-cash

Eddie threatened to go after any Negroes who showed up at the beach.

"What does this have to do with us?" Nate asked. "Why should we care?"

"Well, Valerie is probably going to be with the Negro group that wades in this afternoon," I responded. "And she'll probably have some of her friends from Hyde Park High with her."

"I didn't know anything about this wade-in stuff at Rainbow," Lee confessed. "I don't go to Rainbow too often, but whenever I do, it just seems like a regular beach, no trouble except when the lifeguards go crazy if you swim two inches past their boats."

Nate was more thoughtful. "It's one thing to fight off the gousters. I mean, we're not always great at it, but we do it. We do it to survive. But fighting with crazy whites? That's a whole different ball game. Do we want to be in the middle of a possible riot? Geez, why do the Negroes always have to push into our areas, our neighborhoods, and schools...and now our beaches?"

I tried to shift the discussion from racial politics to something more concrete that they could hopefully relate to.

"You're the one who likes adventure, riding around crazy neighborhoods," I told Nate. "Look at this as the crazy neighborhood coming to us."

He showed a slight smile. To me, the important thing was that neither of them was refusing to help.

"Look, let's try to do what we can," I submitted. "We may not be able to stop the crazies, but maybe we can help keep things from getting out of control."

I was relieved when we shifted into a discussion about where the public phones were located and agreed that I would remain at the beach for as long as possible if trouble broke out. One of them would seek out a pay phone to call the police while the other would try to find a patrolman in the area to alert.

Fortunately, Nate's mom, a very nice upbeat woman, made us tuna salad sandwiches for lunch. She topped it off with Hostess chocolate cupcakes. It was not only a good lunch, but saved us having to buy lunch, and spend from my meager cash reserves, since Maley's hadn't yet paid me.

"It's a beautiful day for the beach, again," she said.

She seemed not to have been listening in on our conversation.

"How are your parents, Jeff? I haven't seen them in a while."

"They're good, Mrs. Higgins."

"I hope they're not planning to move any time soon. It seems like everyone's moving away from here."

"Not that I know of," I said, deciding instantly to lie so as to avoid a protracted discussion about all the hypotheticals and fears being experienced in my family.

On the bicycle ride over, we stopped at the Steinway drug store. Nate wanted to get some Wrigley's spearmint chewing gum. "For nerves," he said as he offered Lee and I each a stick.

47

We stopped first at Rainbow Beach's north entrance on 76th Street to check out the phone situation. There was just one, at a gas station across South Shore Drive. We did better close to the main entrance at 79th Street—came up with four there, and then found another couple right outside the beach, at two restaurants.

Once inside the main entrance, I immediately spotted Drew Boggs, Eddie's friend, standing near one of the three cavernous handball courts off to the side of the main entrance. These were the beach's unofficial social center. On this Saturday afternoon, as on most others, the white-walled courts were each occupied by two or four middle-aged men in shorts and t-shirts in intense competition. A dozen or more other men hung around outside, either watching the guys who crouched and bounced around to hit a small rubber ball off the walls, or waiting their turn for the next set of games.

Drew was notable for keeping a pack of cigarettes in the rolled-up sleeve of his white t-shirt. He was wearing bright yellow Bermuda shorts to complete his beach look, waiting his turn to play handball, likely against one of the wily older veterans of the Rainbow Beach handball crowd.

I motioned Nate and Jeff to go on ahead, and took a deep breath as I approached Drew. "Hey, Drew, how ya doin'?" I tried to sound as nonchalant as I could.

"Hey." I could see from the puzzled look in his eyes that he was racking his memory, trying to place my face with a name. "I'm Jeff Stark."

"Yeah, you're Eddie's friend, right?"

I wondered if he knew that Eddie has disassociated himself from me. For the moment, I decided to assume that Eddie hadn't clued Drew in on any of this. What did I have to lose? If Drew knew, then he'd shut me off pretty quickly, and I wouldn't be any worse off than I would have been had I not tried to win his sympathy.

I shifted the discussion. "Didn't know you play handball."

"My dad got me into it," Drew said, motioning toward another court. "That's him playing over there." A compact but fit man with closely cropped gray hair was scampering around the court in a doubles game, alternately slamming the small ball, together with his equally adept opponents, amid loud grunts and groans. "He's one of the top players here."

"That's a neat thing to do with your dad," I said. I really meant it. I wished my father would have done something like that with me instead of working all the time at Goldblatt's.

"I wonder if there is handball over at the 63rd Street Beach," I said, holding my breath after I said it. There was silence. Drew shifted his gaze from the action on the courts to stare directly at me.

"Who the fuck cares?" he said at long last, mouthing the words slowly, almost as if to wonder how I could have had such a thought. "They can do what the fuck they want at their beach. I don't care. I don't think anybody here cares."

I tried to recover. "Well, I just thought it could be neat, if they do play handball over there, if maybe there was a competition between the best players there and the best players here."

"Yeah, sure," Drew responded. "You know what will happen. They'll just come over here and take over our courts, the whole beach. The way they've taken over our neighborhoods, and schools. They just want everything for themselves, so they can fuck it up and destroy it for everyone."

I needed to tread carefully. "Maybe some of them. But I think there are some that want the same things we want, which is just to have fun and live a normal life."

"Is that what you see over at Hyde Park High?" Drew asked. "Everyone being nice to everyone else?"

So now I knew he remembered me. "No, not by a long shot. There are some tough hombres over there, that's for sure. The gousters. I try to steer clear of them." I was about to tell him about the new Blackstone Rangers gang and how it was making life difficult for Negroes and whites alike, but decided to omit that, that it would only inflame his passions. Instead I shifted to a more positive approach.

"There are also some really nice kids, you know, the Ivy Leaguers. They live the same way we live."

"Sure, there are a few good ones. But you know as well as I do that right after the good ones come in here, the gousters follow. And they'll make life miserable for everyone."

I decided to try yet a different tack. "You know, the Ivy Leaguers hate the gousters as much as we do. If the Ivy Leaguers came in here, they wouldn't want the gousters in here any more than you or I do."

Drew wasn't biting. "The good ones may not want them in here, but once a few darkies get in, the masses follow. Where have you been? How many times has your family moved, to keep ahead of them?"

He continued on, without waiting for an answer. "No, the best thing for us to do is stand our ground here, keep 'em all out, so we at least keep this last beach civilized."

I tried a dose of reality. "You know, we may not want them in here, but if we fight them, the cops will break it up, force us to let them in. Then, all the fighting scares whites away. It turns out the same, either way. By being peaceful, maybe we have a little bit of hope that we can live together, and not have all the whites move away. If the whites stayed, then the Negroes wouldn't have so many places to move to."

Drew still wasn't buying in. "That's a bunch of bullshit. I'd rather go down fighting."

I tried one last desperation tack. "Look, we know they're going to be back here. And the cops will help them. At least leave the girls alone. There's no reason to throw rocks at girls, they can't even defend themselves."

Drew was silent. Then he looked directly at me, with a not-so-hostile look. "Hey, you have some information about when they're coming?"

I decided to be a little forthcoming.

"I heard at school that some may be coming one of these weekends."

"Like today?"

"Today…next weekend. I don't know for sure. I'm not part of any planning. I just hear rumors around."

There was an uncomfortable silence as he continued staring at me, as if he was evaluating my credibility. I decided I had gotten all I was going to get, that it was time to leave him.

"I've got to take off," I said. "The reason I care about this is that some of the kids who may come are in my classes. They're decent kids, not troublemakers. I know Eddie calls the shots on what happens here, so if you could calm him down some, take it easy and make sure no one gets hurt…"

Drew nodded his head slightly and turned back to the action on the handball courts. I wasn't sure if he was agreeing with my request, or simply acknowledging that I was leaving.

48

I rode my bike north toward the less-busy 76th Street entrance. That was where Valerie had said her group would come in to avoid attracting a lot of immediate attention. I was trying to calculate risk, and not liking what I was seeing.

Having just one nearby pay phone seemed very risky because if it was being used when we needed it, Nate would be forced to ride his bike three blocks to the phones near the main entrance, and waste precious time.

We looked around for police who might be directing traffic but didn't spot any. It would be a lot more convenient if a policeman was nearby and we could nudge him in person. He could then alert other cops, who could easily rush over to the beach.

It was about 2:00 p.m. and I hung out with Nate and Lee near the shore where the sand turned into large wading rocks, similar to what existed at the Point. We threw a Frisbee around, tried to look nonchalant.

It was weird because I never saw Valerie's group come on to the beach. I guess I expected some kind of very notable entrance. Maybe they worked it out that they wouldn't come in as a group, so as not to attract attention.

But all of a sudden, around 2:30, I saw a small group of Negroes about fifty yards from where Nate, Lee, and I were sitting. They were sitting very quietly on blankets near the water, talking among themselves. They looked very natural, as if they belonged there.

I spotted Valerie, wearing a white pullover and her yellow two-piece bottom, chatting with a lanky Negro youth who looked to be several years older than her, and whom I assumed was her older brother, Derrick. Everyone among the twenty-five or so people seemed to be speaking with someone else. Whether that was intentional or not, it helped them appear as casual as was possible under the circumstances.

My first instinct was to begin walking over to her group, wave to her, and sit down next to her. Not here, of course. Maybe, just maybe, this would continue to be a normal day at the beach. They'd sit, enjoy the sun and sand, and after a couple hours quietly leave, like the rest of the huge crowd.

After a few minutes of Frisbee, I tried to foster the casual look by pulling out my sketch book from a side saddle on my nearby bike and beginning a drawing of Valerie and her brother sitting together, looking out at the lake.

Alas, it wasn't long before casual was replaced by tension. About twenty minutes after the Negroes arrived, the crowd at our north end of the beach began thinning, with mothers packing up little children, and small groups of teen girls shutting off their transistor radios.

Maybe it was because the people left so quietly, unobtrusively, without loud conversation, that the uninitiated could assume they had simply had enough sun and sand, and were departing, even though it was only the middle of the afternoon on a beautiful warm day. What I also failed to notice, until the trend was well under way, was that most of the people weren't really packing up to leave, but picking up their blankets and towels and dragging them to a different section of beach.

At about 3, some new beachgoers had begun taking up spots on the sand. They were all young men, in their late teens or twenties. Some wore white t-shirts with their swimsuits, and some were bare-chested. It was difficult to say how many there were, because they were scattered about, some sitting on towels or blankets, and some just on the sand.

Damn, everything was happening so quietly and so much differently than I expected that I didn't think to tell Nate and Lee to immediately go off and start alerting the police. Just as my friends were leaving, I heard the taunts.

"What're you doing here?" I heard one of the youths ask the Negroes, directing his question to no one in particular in a voice just a bit louder than normal conversation. The Negroes pretended not to hear, and continued talking among themselves. "You have plenty of beaches. Why'd you pick this one?"

Another voice, louder. "Don't you know you're not wanted here? We don't go to your beaches. Why do you have to go where you're not wanted?"

And another. "Why don't you stay in your own neighborhoods?"

I didn't recognize the guys doing the taunting.

A few moments later, a threat. "Get outta here, if you know what's good for ya." I recognized this voice. It was Eddie.

I spotted Eddie on the periphery of the group of white toughs, who now seemed to number fifteen or twenty. He was wearing a dark t-shirt together with dark shorts, which give him something of a martial look, kind of a beach-goer version of Jeff Fort. He was edging closer to the Negroes with his friend, Drew.

The protesters continued to ignore the taunts. "Don't you darkies understand English?" Eddie called out. "We don't want you here. Stay on your own beaches, stay in your own neighborhoods. We don't bother you in your neighborhoods."

Somehow, everything around me seemed to slow down. I saw Drew engaging Eddie in animated conversation. I saw Eddie shaking his head negative. I saw rocks begin to fly toward where the group was sitting.

I walked over to where Eddie was standing near the water, maybe twenty-five yards from where the group was gathered. I was trembling. "Hey, Eddie" I said as softly as I could, hoping that only Eddie could hear me and no one else. "They're not bothering anyone. Why not keep everything peaceful?"

"So it's big shot Jeff," he replied in a much louder voice, actually more a snarl. "Just who the fuck do you think you are?"

It was much less a question than an assertion.

"Don't mess where you're not wanted. If you aren't going to help us, get the fuck out of here. Go join the women and little girls."

"Don't make a scene," I pleaded. "You don't want to see anyone get hurt."

"Get hurt? They're the ones who are hurting people. Come into our neighborhoods and start robbing people. People who are minding their own business."

"These people are minding their own business, Eddie. C'mon, let's just leave it be."

But he wasn't about to be pacified. "You trying to protect your darkie girlfriend? Is that what this is about?"

"Eddie, it's just about keeping innocent people from getting hurt."

"You want me to start telling everyone about your darkie girlfriend? Is that what you want? That'll protect the darkies, all right. 'Cause everyone will be coming after you. 'Cause the one thing worse than darkies coming into the neighborhood is white traitors, scum like you turning their backs on their own people."

I saw a few of the other white toughs begin to turn toward Eddie and me. And I could see my decision unfolding. Sacrifice myself on behalf of the protesters, or take off and leave the Negroes to survive as best they could. I sensed that if I stayed, I would get it much worse than any of the protesters.

As the options raced through my mind, I took a sudden hard shove from behind, hard enough for me to lose my balance and go down. I was still clear-minded enough to appreciate that I was fortunate to be falling onto sand rather than hard pavement.

Just a couple seconds after I got back up, and was looking around for the culprit who shoved me, there was a slam into the middle of my back, much harder than the shove, almost like a big stick or log. It knocked the breath out of me so that I was gasping as my body lurched forward, and I fell into the sand. As I rolled over, trying to catch my breath, people around me seemed to be slowly spinning. But I caught sight of Tommy Sullivan, standing a few feet away, smiling and not saying a word. Then I saw the white plaster cast on his right wrist and forearm, and realized that he had used that as his weapon against me.

Within a few seconds, he was kicking me in the stomach, chest, and face. The spinning accelerated. I couldn't catch my breath, let alone get into a position to get back on my feet. My ribs ached, and I tasted the sick sweetness of my own blood. The fact that he was wearing Keds softened the impact of the kicks slightly from what they would have been with leather shoes. Another kid had joined Tommie in kicking me, but he couldn't do as much damage as Tommie because he was barefoot.

As I was writhing and rolling and trying to escape the onslaught of kicks, the spinning around me seemed to slow. I caught sight of Valerie, Derrick, and a couple others tending to one of the Negroes. They were holding a white towel or maybe a handkerchief to the side of the man's head, and there was blood all over it, and smeared around his neck. Derrick and another man were helping him stand, placing his arms around their necks as support to him in his semi-consciousness. He could barely hold his head straight. I saw other Negroes getting up and walking away from the shoreline.

Valerie was nearing the place where I was in the sand opposite Eddie. She had left Derrick's side, and approached us, except she was approaching Eddie. Her approach apparently scared Tommy and the other kicker to back off, allowing me to get back on my feet.

She was maybe three feet from Eddie when she stopped. "My name is Valerie!" she said firmly, looking him in the eye. She had much the same pained look she had that day at Riverview months before, when she confronted Vinnie. She and Eddie stared at each other for a few long moments. I sensed he was too shocked by her audacity to respond, just as Vinnie had been. Then, she turned back to where Derrick's friend was walking gingerly with his two helpers.

She hadn't gone more than three or four steps when I saw Eddie look around at his feet, and pick up a rock about the size of a fist, and then stare at Valerie as if he was gauging how far to lob the rock. Instinctively, I lunged forward, like a football tackler focused on Eddie's midsection. He let loose the rock at the moment I made contact with his belly. "You fucking asshole!" I blurted as we both hit the sand. While he lay stunned, I leaped back up and turned around just in time to see Valerie collapsed in a heap.

I darted the few feet to where Valerie lay on her side, tearing at my t-shirt as I approached her. A small dark-red pool of blood was already visible, contrasting sickeningly with the tan sand next to the mop of her disheveled black hair. I gingerly lifted her head a couple inches and inserted the shirt. I looked back and saw Eddie unsteadily climbing onto his knees, mute. Everything went eerily silent, but just for a few seconds, until the sound of police sirens intruded. They were still in the distance, but drawing unmistakably closer. I saw Eddie, now standing, and his pals looking to the north from where the sirens were coming.

"Let's get outta here," Eddie called to several others. They began to back off, and as the sirens were clearly within just a few blocks, the whites turned and ran.

Several of the Negroes were already bent over Valerie. I moved aside as one woman wordlessly wrapped a towel around her head while another man picked her up and carried her toward the beach entrance. She looked as if she was barely conscious, her arms and legs moving reflexively as she was lifted. I resisted a huge urge to join the group around her, and try be more active in comforting Valerie, even if just to touch a hand or an arm. But I sensed I would only inflame the passions of her group, and in any bitter accusations that resulted, delay getting her to medical aid.

The wade-in broke up with a couple dozen police escorting the Negroes out through Rainbow Beach's main entrance. I wanted more than anything to learn more about the seriousness of Valerie's injury. But at that point the police formed a barrier that separated the Negroes from everyone else, and then the protesters disappeared quickly into waiting cars near the entrance. I realized I didn't even have her phone number.

49

I pleaded with Dad to let me use the car that evening so I could swing by the Medici, on the off-chance I'd meet someone from the wade-in group to learn about Valerie's condition. But nothing doing. He just repeated his order, "You aren't chauffeuring schvartze girls around in my car!"

Somehow, my anger at him for his hateful stubbornness had dissipated. All I could surmise was that Dad knew nothing about that afternoon's events at Rainbow Beach, and I certainly wasn't about to fill him in, and launch a new tirade about all the problems being visited on us by the invading Negroes.

So Lee, Nate, and I took the IC into Hyde Park and the Medici that

Saturday evening. But only a few white kids I didn't know, probably from the Lab School, occupied tables.

We left after a short time and plopped ourselves onto a nearby park bench. The three of us re-lived the danger and the scariness of the afternoon's events. Ominously to me personally, Lee had run into Eddie near the north entrance of Rainbow Beach as he was making his getaway. "You better watch your friend," Lee quoted Eddie as saying. "He's helping the darkies take over our neighborhood. He's asking for trouble."

All I could think was that Eddie hadn't expressed the slightest bit of concern about Valerie's condition. He was more cold and callous than I ever imagined.

I explained to Nate and Lee what happened when we first split up and I went alone to the beach entrance, how I spoke with Drew at the handball courts. And then how I pleaded with Eddie during the height of the racial baiting, and watched Valerie confront him, and then tackled him as he lobbed his rock toward Valerie, after Nate and Lee had left to find police.

I could tell from the looks in their eyes that they were impressed. "That was gutsy," Nate said of my tackle. "But I don't know how smart it was. You know what they say about heroes."

I did. It was the mantra that guided much of our lives at Hyde Park High. "Better to be a live coward than a dead hero." They nodded.

"You really like Valerie a lot, don't you?" Lee asked.

I nodded, and felt myself choke up. Just then, I caught sight of Mr. White, the social studies teacher, walking east along 57th Street. He was with a Negro woman, whom I presumed was his wife.

As he caught sight of me approaching him, I detected a slight smile begin to crease his long face. "Hi Mr. White," I said. "I'm Jeff Stark, in your social studies class…"

"I know who you are, Jeff," he said.

"I wonder if you heard anything about what happened at Rainbow Beach this afternoon."

"Yes, I heard that some brave young people tried to use the beach, and had some trouble…" He hesitated. "And I heard that you tried to defuse the situation. I know the protesters appreciated what you did. You put yourself in danger."

I detected some sense of admiration. I had been super alert to antagonism he might be feeling toward me as a white person, but there was none I could detect in his voice, or gaze.

"What about injuries?" I asked. "Is there any word on Valerie? She got hit with a rock. And there was another fellow who was bleeding pretty badly."

"A few people were hit with rocks, but you're right, Valerie was hurt the worst. She was still in the hospital when I left my house. She definitely has a concussion, maybe even a fracture, so the doctors are watching her very closely, to make sure there is no bleeding around the brain. Based on her reactions, her ability to talk and recognize people, they are hopeful she may be okay. But they won't know anything for sure for a few days."

Mr. White then excused himself. "We are meeting some friends for dinner."

As he spoke, I felt a sense of panic, helplessness...and guilt. Strange as it might seem, the words from the conversation that stuck in my gut weren't only "skull fracture," but also the word "tried," that I had "tried to defuse the situation."

In other words, I hadn't succeeded. I had failed. And now Valerie was lying in a hospital, seriously injured.

When I was the one facing racial assaults, Valerie had not just tried, she had succeeded in defusing the situation, in saving me from injury. I had screwed up in trying to do the same for her.

50

The only good news, as far as I was concerned, was that the local media gave the Rainbow Beach blowup minimal coverage. There was a three-paragraph item in one of the papers Dad bought on Sunday, and it highlighted the fact that three people were injured during a demonstration at Rainbow Beach that appeared to be a resumption of the wade-ins that had been going on sporadically since 1960. There was no mention of names. For the newspapers, Valerie was just a statistic.

The minimal coverage meant Mom and Dad likely wouldn't notice what had happened. I guess in my mind, the less they knew about the ever-expanding racial problems, the less likely they would be to pursue moving away from South Shore.

I hid the most visible evidence of the brawl—a bruise high on my forehead—by combing my hair lower than usual. No one seemed to notice. The cuts in my mouth from having gotten kicked in the face and the bruises on my ribs were sore, but fortunately not visible.

At school the next week, which was our final week before summer vacation, Valerie was nowhere to be seen, but she wasn't forgotten. At homeroom, and then later in the lunch room, there was a buzz among the Negro students, and I heard Valerie's name as I passed small groups talking in the halls. I felt angry stares, but I sensed they were directed at all white students, not at me in particular.

I doubted anyone outside of Mr. White had any inkling that Nate, Lee, and I had been at the wade-in where Valerie was injured. I was further encouraged that the anger was contained when lunch passed without plates and cups being thrown at tables with whites, and when neither Booker nor any of his gouster friends came after me.

The low-level tension persisted, though. When I approached Valerie's friend, Tanya, after math class the next day, she looked glum and didn't make eye contact when I inquired about how Valerie was doing. "She's still in the hospital. The doctors and nurses are watching her closely. There's been some fluid around her brain, but it's not bad enough that they need to operate. Everyone's got their fingers crossed."

"What do you think about me visiting?" I asked. "Do you think that would be okay?"

Tanya looked directly at me for the first time. "I don't think that's a good idea, at least not yet. Her family is pretty upset, especially her dad. I'd give it some time."

In social studies later that day, Mr. White started off the class with an announcement that everyone was praying that "the brave young people who were hurt at Rainbow Beach on Saturday will recover fully. They were trying to give everyone the right to use our public places, regardless of race." He hesitated. "One of those who was hurt was a student here, Valerie Davis. She is still in the hospital, but the doctors say she is doing as well as can be expected."

That was it for talk of the wade-in, at least directly. Mr. White then resumed his presentation from the previous class about the U.S. Supreme Court's 1954 school desegregation case. He concluded with the most famous quote from the court's unanimous opinion: "Separate but equal is inherently unequal."

51

My sense of post wade-in anxiety only increased the first week after school let out, when Mom and Dad began an intensive search for an apartment on the North Side. They continued their quest, even after I objected that switching high schools would totally wreck my upcoming senior year.

"We have to do what's best for the family," Mom said. "We can't have Dad putting his life in danger coming home from work, and you going out with Negro girls."

On top of the sudden apartment search, I had no way to monitor what was happening to Valerie, whether she really was getting better as Tanya hoped. When I told Nate about my frustration, he had a simple suggestion: "Why not just go and visit Valerie." He hesitated a moment, then added, "I'll even go with you."

I felt immediately relieved, and grateful. But where to go? We really only had one option—Lying In Hospital—since I didn't have Valerie's address, beyond knowing she lived in Woodlawn. Nate s idea was to try the hospital first, since we'd be likelier to find people with information about her condition, and even if she wasn't still there, people who knew where she lived.

Even though I had never been in the hospital, I sensed it was a big place from the huge building it occupied. But I never knew just how large, and intimidating, it was until early on a Tuesday afternoon, when Nate and I entered the mammoth and bustling lobby and started walking through hallways with seemingly endless patient rooms. Eventually, we were stopped at a nurses' station, and when I explained I was trying to locate Valerie, we were directed to "Patient Services" on the main floor.

I was assuming we had struck out, until we approached the reception desk. The petite young Negro woman at the desk looked familiar, but I couldn't place her. Wait…it was Florence, the budding bride I had sold wedding shoes to a few weeks back at Maley's.

"Excuse me, um, Florence?" She looked up from some papers, and I could tell she was going through the same process in her mind I had just gone through—trying to make sense of the familiar face in front of her. "I'm Jeff Stark, the guy at Maley's who sold you the shoes for your wedding."

Her face brightened. "Oh, yes. What brings you here?"

"How'd the wedding go?" I inquired. I wanted to establish some rapport before pursuing the sensitive business at hand, and besides, I was curious as to how things had gone.

"It was wonderful. It was a very small wedding, but everyone had a wonderful time, including me. You were right about the shoes, they fit perfectly. I was able to dance and my feet were comfortable the whole afternoon and evening."

"That's great," I said. I felt even better about my decision to avoid pushing a PM on her.

"What can I help you with?" Florence inquired, a little more warmth in her voice than the first time she asked.

"Well, I'm trying to find a patient, except I'm not sure she's still a patient."

"Let's see if I can help," she responded.

"Her name is Valerie Davis."

The warm look on Florence's face faded, replaced by a pensive expression. "Why do you want to find her?" she asked, a slight note of skepticism having now entered her voice.

I hadn't expected this conversation to unfold. I decided to just be straightforward. "I'm a classmate of hers from Hyde Park High School. And we're, uh, good friends."

"Do you know why she was in the hospital?" Florence asked. She obviously knew about Valerie, and was now clearly trying to screen me.

I wished I had rehearsed what I should say. "Yes, I was with her when she was injured," I said.

Florence looked surprised. Suddenly it occurred to me that maybe she suspected I was one of the whites throwing rocks.

I paused. "Yes, it was a wade-in, by Negroes who wanted to use Rainbow Beach. Valerie had asked me to come, to try to calm things down with the white guys." I paused again. "Obviously, I wasn't too successful, because Valerie and a couple other people were injured…I was hoping to visit Valerie, see how she is doing. I wasn't even sure she is still here, but I don't have her address..." I felt myself tearing up.

I saw Florence reach for a sheet of blank note paper on her desk. She wrote something down, and folded the sheet in half. She looked up at me, and spoke softly. "You are right, Valerie isn't here. She was discharged two days ago. That's good news, because she was greatly improved. She still has to take it easy, though." Florence handed me the folded paper.

52

I waited till Nate and I returned to our bikes locked outside before opening the folded paper. Silently, I handed it to Nate. Neither of us said a word. It showed an address at sixty-second and Kimbark, five or six blocks away, but smack dab in the middle of gouster and Blackstone Ranger territory.

"Let's just go," I finally said to Nate. "We've come this far. It's still early in the day, so fewer tough guys around. You can stay outside and watch the bikes while I go inside to try to find Valerie's place." He nodded his agreement and we took off.

The address on Kimbark was a three-story gray stucco building, which looked as if it might have been elegant at some point in time, but at this point in time appeared tired, in need of patching and painting. There was old trash—newspaper pages and food packaging—scattered around the front yard, just as there was in most front yards in Woodlawn. Inside the vestibule, I scanned the mailboxes and buzzers looking for "Davis." The problem was that instead of the three or maybe five or six mailboxes I was accustomed to in a three-story apartment building, there were more like twelve or fourteen here. And some had multiple names hand-written on tiny pieces of paper taped to the brass. When I found "Robert Davis" for apartment 7a, there was more confusion because another name, "Knight," was immediately below it, suggesting another family might share the apartment.

I pressed a buzzer I thought was the right one and held my breath. No need for waiting, I quickly realized, since the lock on the vestibule door was broken, and I just pushed into the hallway. "Who's there?" a woman's voice shouted down from what seemed like the second floor.

"My name's Jeff, and I'm a friend of Valerie's," I called back up into the near darkness, since I couldn't see anyone.

Just then, I caught sight of a slender middle-aged woman leaning over a bannister at the second floor landing, trying to give me a quick look over. "Come on up," she said curtly.

Once I was on the second-floor landing, I could see a definite family resemblance in the woman's mouth and eyes to Valerie. She was dressed plainly in a faded checked brown dress. But there was no introduction or small talk. And fortunately no question about how I found the apartment. "Valerie is resting. I'll tell her you're here and see if you can go in and see her. She mentioned you might come by."

Then a man's voice interrupted from inside. "Who is it, Gloria?"

"It's a friend of Valerie's."

Valerie's mom led me into a small living room that felt dark and crowded with dark-green and brown furnishings. The man was sitting in an easy chair, listening to a soft man's voice coming from a radio on a table next to him. As I walked in, he looked up, and I could feel the glare even without looking directly at him.

"Wait here while I check on Valerie," she said. There was no invitation to sit down, no introduction to Valerie's father. So I stood there, the only break in the silence coming from the soft male voice on the radio, who was saying, "We have no record of the black man's birth. We know he was the first aboriginal man. But how is it we have no record..." I assumed the voice belonged to Elijah Muhammad, the radical Negro leader Valerie had told me her father admired so much. It sounded so strange to hear someone refer to Negroes as "black."

The uncomfortable seconds turned into minutes. I didn't want to interrupt his listening, but I just felt I should say something to acknowledge the injury to Valerie. "I'm really sorry about what happened to Valerie," I said to her father, who looked smaller than his gruff voice had suggested. I'll never really know what he might have said in response, because about five seconds after I said it, Valerie's mom was back out.

"Okay, you can go in, but just for a couple of minutes. Valerie is supposed to take it very easy until her headaches and dizziness go away. But she did want to see you." I was encouraged she had told he mother I might come by, and that she wanted to see me. Her bedroom was the first in a short narrow hallway that looked to have one more bedroom, and a bathroom. The whole thing was probably one-half or maybe even one-third the size of our apartment. It was hard to tell exactly how big the bedroom was because it was dimly lit, and the two window shades drawn. Valerie was sitting in a small easy chair in a corner dressed in a checked gray robe pulled up around the neck. She looked like herself, except her bouffant hairdo was gone, apparently shaved off to treat her injury, and replaced by scraggly hair only an inch or so long. She looked a little drawn, like she had lost some weight. A big white bandage was taped snugly to one side of her head, presumably where the rock hit and cut her.

"Hi, so how is the patient?" I asked, trying to inject cheerfulness into my voice, and not show the shock I felt at seeing her in an injured state.

"I'd be a lot better if I could get rid of my headache, and if things wouldn't spin around when I stand up. But it's so much better than being in the hospital, being in my own bed."

She paused. "And how about my new hairdo? Pretty high fashion, huh?"

I nodded and chuckled. "Maybe Ebony wants to do a feature. Have any friends been by?"

"No friends were allowed to visit in the hospital. I've only been home for two days. But Tanya was by yesterday. And a couple other girlfriends are supposed to come by later this afternoon. Speaking of visiting, how did you figure out where I live?"

"Hmmm. It's a long story, but let's just say I got some help from one of my customers at the shoe store."

I wanted to tell her how badly I felt about the Rainbow Beach violence, but I wasn't sure I should risk upsetting her—she seemed so fragile. I needn't have worried. Valerie's mind was elsewhere. "I want to get outside, get Derrick to take Tanya and me over to the Point in the next few days. Get some sun, and fresh air. Maybe bring a sandwich and have lunch."

"I'll try to get over there," I said. Just then, Valerie's mother opened the bedroom door and poked her head in. "I think Valerie needs to nap some. She's not supposed to spend too much time talking."

Valerie looked at me with a mock serious look, put a hand up to the side of her mouth and spoke in a near whisper. "I've got some things to tell you." I nodded and gave her a smile. I put a hand softly on one of hers and she smiled softly.

Visit over. No words from her dad, and a polite good-bye from her mom.

Fortunately, Nate's time watching the bikes had been uneventful, and we rode quickly back to South Shore. I told him about Valerie's fragile state. I also told him about my discomfort with Valerie's parents.

"You didn't expect them to welcome you like some kind of hero, did you? Their daughter was badly hurt by white guys, they've probably been worried sick about her. It's pretty amazing they allowed you to visit at all."

I knew he was right, especially about how they let me in to visit Valerie. My mind, though, was on the last thing Valerie said, about having things to tell me.

53

As we rode back into South Shore, I decided to ask Nate point-blank about his family's moving plans. It was one of those subjects that frequently hung out there with friends, but rarely got talked about outside family circles.

"Yeah, my parents talk about it. Remember, my mom asked you about it before we went over to Rainbow Beach for the big blowup? I don't think it's going to happen right away, though. They seem to think the Highlands might stay mostly white for a few more years, because the Highlands are houses, and it's harder for people to just pick up and move like they do from apartments."

That made some sense. I felt envious of him for not having the prospect of moving hanging over his head seemingly every day, like I did. If only Valerie and I hadn't gone to LaRabida that night. If only the cops hadn't come by when they did. If only the cops hadn't called my parents. If only Valerie hadn't decided to join the wade-in. If only, if only.

I wished it was just my imagination, all the worrying about when we might move, but every day seemed to bring the possibility a little closer. Two days after my visit with Valerie, one of the three remaining white families in our building moved out. Which family would be next? We didn't know the remaining family well, but I imagined we'd now be looking each other over closely, searching for small clues about intentions. Maybe someone was collecting cardboard boxes from liquor stores and supermarkets. Or maybe someone had a mover looking over the stairs and doorways to give an estimate.

It was almost anticlimactic when Dad broke the news the next Tuesday, at the close of a steamy July day, over dinner.

They had found an apartment in Rogers Park on the North Side. It wasn't far from Devon Avenue. "Like Werner says, it's a lot like 71st Street," Dad said. He tried to sound upbeat, as if this point of familiarity would make everything okay.

Then he stopped, as if he was waiting for Emily or me to inquire about the schools we would be attending. No way was I going to voluntarily engage in any such discussion. I was too pissed. Emily broke the silence. "Which schools will we be going to?"

"Jeffrey will be going to Sullivan High School. You will be going to one of two elementary schools, we still have to figure out which one includes our neighborhood."

"When do we move?" Emily asked.

"In ten days, a week from this Saturday."

I had to speak up. "It's all because of Valerie, isn't it?"

"Valerie?" Mom asked.

"Yeah, my friend from Hyde Park High does have a name. It's because I went out with a Negro girl that we're moving, right?"

Dad intervened. "No Jeffrey. It isn't any one thing. It's just so many things that have made us unsafe here. Your run-in with the police didn't help. But your mother and I just feel we've run out of places to move on the South Side. It's all turning. We need to leave while we still can."

I considered yet again telling them about Valerie's injury at Rainbow Beach, but yet again decided against bringing it up. It wouldn't do anything except give them more ammunition for their perverse arguments that Negroes brought attacks on themselves by pushing to get into white neighborhoods and white beaches.

It was clearly useless to argue any further. The only thing I could think to do was to let friends know the bad news. Nate wasn't surprised. Lee said he was, though in the next breath he said his parents were talking more about possibly selling their house. George said his parents had sworn him and a brother to secrecy, that a move could be imminent. The next week passed in near silence at home.

54

I try to put the moving truck and Mom and Dad and Werner out of my mind as I approach the rocky 67th Street Beach, with its sparse crowd, on my bike. The cooling breeze off the lake helps ease my mind.

On some sort of impulse, I turn left, and ride north along Lake Shore Drive, toward the Point. As beautiful a ride as it is sure to be, I can't remember ever having taken this route before, because smack in between the 67th Street Beach and the Point is the 63rd Street Beach, and its huge crowds of Negro beach goers. But I am pretending such obstacles don't exist on this last day of living on the South Side.

Fortunately, most people enter the 63rd Street Beach via a pedestrian bridge over Lake Shore Drive, so my ride through this all-Negro area is uneventful. Before long, I am circling the Point's perimeter. At first blush, it looks like a normal summer day, with a handful of people sunbathing on the large white rocks along the lake, while others play Frisbee on the inner grassy area.

I'm making a beeline for Valerie's favorite spot on the rocks overlooking Lake Michigan. Sure enough, there on the same giant white limestone boulder where she sat a few weeks earlier, I catch sight of someone sitting, knees up, head tilted slightly to the left. As I draw closer, the giveaway that it's Valerie is the white bandage, now just a third the size of what I saw at her apartment, on the side of her shaved head.

I get off my bike and walk toward her, terribly grateful for having gotten the shock of seeing her injured out of the way the previous week. It's still a shock to see her with the closely cropped hair pushing through around the white cloth. To my relief, she flashes a smile. "I'm glad you were able to find me."

"What are the doctors saying about how you're doing?"

"They are getting more positive. At first, they were giving me medicine to keep me asleep a lot. It was just as well, because whenever I was up I'd have terrible headaches, and be dizzy. Now, I don't have headaches and dizziness all the time. Like now, I feel okay. But it's not like I can just start running around and playing frisby. The doctors say it will take time before I can be myself again." She looks out over the glistening Lake Michigan water.

If feels like as bad a time as any to talk about Rainbow Beach. "I'm so glad you're better. I couldn't believe how out of control things got at the beach."

"I couldn't believe how much they could hate us." Valerie is still looking out over the water. "I guess I always knew there were some who hated us. But even when we were in Cicero and got firebombed, I never saw the people who threw the firebomb. I guess it's probably easier to throw a firebomb when you don't see the people you are throwing it at."

She pauses, and looks at me momentarily. "I never heard so many people so angry at us, never saw such hatred right to our faces. How can we ever live together if we can't even go to the beach together?"

I can't think of anything to say in response. I think of saying something about how those few don't represent all white people, but I sense it would sound trite, demeaning.

There clearly were a lot of whites who hated Negroes, wanted them out. Not just the guys like Eddie and Tommy and Drew throwing rocks, but all the people who had moved their blankets that afternoon to get away from the Negroes, not to mention those who had moved their families away from Hyde Park High School to South Shore High School, or who had fled South Shore entirely.

"Do you think we'll ever learn to live together?" I just blurt the question out. "It's all so crazy. There was Tommy Sullivan, who hates Jews, joining up with Eddie, who is Jewish, to throw rocks at Negroes. I don't get it."

She looks at me with sorry eyes, tears forming. One runs down her cheek.

"Derrick is going to be back in just a few minutes to take me back home. They're still treating me like an invalid, but I guess I have to rest and take it easy for a while." She hesitates, as if she has something important she wants to say, but is searching for the right words.

"We're moving..." She avoids eye contact. "Probably in a couple weeks, when I'm a little stronger. We're going to Drexel. The Rangers aren't over there yet. Daddy is hoping that James, my younger brother, will be able to steer clear of the gangs there. Plus, no crazy whites."

Now it's my turn to break news, and I'm the one avoiding eye contact. "We're moving, too—to the North Side—the all-white North Side." I pause, hoping for just a slight smile acknowledging my dark humor, but she just stares at me. "I fought it, but my parents say too many of their friends and relatives have left and they're tired of fighting off gousters."

"When are you moving?" Her eyes are penetrating.

"Today...right now. The moving truck is waiting. I just left them and took a chance I might find you here...I have something for you." I pull a folded sheet of paper out of my rear pocket. "It's the drawing I was doing of you sitting on Rainbow Beach, before everything went crazy."

She opens it and scans it quickly, before turning away. She dabs at one of her eyes with a cloth. "Uh-oh, Derrick is coming for me." She gestures her head toward a figure a hundred yards away walking slowly toward us. We both get up slowly from the rock. Once she is standing, I move closer to her. "I have one other piece of news," I say. "I've decided to go to the University of Illinois in Chicago. So I'll be looking for you there when I'm a sophomore." She smiles slightly. I can barely see any more, so full of tears are my eyes. I put my arms around her, tentatively because she seems so fragile. But she is fine, and puts her arms lightly around me, and we kiss. She closes her eyes, as do I. When I pull back after several seconds, she turns without a word.

Then she is gone. And so am I.

Afterword

I wish *Gouster Girl* was more of a feel-good happy-ending coming-of-age story. Unfortunately, the racial turmoil that gripped the South Side of Chicago during the late 1950s and early 1960s wasn't feel-good happy stuff. As wonderful as growing up in South Shore was in so many ways, it was also terrifying, even traumatic, not just for me but for many others, white and black alike.

It took me a long time after leaving South Shore as a young adult to appreciate that, in a very real sense, the racial and social tensions that intruded on life in the late 1950s and early 1960s also marked the launch of an extended period of violence that has defined subsequent decades of Chicago's history. I only began to understand much later that the South Side's racial upheaval wasn't the result of blacks wanting to take over neighborhoods and kick whites out, as many whites assumed.

Housing discrimination and the contract sales of real estate to blacks occurred because of political and policy decisions made by the city's white power structure. The Second Great Migration of blacks from the South to Chicago and other northern cities occurred because of brutal racial suppression in the deep South. The gangs that took hold in the early 1960s were the result in significant measure of Chicago's failed education system and assaults on the black family dynamic. The disgust of middle-class blacks with the criminal and gang activity of the gousters was much the same as it was for middle-class whites.

By now, of course, the rest of the country knows about the downward spiral of the South Side, driven as it was by white and middle-class-black flight and expanding gang violence. Michelle Obama, in her 2019 book *Becoming,* chronicled the discouraging decline she witnessed as a youngster and teenager growing up in South Shore during the 1970s, just a few blocks south of where Jeffrey Stark and his family had lived.

"Racial and economic sorting in the South Shore neighborhood continued through the 1970s, meaning that the student population only grew blacker and poorer with each year," she recalled. She recounted "families who watched their better-off neighbors leave for the suburbs or transfer their children to Catholic schools. There were predatory real estate agents roaming South Shore all the while, whispering to home owners that they should sell before it was too late, that they'd help them get out *while you still can* (author's emphasis). The inference being that failure was coming, that it was inevitable, that it had already half arrived. You could get caught up in the ruin or you could escape it. They used the word everyone was most afraid of—'ghetto'—dropping it like a lit match."

By the time she was to attend high school in the late 1970s, her brother was already attending a private Catholic school. There apparently wasn't even a discussion about whether Michelle Obama might attend nearby South Shore High School. She describes how she took a test and qualified to attend a magnet school on close to Downtown Chicago. After age fourteen, her body may have been with her family in South Shore, but her mind was on college and law school in the East and career opportunities awaiting her in Downtown Chicago.

As time has gone on, ever-more-violent gang activity has turned much of the South Side into an urban killing field. Endless community efforts to re-energize the education and law enforcement systems seem to peter out.

Alex Kotlowitz, author of a 2019 chronicle of gang violence in Chicago, *An American Summer: Love and Death in Chicago*, described it this way in his promotional material for talks he gave to civic and other organizations: "The numbers are staggering: over the past twenty years in Chicago, 14,033 people have been killed and another roughly 60,000 wounded by gunfire. What does that do to the spirit of individuals and community?"

I'm not sure what it is about Chicago that fosters such ongoing failure and violence. It seems like something akin to what we have witnessed in El Salvador and Honduras, where gangs have filled the institutional void left by an impotent power structure and failed education and law enforcement systems.

In any event, trying to reconstruct the racial pressure cooker that South Shore evolved into in the late 1950s and early 1960s required lots of help beyond my own growing-up experiences.

A landmark 2009 book about housing discrimination in Chicago, *Family Properties* by Beryl Satter, was in retrospect a key motivator for me to finally think seriously about writing *Gouster Girl*. Her book chronicles the experiences of Beryl's lawyer father, Mark Satter, in fighting legal battles on behalf of blacks who tried to buy apartment buildings and homes using contract sales. He lost many of those cases, but in the process of arguing vehemently against the injustice of Chicago's discriminatory housing practices, set the stage for the eventual reform of those practices.

Another important resource was Tim Black, a social studies teacher at Hyde Park High School in the 1960s. He went on to become an important Chicago civil rights activist and community organizer in the years after and helped mentor Barack Obama in his community organizing days on the South Side in the 1990s. I was fortunate to have had him as a social studies teacher, to meet him periodically when I visited Chicago, and then to be able to spend time with him when he appeared at my Hyde Park High School fiftieth reunion in 2014, at age ninety-six, and explore his recollections of, among other things, trying to convince (unsuccessfully) Blackstone Rangers leader Jeff Fort to stay in school. He celebrated his one-hundredth birthday in 2018, and has left a rich legacy of video recollections available on YouTube, which helped me immensely in my research for this book.

One of the challenges of undertaking a serious writing project like *Gouster Girl* is getting honest feedback to help in the inevitable revising that is required. I am grateful to a number of friends willing to be straightforward, and constructive. Beryl Satter, the author who is also a historian teaching at Rutgers University in Newark, provided me with key feedback as I was revising.

I received important feedback as well from former classmates of mine at Columbia Journalism School, including Alan Ehrenhalt, author of a 1995 book, *The Lost City*, about community life in Chicago in the 1950s; Larry Leamer, author of *Mar-a-Lago* in 2019, among other books about the rich and powerful; Carla Fine, author of the 1996 book, *No Time to Say Goodbye*, about the suicide of her husband; and Dotty Brown, author of *Boathouse Row*, a 2016 account of the history of rowing in Philadelphia. Caryn Amster's 2004 book, *The Pied Piper of South Shore*, about the murder of her father in his South Shore toy store by a gang member, provided important insights, as did Carlo Rotella's 2019 book about South Shore's challenges as a community, *The World Is Always Coming to an End*.

Other writer and teacher friends and associates who provided me with feedback included Al Furst, Michelle Jay-Russell, Jill Richardson, and Narayan Liebenson. And then there were friends from Hyde Park High School days who shared recollections from that long-ago time to help in recalling key details, including Jerry Sabath, Lee Johnson, David Satter, Roger Bash, and David Israel. Thanks also to editors Dawn Michelle Hardy and Debra Ginsberg for invaluable input. I also should thank members of my family who reviewed versions of the novel at different times and were always cheerfully frank—my wife Jean, and children Laura Wintroub and Jason Gumpert.

I want to thank as well, Lauren Grosskopf, a talented graphic designer, for developing the book's typographical format and wordsintheworks.com for producing the book in its final design. To the many others who provided input, sometimes without even being aware of how helpful they were, thank you.

About the Author

David E. Gumpert grew up on the South Side of Chicago, in South Shore and Hyde Park.

In the years since graduating the University of Chicago, he has attended Columbia Journalism School and worked as a reporter for *The Wall Street Journal* and an editor for the *Harvard Business Review* and *Inc.* magazine.

He has also authored ten nonfiction books on a variety of subjects—from entrepreneurship and small business management to food politics. His most prominent titles include *How to Really Create a Successful Business Plan* (Inc. Publishing); *How to Really Start Your Own Business* (Inc. Publishing); *Life, Liberty and the Pursuit of Food Rights* (Chelsea Green Publishing), and *The Raw Milk Answer Book* (Lauson Publishing).

He spent ten years from the 1990s to the early 2000s researching his family's history during the Holocaust. The result was a book co-authored with his deceased aunt Inge Bleier: *Inge: A Girl's Journey Through Nazi Europe* (Wm. B. Eerdman Publishing).

David is an avid swimmer, cross-country skier, and walker. He lives in the Boston suburb of Waltham, and also spends time in New Hampshire's Upper Valley.

Made in the USA
Monee, IL
25 September 2020